STRAYS

STRAYS

Remy Wilkins

canonball
B O O K S
an imprint of canonpress

Moscow, Idaho

Published by Canonball Books, an imprint of Canon Press
P.O. Box 8729, Moscow, Idaho 83843
800.488.2034 | www.canonballbooks.com

Remy Wilkins, *Strays*
Copyright © 2017, 2022 by Remy Wilkins
Second Edition

Cover design by James Engerbretson
Cover illustration by Forrest Dickison
Interior design by Valerie Anne Bost

Library-of-Congress publication data
Wilkins, Remy, author.
Strays / Remy Wilkins.
Moscow, Idaho : Canon Press, 2017.
LCCN 2017045071 | ISBN 9781954887343 (paperback : alk. paper)
Subjects: | CYAC: Demonology—Fiction. | Loneliness—Fiction. |
   Uncles—Fiction. | Secrets—Fiction.
Classification: LCC PZ7.1.W544 St 2017 | DDC [Fic]—dc23
LC record available at https://lccn.loc.gov/2017045071

22 23 24 25 26 27 28 29   10 9 8 7 6 5 4 3 2 1

To My Sons

Stephen Archer
Jaiken Montaigne
Oz Maethelvin Anderson
Tallis Jove
and
Regis Augustine

My Reason for Writing

CONTENTS

♍

CHAPTER ONE

A MIGHTY FORTRESS

Out of the hills in the early evening, where finally the Appalachians roll to a rest in northern Alabama, descended a gray van, a trail of dust signaling its arrival. The nearby mountain had many names, including Gategwa or Oostanaula, though most of the locals called it Skeleton Mount due to the stone snake effigy built like a spine atop its peak. For the passengers in the gray van, the mountain was the tombstone to their journey.

Inside the van was the Niemand family—or two-thirds of the Niemand family, for Mr. Niemand had recently left Virginia, his wife of thirteen years, and his son Rodney in early spring to make a name for himself in the City of Angels.

Rodney thought his dad was already off to a bad start if he wanted to make his name in a town called that.

Their destination was at the foot of Skeleton Mount, a little town once called Etowah but now known as Twin Rivers, where Rodney was to spend the summer with his weird Uncle Ray.

The first of these "twins," the Snake River, flowed alongside the mountain before curling off and corkscrewing through the farmland outside the town. The second was simply named the Second River, and it flowed down Skeleton Mount in buoyant leaps and waterfalls. These two rivers gradually drew nearer until they united as they left the county. The van outlined the Snake River before crossing over a bridge to town.

Rodney brushed back his thick brown hair and settled his red ball cap back to its usual place. They drove down Main Street, where most of the businesses had already closed. Here and there the bright signs of a diner or coffee shop or cinema would add their light to the late afternoon sun. Rodney plucked out his earbuds. "For real, he doesn't have a TV?"

"For real," she said, moving her hand to flip her hair over her shoulder, but finding only a shorn sandy brown wisp.

"I thought he hid one in his bedroom."

"Nope. Sorry, kiddo."

"How far outside the city does he live?"

His mother laughed. "I bet you could walk from his front door to this gas station in an hour. Less if you use your bike."

"I'm going to need more video games," he muttered to himself as they left the town and followed the curve of the mount westward. On the right were rows of cotton plants, about a month or so into their growth, green and hardly knee-high. On the left side of the road, a wall of trees grew thick up the toe of Skeleton Mount.

Rodney's mother slowed as they arrived at a gravel road that led into the woods. The road was marked by a wood barrel mailbox. The final stretch to Ray's house was a long driveway that looped around a steep hill. The gray, moss-covered trees slumped, and the roof screeched as their low branches scraped the top of the van.

"I think it will be good for you," said his mother, picking up the discussion they'd had the last two weeks. "He used to play baseball. He could probably help you."

"I hate baseball." He kicked the bat lying at his feet, still looking new despite a full year of use.

"You're still learning. It'll be more fun when you get better at it."

"Dad made me play. I didn't want to."

"It's good to get some sunshine."

"Ugh, I hate sunshine."

"Rodney Abner Niemand." Her voice was a crisp even tone, not angry, but as if she were invoking an historical figure. She shot him a mirthful look from the rearview mirror. (He'd chosen to sit in the back.) "You don't get to talk like that. Tell me you love sunshine."

Rodney pulled his hat low. "I love sunshine."

"What was that?"

"I love sunshine."

"You need to keep practicing. It sounds like you don't mean it." She playfully stuck her tongue out at him. He tried to smother his smile with a shrug.

She flipped on the headlights to see through the shadows and slowed the van to creep over a washed-out section of the road. Potholes made the whole van shiver.

"Ray's got rabbits. He'll let you play with those. And you've got the woods to explore."

"Uncle Ray's always so busy, Mom. He's not going to play with me. Besides, he talks to himself."

"Oh, he's just joking around," she said, catching his eyes in the mirror to gauge his reaction. He drew his lips into a straight line, noncommittal, like his dad. Balanced between smart remarks and sincerity. "He's doing us a big favor."

"Doing *you* a favor."

She slowed the car down to a crawl. "Rodney," she said more sternly.

His voice leaped a measure, to the tone of pleading, but short of whining. "I want to go with you. Why can't I go with you?"

"Rodney, I've told you. We're starting a new life. A new everything, new city, house, job, friends. I need to get some things settled first, and then you can come."

Rodney crossed his arms and muttered, "Abandoning me."

She paused to let the argument die. They'd spoken these same words again and again. She increased the van's speed and the gravel took up the complaint.

"What am I going to do with rabbits?"

"Hey, maybe you could help make a rocking chair. That'd be good for you to learn."

Rodney picked at the loose threads of his shirt. "Yeah, I guess. If I get to use knives and other things." He chopped at the stray threads with his hand. They rumbled across the wood bridge that spanned Second River.

"Rodney, Rodney, Rodney," she said, " . . . you'll be happy."

Uncle Ray only invited them the week after Christmas and on Easter Sunday. Rodney had never stayed there longer than a couple of nights. He usually spent the whole time on the couch playing his video games or reading. When he was younger he'd lie on the rug and push cars across it.

They lived an hour and a half away in Rome, Georgia, but Ray never visited. His mom would always invite him, and his dad would always give her a look, but Ray stayed home tending his garden and making the rocking chairs he sold online. Both the governors of Alabama and Georgia had bought one. Another was in a museum somewhere. It made the newspapers. "Recluse woodworker," they called Ray. He had to look up that word—*recluse* meant a person that had withdrawn from the world to live alone.

"Mom?" he looked up to find her eyes in the mirror. "Did Ray go crazy?"

She kept her eyes on the road as she answered. "No, of course not."

"Dad said he did."

"Your dad . . . " she slowed the car till they almost stopped. "Ray is just a little lonely."

Rounding the last bend, they descended into a clearing where the house sat. Though the sun was at a low angle in the sky, the two light poles out front were already on, emitting a soft yellow light.

His uncle had built his house as a series of interlocking honeycombs, each room a hexagonal cell. Ray had named his home Corleonis, Heart of the Lion, but the locals simply called it the Honeycomb House. The first floor was in a flower pattern with six petals around a central stair room that held a grand spiral staircase. The second floor held three bedrooms—Ray's and two guest bedrooms—plus two bathrooms. A more modest spiral staircase climbed to the third floor, which was an observatory. Last Christmas Ray had tried to get Rodney interested in looking at stars, but after ten minutes of staring at white dots he'd had enough of that for a lifetime.

Next to the towering Corleonis was Ray's workshop. It was a great wooden hall with a concrete floor and a high ceiling, crossbeamed throughout. It held whispers like regular speech and speech like shouts. Rodney could hear the whine of the circular saw reverberate through the walls. Inside you could feel it with your teeth.

Between the house and the workshop was Ray's car. It was a beat-up yellow Honda Civic Wagon, an "old hoopty," Ray called it. It had long ago lost the "da" at the end of "Honda" and his mom had pried off the c-v-c from "Civic" so that it would read "Hon i i" and was henceforth called the Honey Pot.

Rodney's mom parked the car, and he began gathering his belongings: a stack of comic books, his baseball glove and bat, and a slingshot his mother rarely let him use back home. Rodney waited until the whine of the car died before he opened his door.

Ray was standing on the porch to greet them. His beard, salted with grays, hid his neck. His nearly shoulder-length hair was without the ponytail today, but he wore one of his signature tie-dye shirts. His tie-dye shirts weren't spirals; they were

CORLEONIS, THE HONEYCOMB HOUSE

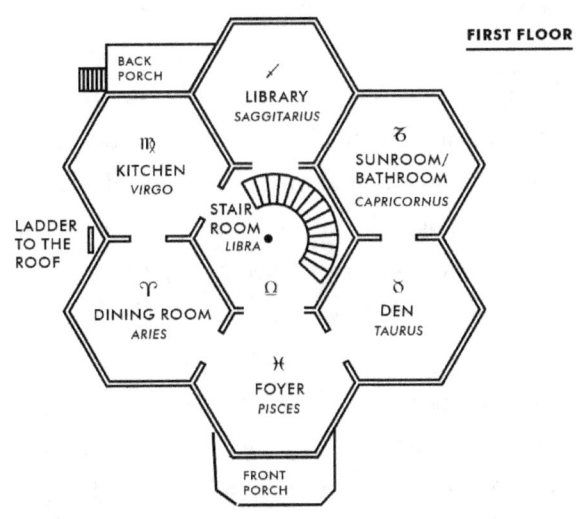

FIRST FLOOR

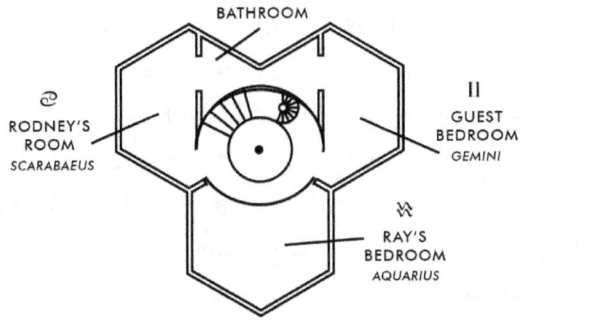

SECOND FLOOR

THIRD FLOOR

vertical pillars of color with purple in the middle and reds, greens, yellows, and blues flowing out of it.

He snapped the black suspenders spanning the length of his stomach and smiled as Rodney trudged around the van. Then Ray rumbled down the steps, swatting the air in front of him and saying, "Out of the way scalawag—let me greet my nephew." He put a hand on Rodney's head and gave him a rough hair tousling, knocking off his cap. "Rodney, my man."

"Hi, Ray." Rodney straightened his hair and picked up his cap, settling it more tightly.

Ray took the suitcase his sister pulled out of the trunk. "Need some supper, Ginny?"

Ray called her Gin or Ginny, short for Virginia (only her co-workers called her that). Sometimes Ray called her Spica. Rodney was in the dark as to why, but his mother would brush it off as from some forgotten story. His father assumed it was racist.

"No, we got something on the way." Rodney's mom pulled out his bike from the back and wheeled it to the house. She leaned it against the wall beside the front stairs.

"Aw, at least have some winter apples. They're just starting to peak. I put 'em up as soon as I harvested them, and they've got this perfect sweetness to them now."

"Are they from Daddy's trees?" she asked.

"Yup, and I got this great apple peeler too." He led them up the front steps. "Mind the hooligans," he said, gesturing to nothing as they entered.

They dropped Rodney's stuff on the floor of the foyer. Carved on the floor was a sign like two crescent moons back to back with a bar connecting them, like an H. This is partly why most called it the Honeycomb House, yet the walls were decorated with little fish.

The wood floor creaked as they walked into the dining room. There, carved on the wall between the windows, was a charging ram. Its head was down like it wanted to burst through the wall into the kitchen. Rodney couldn't help but touch the intricately carved chairs and table as he passed. His uncle had spent years "doodling," as he called it, etching symbols, scrolls, and pictures into the wood surfaces. They entered the kitchen. The panel over the back door was of a woman holding two wheat stalks in her outstretched hand.

"I've got you in the Scrab bedroom this time, Rod, since it's closer to the stairs."

"Okay." Rodney didn't like that room because it had beetles carved into the wood that looked like sinister baseballs.

Ray pulled out wood bowls from the cabinet and set them on the counter. He reached into the fridge and took out a wood bowl with reddish-yellow apples in it.

"Rodney? Would you like one?"

"Sure."

He brought out a metal contraption with a wide wood base from one of the cabinets. It had a long screw with a crank at one end and three prongs at the other that passed through a sharp metal hoop. The hoop removed the apple core, while another blade cut the apple meat into a spiral.

"These babies are Stayman-Winesaps," he said as he pressed the top of an apple into the prongs. "A tad tart when you harvest them, but if you store them right, they take on a bit of sweetness over a few months." He began turning the crank, which pushed the apple into the skinner. The apple skin was spit from the peeler and spilled to the counter with a wet slicing sound.

When the apple had passed through the hoop, Ray pulled it free, leaving the core impaled on the prongs, and pulled apart a perfect slinky of apple. He handed it to Rodney.

"Eat hearty, me lad."

"Cool," he said as he played it like an accordion. "Can I do one?"

"Do two, so I can have one as well." He pulled off the core, unwound the crank so that the screw returned to its starting point and stuffed another apple on the prongs. He stepped aside so Rodney could turn the shaft.

The crank required more effort than he expected. Not wanting to look weak, he turned his shoulders into it and the apple shot through the bladed ring, sending out a rooster tail of apple peel.

"That was fun," he said as he finished. He pulled the fruit free and handed it to his mother. She put the head of the spiral into her mouth and bit. The crack of the apple was like fingers snapping.

"Mmmm," she said. She raised the fruit, letting it dangle from three fingers, closed her eyes and said, "I love apples, I love apples, I love apples."

Rodney finished an apple for Ray, picked one of his own, and announced, "I'm going to look at the walls."

"Hey, check out the library," Ray called as the boy pushed through the swinging door into the stair room. "I just put in some wildlife to go with the hunter."

With his eyes, Rodney followed the thick central beam way up to the third floor. Ray joked that if it was run into hard enough the whole house would come crashing down. The pillar was about the only thing that was untouched by his carving knife.

He approached the strange clock that was built into the wall under the stairs. It was a pendulum clock with symbols instead of numbers, gold set in a blond wood so finely grained that it looked like the Aurora Borealis. The little hand was pointing between a symbol that looked like an H with two fish behind it and one that looked like a Y, where the seven and eight would be, and the long hand was pointing to squiggly lines over a picture of flowing water, where the six would be. The second hand circled over the other marks, a horseshoe, the letter M, an arrow, and other weird symbols.

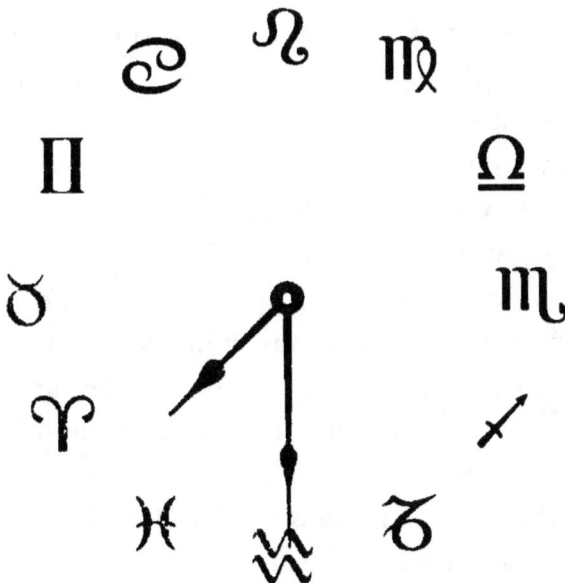

Below the clock was the only phone in the house. A little shelf was built into the wall with a piano bench pushed underneath. Years ago, Rodney would tuck himself into this cubbyhole to play with cars or action figures. He could lie curled up and watch the ankles of others as they walked through the house.

He heard his mother speaking in a secretive tone. Though it was quiet, it sounded like a siren in his ears: *Grown-up talk. Pay attention.* He moved nearer to the wall to listen.

"Ray, I'm thinking about going back to my maiden name."

"Did you get papers?"

"Yeah, last week. I'm not going to contest. He doesn't want anything. It'll be official in thirty-one days."

Rodney slouched to the floor, his back against the wall, knees to his chin. Turns out his mother wanted to make a new name for herself, as well. He felt like the last Niemand alive. The thread of his mom's voice pulled him out of his thoughts.

"But what about Rodney?"

"What about him?"

"What should I do about his name?"

"Have you talked to him about it?"

"I don't know what to do. I don't want him to feel like his last name is bad. I also don't want him to feel abandoned. He's only twelve." Rodney only ever heard his mom speak this way when he was out of the room. To him she was as cheerful as ever.

His uncle cleared his throat. "I could ask him about it." Then Rodney heard the wood bowls clink and the faucet turn on. He stood and tiptoed into the library. The walls were bookshelves stuffed with books, and across from him were two small windows looking out into the backyard. He slid the door shut behind him and noticed an archer carved into it, an arrow strung on his bow. He scanned the walls for what the archer hunted, but could see only rabbits and a single snake carved at the foot of a tree.

His eyes were drawn to a shelf of brightly colored paperbacks. He ran a finger across the cracked spines, silently reading their titles: *The Order of Angels, The Flood of Demons, The Cloak of Colors.* They were well worn, probably read yearly. Ray was rarely without a book in his hand or a potboiler tucked into his back pocket. He and his mother would quote comedic lines to each other from stories they'd both read. They could go for hours.

The phone rang, its rattle springing into his ears. He returned to the stair room, pulled out the little bench below the telephone and sat. In all his visits to Twin Rivers, Rodney could never remember the phone ringing. He thought the only person that called Ray was his mother. He waited for another ring before answering.

"Hello?" he said and held his breath.

" . . . Rodney? That you?"

"Dad!" Rodney looked back at the kitchen door to see if his mom or Ray had entered behind him. No one stirred. They must have known who was calling.

"Hey, buddy. How ya been?"

"M'okay. School's out."

"Yeah, I heard Mom's dumping you at Uncle Ray's for the next month or so."

"Yeah. Until she gets things settled."

"Sorry about that." There was a slight pause, Rodney held his breath again. Finally his father spoke, "He still crazy?"

Rodney checked for Ray again. He gave a whispered laugh. "Yeah, he is."

"Crazy with a capital R-A-Y." This was an old joke. Rodney laughed softly again. His dad continued, "Sorry I couldn't take you with me. You understand, right? Sometime, when I'm more settled, you can come out." After another pause he added, "To visit. Would you like that?"

"Sure."

"Alright, buddy. Just wanted to check in. Hate that mom left you there. Don't go cra-ray-zee."

"Okay."

"See ya, bud."

"Love—" Rodney heard the click on the line as his dad hung up.

The last day of school followed by the drive had sapped his energy. The shadows moved, and Rodney shook his head to keep his eyes from playing tricks. He returned to the library to sit in the last of the sunlight.

The thought of being here all summer settled heavily on his shoulders. The house was musty, and creaked and groaned when the wind blew. He didn't want to be abandoned in a house like this. Maybe if there was a television to dull time and shrink it to nothing. Or if there were other kids to distract him with talk of their father's jokes and their mother's cooking. The last thing he wanted was to stay with a man who talked to himself and wore too much tie-dyed clothing.

His mother entered and read his mood. "You'll have a good time, Rodney. You'll see."

Rodney angled his back to her. "You're abandoning me."

She stood silent. Rodney put his hand on the books in front of him. He read the title of the volume his hand rested on: *The Jawbone of Heaven*. He knew his mom was fighting back tears, something that happened a lot in their recent exchanges. They were both so full of wounds that every hard word was like salt to them.

He pulled his hand away and the book toppled off the shelf and crashed on his foot. The book's pages were splayed open, making a tent over his shoe. He was angry at himself and felt anger and sorrow for his mother.

She moved closer and put her arms around him. He felt her breath in his hair.

Without turning his head he said, "Please take me with you."

She whispered back, "You need to be here."

"Please don't leave me."

"I'm sorry," she said.

Rodney kicked the book off his shoe and turned to put his arms around her.

She pulled back and looked into his eyes. "I'm sorry." Her voice entered softly. He pulled out of her arms and left the room. He went straight through the stair room into the foyer and out the front door.

Leaping off the porch and into the thick grass of the front yard, he felt tears welling up, so he took off in a sprint to keep his eyes fierce and alert. He ran straight for the woods.

Rodney stumbled up the slope and entered the trees, pushing past the undergrowth. He was already beginning to slow, his lungs burned and his eyes itched with sweat. The last dregs of the day were swallowed, and a darkness settled around him.

His mom would be leaving first thing in the morning to travel to Nashville. She was taking a nursing job at some hospital. A new start for them both, but it would be starting without him. It was only fair that their old life would end without him too.

He trudged and tripped through the brush. As he walked, he realized why the driveway looped. There was a steep incline that dropped to a ravine where the river ran. There was a twelve-foot waterfall upstream, spattering as it sloshed against the rocks.

The water seemed slower at the bridge and more shallow. Here, however, the water boiled and bubbled. Rodney sat to slide down the embankment to the water below. He started slipping so he fell back, sprawling against the turf to slow down.

"Jeez!" He scrambled for a foothold. A root like a jutted lip stopped him short of the water. A coolness moved across him. "Jesus," he said more carefully. He felt the absence of his father again, who would say that name at any slip or stubbing. His mother would hiss and make mean eyes at his dad, but if she heard Rodney say it, he'd be in a heap of trouble. He stood and placed his foot on the nearest rock peeking out of the stream. Soon he was drenched in the waterfall's spray. In the dim light he couldn't see the mist, but could feel it pulsing over him.

The cool of the water was soothing and seemed to cut through the grime he had gathered in his run through the woods. He felt refreshed, and the heat of the night had been swept back.

It took three leaps, stone to stone, before he made it across and clambered up the other side. From this point, he could hear the whooshing of cars speeding down the road. He continued his walk and soon stepped out of the woods. Ahead of him was Ray's mailbox. He walked up to look into its dark mouth, but it was empty. Not quite ready to follow the road back to the house, he crouched down in the gravel. The thrum and siren of the cicadas awoke in his ears, a chorus he'd blocked out till then.

Down the road, the lights of a small car appeared. Rodney watched as it slowed and turned off the road in front of him. The car kept running as the door opened and a wiry man stood up.

"Who are you? What are you doing?" He sounded afraid.

Rodney stood. "I'm Rodney."

"Oh," his tone changed. "Do you know Raymond?"

"He's my uncle."

"Staying with him, are you?"

Rodney nodded. "For the summer."

The man reached into the car and withdrew a stack of letters, magazines, and fliers wrapped in a rubberband. "I'm Otis, the mailman." He took a few steps toward Rodney and handed him the mail.

"It's late. Did you have a lot to deliver today?"

"No, but I live up the road a bit. I drop Raymond's stuff off last. He don't mind."

Rodney nodded again.

Otis put his foot back in the car. "You don't seem too happy about being here for the summer?"

Rodney shook his head no.

Otis looked up the winding gravel road before speaking again. "If you find yourself in any sort of trouble, you just let me know." His tone was hushed.

"What kind of trouble?"

Otis gave a wan smile. "Haven't you heard? Your uncle is a bit of a troublemaker."

"Mom says he's just lonely."

"Listen, I'm not talking bad about the man, but just keep an eye on him. Something happens, anything, you call me. I'm right down the road."

Rodney stood silently. He knew people considered Ray weird, but this was the first time he'd heard that Ray was trouble.

Otis sat down and shut the door. He stuck his head out of the window. "You wouldn't understand. Forget I said anything." He stopped. "And don't tell your uncle. He don't like me, neither. Just be careful."

He drove off before Rodney could ask anything else. He followed the red lights of his car until it turned off the road. In the distance he spotted the lights of Otis's house.

Rodney turned and started the trek back to his uncle's house, his thoughts growing as dark as the night around him.

Ω

CHAPTER TWO

OUR ANCIENT FOE

It was past nine when Rodney got back to Ray's house. The walk in the dark wasn't nearly as daunting as the prospect of spending the summer here. He had never felt this sense of foreboding when he had visited before with his mother and father. There was something more ominous about the house now.

He went upstairs to his room without looking for Ray or his mom. Flipping on the light, he flopped on the bed and stared at the beetles carved on the wall. Scarab beetles, Ray had explained to him years ago. At first Rodney was scared of the horned bugs ascending and descending the walls. Some with

wings outspread, others bearing circles which Ray mysterious-
ly said were suns or balls of dung.

He spotted his things near the door where Ray had depos-
ited them. He began unpacking. He stuffed his clothes into the
dresser without much care, socks with shirts, socks with pants,
underwear going anywhere.

When he was little, his dad would sweep him into his arms
to crush him. "Too big for the bed," he'd say as his arms would
tighten around him. Or he'd say, "Dreams are in your bed. Go
get them." Every New Year's Eve he'd tuck Rodney in bed and
say, "I'll see you next year."

"Don't go," he'd say to his dad.

"I'll be back next year though."

"Don't go." He'd cling to his dad's arm.

"I'll miss you," his dad would say as he shook himself free.

Rodney put his comic books and electronic distractions in
the cabinet next to his bed. He let his bat roll underneath and
tossed his glove after it to keep it company. He hoped they'd
stay hidden all summer.

When he lifted his empty suitcase to toss it into the closet
he found a wood bat underneath. He picked it up and ran his
hand down the shaft. It was smooth and a deep red color. He
held it out and noticed that it was warped. It was humped in
the middle, just a slight curve. On the barrel of the bat the
word "Libra" was carved.

"Libra means Balance."

Rodney looked up to see Ray standing in the doorway. "Huh?"

"The name of the bat."

"Why would you name a bat?"

"Your bat is named."

"No it isn't."

"Sure it is, look, says there its name is DeMarini."

Rodney turned and saw that the bat had rolled back from underneath the bed. "That's who made the bat."

"Oh, does it say anything on the other side?"

Rodney spun it with his toe so that he could see. 'Vendetta' was printed on the side in wide red letters. "Yeah, I guess it does have a name."

"I put the name of my company on your bat too."

Rodney spun the wood bat in his hand to find a symbol of two lines, with the top line humped in the middle like a sunset. Underneath were the words "Ray of Hope".

"When did you start making bats?"

Ray grinned. "This afternoon."

Rodney gripped it till his knuckles went white. "Not bad, it's hardly wonky at all."

"Yeah, but you should see the other bats. They're way worse. They look like gnarly wizard wands." Ray laughed, then placed his finger on the sunset lines. "That's the astrological symbol for Libra."

"The what?"

"Astrological symbol for Libra." Rodney's face was as deeply grained as the bat he held. Ray laughed.

"Don't you know your constellations?"

Rodney continued frowning. "No."

"Patterns of the stars?" Ray whirled his finger around above his head. "Pictures that guide us through the year? Sagittarius, Capricorn, Taurus . . . ring any bells?"

"Is that like the horoscope? Mom says that's stupid."

"It is stupid, but that doesn't mean the constellations are. We'll play with the telescope some night."

"Okay." Rodney stretched, signaling to Ray that he was ready to be alone.

"I can see you're tired. Long day, I know."

Rodney toed his shoes off, stepping on the heel to peel his foot out. "Yeah, thanks for letting me stay here, Ray. Even though you didn't want me to."

"What? That's crazy. Who told you that?"

"I heard Mom. She had to convince you to keep me."

"Hey, hey, that's not how it is, bud. It was never about you."

"But you didn't think it'd be good for me to stay here, right?"

"It's not you I'm worried about." They both nodded at each other, unsure of how to continue.

Rodney sensed a deep conversation coming. Perhaps someone would finally talk like an adult to him about his dad leaving. He was past ready to be angry about it, past being sad, but he felt a fist well up in his throat.

Ray scratched his beard with his mouth agape. Finally he spoke, saying each word slowly, "I don't know how to say this."

Rodney blinked away the wet in his eyes and flopped on the bed. He pulled his hat off and set it in front of his face. He took a deep breath, smelling the salt of his sweat.

"You're a brave kid," he finally said.

"Thanks." He waited for Ray to say more.

"We'll talk more." He nodded his head once. "'Night." Ray turned. Rodney listened to him descending the stairs. There were stumbling, heavy stomps on the steps. He heard Ray bark, "Spit-thicket, bah!"

He tried to recall all the weird things he'd heard about Ray. His dad never liked Ray and called him kooky, but he didn't remember any reasons aside from his constant comments to no one. His mom called him strange, but seemed to mean his lonely lifestyle. He had no friends that Rodney had ever seen or heard about, and he only visited town for food. Everything else he needed he received by mail.

He heard his mom entering the bathroom that connected their rooms. He rolled over and began to feign sleep in case she decided to peek in. He heard the shower snap on and the white noise of water rise. His eyes felt thick and the warm night packed him away into a dreamless sleep.

* * *

When he woke, the house was quiet and the lights were off. His stomach growled, so he decided to slip downstairs to find a snack. Maybe spin out another apple. The clock in the stair room indicated that it was just after midnight. The night was alive and aloud with bugs and frogs; the wood of the house shifted and groaned, but other noises caught his ear. There was movement in the library.

He crept closer and heard Ray as he flopped into a leather chair with a groan. Through the door he heard Ray say, "Do you have to break my light bulbs every time you come?"

Rodney was startled at the crackling voice that responded. "Do you insist on fouling the air with light?" It was like gravel being crushed.

"It's a fifteen watt bulb, the dimmest I can find." Ray responded, clearly annoyed.

"Your obsession with light is not shared by the diaboloi."
The figure shifted, Rodney could tell he was standing in front
of the far wall by the windows. The boards creaked under the
weight of the mysterious figure. "Now what is the reason for
this summons?"

"The deal is still on, but my visitor is here. I want you to
leave him alone. I've already talked to the minion that will be
following him around. Make sure your other flunkies stay out
of the way."

There was a swooshing sound like the visitor had slashed
the air with a flag. "That is not a part of the terms. The diaboloi
have free reign here. That is the deal." The last sentence was
punctuated with a menacing pause between each word.

The squeak of leather and shift of the wood flooring signaled that Ray was rising to his feet. Rodney scrambled to the
clock and hid beneath the bench. He knocked his knee against
his lip as he curled up in the cubbyhole. It was a lot smaller
than he remembered.

His clamoring was covered by the library door being pulled
back. Ray stood at the door to say one last thing over his shoulder, "Listen fella, I'm not asking permission, I'm telling you.
There's a guest, a boy. He doesn't know the rules, he doesn't
know the agreement. Encounter him at your own risk." Ray
turned and marched directly upstairs.

A long shadow was cast on the floor, and Rodney could
hear the figure in the library breathing. There was a loud clatter and the tinkling of broken glass as the last light went out.

Rodney held his breath and heard a low murmuring from
the library. "The risk is yours, foolish adam."

A chill went up Rodney's spine. He heard a click like the sound of a dog's toenails on the wood floor and the scuffing of the window being opened. There was the sound of wind and then quiet. Rodney lay in his alcove long after the only sound was the crickets and the croaking toads.

* * *

The morning light was a dim halo at the horizon when Rodney woke. He sat up in his bed and began patting his hair down. He slid out of his bed and tiptoed to the bathroom.

Last night he had waited until he was certain that Ray was in bed and whoever or whatever was in the library had long ago abandoned the premises. He'd pulled himself out from under the clock in the stair room and made his way back to his room. He lay in bed with the sheet up to his nose trying to still his shivering legs. He drifted off without ever feeling sleep creep up.

In the new day, the house had lost its menace. What had happened or what he thought had happened last night seemed like a dream. He made his way loudly down the stairs and stretched his arms and legs, stretching his back and joggling his head as he went.

He turned at the sound of movement. Ray was scuffing his way toward him wearing a tie-dyed bathrobe and blue bunny slippers, both ragged with use.

"There he is, prince of the beetles." Ray was always coining dumb nicknames.

"Morning," Rodney mumbled.

"Night not have enough sleep for ya? Had to spend some of the morning to catch up?" Ray knocked the wet tail of his braided hair off his shoulder.

"I guess."

"Your mom already left. Said she'd give you a call tomorrow."

"She didn't wake me?" He followed Ray into the foyer.

"Said she stuck her head in and said goodbye. Apparently you muttered a goodbye back."

Rodney shrugged. "Don't remember that."

"I was just about to get you; I've got breakfast on the way. My morning is all wonky. Haven't even picked up the paper." He raised his arms in the air looking like Moses at the Red Sea. "How will I know what to think if I don't read the paper?" He laughed.

Rodney ran the side of his hand under his nose. "Want me to go get it?"

Ray turned and waved him to follow. "Nah, the paper will be at the road. Otis doesn't like driving up to the house."

"He delivers the paper, too?"

"Yeah. How do you know Otis?"

"I met him when I, uh, when I went to get the mail yesterday." They passed through the dining room.

"Otis, Outis, Odi, Odiferous." Ray chanted. "I saw the mail this morning. Thanks. I usually wait and pick it up when I get the paper."

He followed Ray into the kitchen where the smell of breakfast had already complicated the air. There was a chorus of over-easy eggs accompanied by the applause of sausage sizzling next to them. Boiling on the stove was a pot of grits and, as they entered, there was a pop announcing toast. His stomach chimed in.

"What time is it?" he asked as he gave the sausage a closer sniff.

"Just a hair before nine o'clock. Grab the juice out of the fridge for me." He gave the grits a stir.

"Guess I was pretty tired." He pulled open the door and found a pitcher with orange juice. He set it on the counter behind him.

"I usually get going a lot earlier, but I thought I'd wait till you were up before starting breakfast. Couldn't let you eat alone on your first day here."

Rodney pulled a jar of red jam out of the fridge. He held it up. "Cherry?"

"Strawberry," Ray answered. "I grew them myself." He lowered the heat and put a lid over the grits. His hand brushed the empty stove burner, and he jumped and snatched his hand back. "Fibditch, rapscallion." Then he turned off the burner. "Always looking to burn me," he muttered with a slight smirk on his face.

Rodney ignored the comment and pulled out two cups to fill with the frothy juice.

"I usually start the grits too late, but I think I timed it perfect today. They'll be ready as soon as we get the table set."

They bustled in and out of the kitchen setting up plates and forks and knives. When they finally sat at the table there was a tower of toast, a mound of eggs, a fallen forest of sausage, and a pond of grits.

Rodney's eyes popped at the spread before them. "I've never seen so much food for breakfast."

Ray cut tiny tires of sausage with his fork. "That's because you normally sleep too late when you come to my house. Besides, you prefer cereal."

"I never knew you did this for breakfast, though." He watched as Ray began spreading butter on the toast like he was sharpening a knife. He accepted two planks of toast offered to him and took a sip of cold juice.

Ray leaned back with a hunk of sausage on his fork. He held the fork up and closed his eyes, "I love sausage. I love sausage. I love sausage." He put it in his mouth and smiled as he chewed.

Rodney laughed. He dissected his sausage while maintaining the demarcation between grits and eggs. Ray sat back with his coffee and watched him.

"You eat just like your dad. You're very precise in your bites and while you chew, you look like you're planning your next one. Like a chessmaster, you're two or three plays ahead."

"Sorry."

"No, it's just funny."

They sat in silence and ate. The sun angled through the window in its slow hoist into the sky, like a pole-vaulter planting his beam.

"I don't think I ever watched my dad eat," said Rodney while staring at his food. He spread his grits over the plate with his fork in slow swirling motions. "I don't think I've ever noticed how my mom eats either."

Ray chuckled, his smile causing his beard to bristle. "Talks to her food too much, ya ask me." He caught Rodney's eye and gave a wink. "Come on, let's go get the paper. I want to show you the stone snake, and a walk'll do us good before the drive."

* * *

Rodney and Ray followed the road as it looped around the ridge. The air was still cool, but already the day had begun to shift. The moss canopy grew thicker as they went deeper into the woods and the branches stretched almost to the ground.

As they approached the bridge Rodney asked, "Why do they call it the Second River? And don't say 'because there's two.'"

"Well, that is the reason, but you're right that wasn't what it used to be called."

"What was that?"

"I don't know its original name or anything, but it was once called the Wine River."

Rodney peered over the rail into the dark water. "The Snake and Wine Rivers." Rodney nudged a rock off the edge and watched it plop into the water. "Why'd they call it that?"

"I don't know. But what people don't notice is that when the two rivers join, it's the Snake that's swallowed up by the Wine, yet it's still called the Snake River." He snorted and shook his head.

"Why did they change the name to Second River? Wine River is way better than that."

"It was during a time when people thought that wine was bad. So they changed it."

"But snakes are bad. Why didn't they change the name of that one?"

Ray laughed and turned to keep walking. "Some names don't seem as dangerous as others."

Rodney jogged to catch up. "What about my name?"

"What about it?"

"I think Mom wants me to change it."

"Does she?"

"But I don't know what to change it to." Rodney picked up a stick and snapped it in half.

"Your mom is thinking about changing her name back to Lauter."

"Virginia Lauter. Virginia Niemand." He slashed back and forth with the two stick fragments. "I don't get it. What's the big deal?"

"Names are important."

"Is that why you named my bat?" Rodney flung one of his sticks into the woods.

"Of course."

"How long did it take you to think of a name you liked?"

"Not long. I was holding it and I thought it was well balanced."

"Libra."

"I'm an amateur astronomer."

"I don't think I've ever paid attention to the stars."

"Maybe tonight I'll take you up to my observatory."

They arrived at the mailbox. Ray reached into a plastic tube fastened underneath the box where the paper was put. He slapped it against his palm and on a whim he opened the mailbox.

"Hup, ya missed one last night." He pulled out an envelope and turned it over. "It's for you. Wow, been here a night and already you're getting mail." He handed the letter to Rodney.

"That's weird. Otis didn't put anything in the mailbox, he just handed it to me." The letter was addressed to Ray's Nephew, but no sender and no return address or even a stamp. It must have been slipped into the mailbox after he had returned to the house.

He flipped it over and saw an "O.S." written in pencil on the back. Rodney slid it into his back pocket not wanting to open it in front of Ray.

"Come on, let's hustle back before it gets too hot. The mountain awaits!"

* * *

The drive to the park at the apex of Skeleton Mount took an hour; it was a slow slithering up the north-facing slope. The rattle of Ray's car was muffled by Ray's choice of music or, in his words, "the dulcet tones of the Iron Maiden." At odd moments Ray would rattle off a few lines and then stop, as if that were all he could remember. He'd thump the steering wheel in time with the guitars. Occasionally, when the drums were especially moving, he'd strike the wood beads that hung down from the rearview mirror with a finger.

Ray wore denim coveralls over his tie-dye shirt while Rodney had opted for a T-shirt and shorts. Ray howled the chorus "Fly on your way, like an eagle!" while Rodney fiddled with the air conditioner.

"Hot?" Ray asked, while turning the volume down on the music.

"Little bit."

"Do ya like the music?" Ray bit his lower lip and jostled in his chair to the beat of the song, pumping his head to the beat.

"No."

Ray laughed. "Yeah? Hm." He turned the volume down till it was a low hum, just beneath the rumble of the groaning engine. "I guess it's an acquired taste."

The park had been built in the late seventies to capitalize on the historic stone snake and the nearby scenic waterfall. There was a small visitor center with bathrooms and information about the stone effigy as well as a picnic area and a gift shop selling snake trinkets and food. In the play area there were see-saws, monkey-bars, swing sets, and a rusty old merry-go-round.

The parking lot was about half full, fifteen cars scattered about the gravel lot. They got out and stretched. Rodney noticed that Ray performed the same ritual as his mother; arms held out in a T, then raising them above his head he performed a deep bow. Rodney added a few toe touches and then trotted after Ray.

Ray began his informal tour of the park. "That's the Second River. It comes from a lake northeast of here called the Wedowee Lake. The name means Old Water."

Rodney followed him as he veered away from the visitor's center and the playground. "Where we going, Uncle Ray?"

He glanced around. "Stone snake's this way. That stuff's just for tourists." He made a dismissive gesture with his hand and continued on the dirt path that led into the trees. He continued the history lesson. "The story goes back ages—over two thousand years ago, a Thunder Snake was caught here."

"Thunder Snake? That like a dinosaur?" Rodney kicked a twisted pine branch out of his way.

"Maybe. The story says that the Paleo-Indians 'round these parts built a stone wall to mark its death, right where it fell."

"Paleo-Indians?" Rodney asked with an eye squint.

"Ancient. Here-before-the-Indians Indians."

"Ah," Rodney said, not sure he understood. Ahead he saw a wood sign, and behind it the beginnings of a stone wall. He ran ahead, nearly falling over when a stick snared a sock.

"Watch it, don't brain yourself against the snake," called Ray.

The snake was a tightly packed line of stones with a zig between two small zags, like a V with tiny wings. The V was broken down, crushed and toppled by time. All along loose stones had fallen away like it was molting.

Ray picked up his monologue. "If you stretched it straight, the whole thing would be almost two football fields."

There was a series of iron posts beside the path, connected by a heavy chain, partitioning the snake from the visitors. Signs requested people to stay on the path. They walked toward the head of the snake, drawing nearer to the river.

"I can't imagine killing something this big. Does the story say how they did it?"

"Well, reports differ on that point. Some say the earliest people in Alabama brought down the great Thunder Snake with a song. Others said the enemy of the great serpent, the Warrior of Light, threw it down from the heavens."

"The Warrior of Light? Cool." They arrived at the river and stopped. It was slow-moving, a brackish brown. He looked to see the waterfall, but a bend obscured it.

The head of the serpent was a huge, solid block of stone that was nearly six feet high. There was a split at the bottom that gave the serpent a mouth, perhaps carved. Rodney leaned against the chain to see if he could touch it. His fingers were a mere flicker of a stone tongue away.

"So the Warrior of Light beat it up and threw it down to earth. Did it scare the Indians?"

Ray plucked a weed from the ground, broke off the end and stuck the stem in his mouth. He made a sucking sound before continuing, "The version of the story I like is that there was a corrupt medicine man, a person who can communicate with the spiritual world, and he called down the Thunder Snake."

"What for?" He turned, leaning back on the chain.

"What? Calling down the Thunder Snake? For power, of course. Make a deal with the devil, you know." Rodney nodded his head. Ray went on, "But before the Snake made it to earth, the Warrior of Light fought it and imprisoned it in stone."

Rodney curled his lip and hung his mouth in a look his dad called the Hayseed, usually following with his own mocking rendition. "How do you capture a giant space snake in a rock?" He held onto the chain and began swinging.

Ray bent down in front of Rodney, putting his hands on his knees. "Don't you know? Demons are subject to stone."

"That's dumb." He rocked himself to his feet. "So the Thunder Snake is like a demon that can be captured in stone if the angel does it? Lame."

"Whaddya mean 'lame'? That's *cool.*" Ray's eyes seemed to leap with imagined stories.

Rodney went to the river and instinctively began looking for rocks to toss. "Nah, I like the Warrior of Light and the Thunder Snake fighting, but it'd be cooler to kill it with a sword."

Ray joined him in rock tossing. "You've obviously never fought a Thunder Snake. The Warrior of Light was overwhelmed, and she was the only angel there to fight it, because she was the guardian of the Thunder Snake."

"Wait, the angel's a girl?"

"Or a guy." He looked over at Rodney before launching another pebble into the dark flow of water. "It's just a story. So the Warrior of Light, in an act of desperation, captures the serpent in stone. This is a bad idea because now the Thunder Snake is in the physical world. If it ever escapes the stone prison, she, the angel I mean, won't be able to fight it."

"How does a Thunder Snake escape from rock?"

Ray gave a scratch to his beard; Rodney could hear it above the plips and bloops his pebbles made as he slung handfuls into the air, watching them fall like comets into the water. "Um, I think that if you smash the head it becomes free."

"Smash the head?" Rodney turned to look at the head stone of the snake effigy. "Seems like that'd kill it."

"Yeah, probably. Maybe blood sacrifice. Evil loves a good bloody sacrifice."

Rodney nodded as if he knew.

"But those're just some guesses. The story goes that the Warrior of Light must stay here and drive away anyone that comes to free the snake."

"That's a cool story, I guess."

"Now let's go get some snake sandwiches."

Rodney looked at Ray to gauge his seriousness. "What? That's gross."

Ray nodded. "Snake sandwiches. 'Swhat they call hot dogs here at the park." He put his arm on Rodney's shoulders and directed him back to the visitor center.

"Does everything have to be so weird here?" Rodney said as they retreated from the river, following the long-dead stone serpent back through the woods.

CHAPTER THREE

THIS MORTAL LIFE

The "snake sandwich" was no better than any of the hundreds of hot dogs Rodney had eaten in his lifetime. Ray tried to get him to load up on condiments, but he wanted only a single stripe of mustard. He carefully ran a thin beam down the length of the sandwich and held it up to Ray for approval.

Ray ate his first snakedog in two bites, licked his fingers clean and raised his second to his mouth before he turned and grinned. "I luff dese," he said, with his cheeks bulging.

They were in the car and heading down the mountain before Rodney had tucked the last nub between his lips.

Rodney entered the Corleonis slump-shouldered and hot. He kicked off his sneakers, leaving them on the floor behind him, and wandered into the living room. He lay down on the cool couch and closed his eyes.

He could still feel the weaving of the car down the mountainside, the roll and bounce and jostle. He'd suppressed nausea the whole way back as Ray burped up the onions he'd stacked on his third and fourth snakes. A creaking of wood heralded Ray's entrance. Rodney rolled over onto his back.

Ray closed his mouth on another burp and rolled his shoulders. He beat on his chest before speaking. "Whew, ugh, shouldn't have had that fifth snake. Can't help myself sometimes."

"Yeah, the sauerkraut wasn't a good idea."

"Ergh, nor the chili. So, needless to say, I won't eat dinner, but let me know when you want something."

"Alright." Rodney felt something underneath him and he rotated to pull it out. His hand closed on the letter from this morning.

Ray turned and held up a hand. "I'll be in the library sleeping underneath a book."

Rodney turned over the letter to examine the "O.S." on the back, then slid open the flap and withdrew the page inside.

> Kid,
>
> My name is Otis, the mailman. I hope I didn't frighten you with my concerns about your uncle. If you want to talk, feel free to come to my house. I'm just down the road, first turn on the right. No big deal if you don't want to. Just watch out.
>
> Otis Schlange

"Otis Schlange, O.S." he said aloud. He wondered what sort of trouble Otis thought was going on. Perhaps he knew more about some crazy things Ray did. His dad always needled his mom about this or that oddity, such as sprinkling a pinch of salt on his shoulder or blowing on your face before bedtime.

There was talk about a controversy at the church Ray attended in town. He had heard his mom whisper about it when he was out of the room: Ray had been kicked out. Perhaps Otis had more information on that. He considered dropping in for a visit and stuffed the letter into his pants pocket. He heard Ray bark from behind the closed library door, "Beat it, I'm sleeping, knucklehead. The sun still shines." Rodney waited for more but it seemed that Ray had settled back into his chair and resumed his nap.

It was like he was addressing unseen spirits, but it was always with an insult. *Scoundrel, varmint, sucka,* occasionally he'd let fly a *nerd* or *potlicker* whenever he stumbled or entered a room. Rodney would laugh, his mom would roll her eyes, but his father would grit his teeth. These outbursts confirmed all manner of mental problems in his father's eyes. More and more, they convinced Rodney, as well.

He spent the rest of the day wandering around the grounds, fighting the urge to play video games. His mom had counseled him to resist that activity as much as possible, but after walking around the workshop, examining the odd scraps of wood in the junk pile, and watching the rabbits hop around in their pen behind the house, Rodney gave in to the temptation.

He grabbed an apple on his way and clomped upstairs to his room. He took out his handheld console and turned it on.

The screen flickered bright and soon the bleats and whoops of his game nailed his ears shut. He played with his leg kicked up against the wall and his eyes stuck to the screen.

The game was Wombatter, the last thing given to him from his dad. You were a character that knocked out monster wombats with your handy bat. If you hit a wombat enough it would explode, destroying the town and revealing treasure and secrets. Some were so big you'd have to knock other exploding wombats into them before they themselves exploded.

Rodney knocked wombats and blasted the city flat, earning gold and increasing the power of his weapon. He went on a rampage with a flaming bat, sending the screen into bright convulsions of explosions and stars. The level was almost clear when the screen went dark, and the lights above him snapped off.

Weird. Rodney sat up, bringing his leg down from the wall. It tingled as blood rushed back into the forgotten limb. He rubbed it and stood. "Uncle Ray?" he called. "I think the power's out." He paused, listening.

There were footsteps out in the stairwell. Rodney hobbled to his door limping from a sleeping leg. He opened the door to the darkness. The sunlight from the window was added to the room, which only caused the shadows to leap and lean. He heard a rapid patter down the stairs.

"Ray?" He went out into the hall, reaching for the rail to guide him down. "Ray?" he called again. The floor squeaked as someone moved away from him. He reached the bottom level, listening to the ticking of the clock. His heart kickstarted and roared in his chest. His face grew hot with adrenaline.

The door to the library was shut, but the red light of the setting sun gleamed underneath. He tiptoed toward it with his hands out. He felt the wood of the sliding door and drew it back.

The chair was empty. Ray was gone. Out the window he could see the declining light of the sun as if it had been captured and dragged down by the black forest behind the house. He spun around at a clatter in the kitchen—some pots jostled. The urge to run was strong, but he forced himself toward the noise.

"Ray?" he couldn't help the panic that crept into his voice. His face was beaded with sweat, and his shirt stuck to him. The a/c must be off, too. He shivered despite the hot and put his hands to the swinging door of the kitchen.

The curtains were drawn, sealing the room in blackness. Rodney entered, but the eerie touch of spiderwebs across his face caused him to sputter and back away, slashing the air in front of him with his hands.

The heel of his foot caught the edge of something, and he fell. The noise from hitting the wood floor sounded like an alarm; the whole house rang with his fall. He caught up his breath and listened for any movement. Nothing.

Rising, Rodney felt a breath at his ear though only the clock was behind him. He spooked and ran into the library, to the window. His fingers clawed at the bottom, trying to raise it up. There was a sound, a gurgle, a voice. Rodney searched the darkness behind him, but felt the window give and lift.

He pulled it up and put his foot to the sill. He ducked under to get his head out and launched himself away from the house. He misjudged the ground, falling farther than he expected, and landed badly. His body registered injuries as he rose, but he ran before the ache of his hands, the pain of his knee, and the sting of his ankles swarmed him.

He ran, looking back at the house. Nothing pursued. He turned his head in time to see the low wood fence before him. He collided with it full speed. The slats cracked, but the crossbeam held and Rodney was thrown to the ground.

He groaned and coughed. In the darkness he saw a figure leap. He stumbled back. The figure jumped again, this time landing on his chest. It was small and furry and he felt claws dig into his shirt. He screamed and rolled, the creature jumped free, and Rodney hobbled away, limping from a banged knee on one leg and a turned ankle on the other.

He spun to defend himself, but noticed only a golden rabbit, fat for a rabbit, staring at him with its ears erect. Rodney flushed with embarrassment and relief: Ray's rabbits. He couldn't remember the name of the fuzzy sun hopping away from him, Trumpet-something. Rodney huffed and felt the urge to cry.

Freaked myself out, he thought as he walked back to the house. He went up to the back door of the kitchen, but it was locked. He walked around to the front; the shadows were already cooling the day.

Rodney noticed Ray's car was still there, next to his workshop. He hobbled up to the front steps, lifting his head. His throat seized up. Before him stood a black figure just over two feet tall. His eyes were a deep black, blacker than the black around him.

The creature opened his mouth, showing a glinting of teeth. A smell of sweet rot filled Rodney's nose. His insides churned and clenched. The figure lunged at him with a shriek, striking his head. Rodney fell.

The creature disappeared into the darkness, somewhere into the woods. Rodney shifted to his elbows and vomited. His shoulders rolled as he expelled the contents of his stomach. He emptied, but his stomach still struggled to eject the void inside him. He lay on the ground, panting before the pool of his throw-up.

The door behind him opened and Ray came out. "Rodney?" He saw him, bowed down and quivering. "Whoa, you okay?"

"I got sick," he managed.

"Those snakes speaking to you too, huh?"

"What?" Rodney looked up at him, wiping back his wet mop of hair.

"Those snake sandwiches. Hot dogs. Had a few words with them myself over the porcelain pit."

Rodney stood. His knees felt wobbly. "What are you talking about?"

"The toilet, man. I was puking my guts out, too. Come on, why don't you relax a tad?"

Rodney followed him in. The lights were back on, but Rodney was too tired to ask about it or mention his weird encounter, if it was an encounter. Maybe he was feverish.

He stopped in the kitchen for a swig of water and then went into the library to flop down on the couch across from Ray's reading chair. The window was still open. He wondered whether the thing he had seen was what Ray was always talking to, rapscallion or scalawag or any of the innumerable names he blurted out every day.

The air was cool, and he shivered. Rodney rose to shut the window. He placed his hand at the top and pulled down. As the frame met the sill, the phone rang from the stair room.

It was a rare thing for the phone to ring. Ray joked that he spent more time talking to the phone than into it. "I got it," Rodney called out as he jogged to it.

He checked the time on the clock above where the phone rested. He ignored the symbols of the clock and focused on the position of the hands. It was nearly 8:30.

Rodney lifted the phone, "Hello?"

"Hey, sweetie."

"Hi, Mom." A cloud gathered at the back of his skull and he felt the sting of being left behind again.

"How are you?"

"Okay. I threw up."

"I'm sorry. Are you sick? Was it something you ate?"

"I just want to leave." He bent forward to rest his head against the wall as if onto his mother's shoulder. The ticking of the clock was like a heartbeat. He closed his eyes and imagined she was brushing his hair back, trying to tame its unruliness.

"I know, but the summer will go quickly and I'll come get you then." She went on describing the town, the school he'd attend in the fall, and their housing options. He let her drone on without interruption and offered nothing when she asked if there was anything else. He barely grunted when she said, "I love you, bye."

He held the receiver to his face for a second longer before setting it back on its cradle. He watched the second hand cycle over the strange clock. His face was like the face of the clock, full of strange things, symbols, mysteries, but he let the hand wipe them free and clear of his mind.

His shoulders sagged and he felt the pull of his bed. He lumbered up the stairs to his scarab-cluttered bedroom. His fingers trailed along the wall, feeling the scrolls and curls of Ray's symbols. In the stair room there weren't any creatures, only waves and strange squiggles like words. He imagined being able to decipher them through his touch.

At the top of the stairs he let his eyes follow the central beam as it continued up to the third floor. He slid his hand on the railing, passing by the bedrooms until he arrived at the small spiral staircase that went to the observatory.

When he was younger, he had been afraid to climb those stairs. The gaps seemed child-sized, the ascent was too steep, and it just led to the ceiling. Pushing through the trapdoor to enter the observatory seemed like great fun until you were pressed against it, straining against its weight, standing perilously on a thin step at the top of a great fall.

Ray seemed to think that it was interesting or important to gaze at the stars. Rodney had spent more time gazing at the stairs than the stars.

He was about to turn to his bed when the floor above him shifted. He looked up and listened. He heard Ray speaking, indistinctly. He took two steps to see if he could make out any words.

Ray's voice got louder and he heard: "I brought him into this world. I can take him out." Ray sounded angry, but he paused as if waiting for a reply. If there was one, Rodney couldn't hear it. Then Ray broke in again. "You do your job, and I'll do mine. We'll bring this whole thing down on his head."

Rodney's mind swirled with confusion and anxiety. Ray's voice had calmed and become quiet. All he could hear was a low murmuring until the floor shifted again as Ray moved across it. The trapdoor swung open. Rodney slipped back to his room as Ray descended. He shut the door, but leaned against it and listened. He heard the slam of Ray's door and then silence.

Rodney cracked open his door. After a minute of silence there was a sob, a gasp of sorrow that came from Ray's room. Or so he thought. Perhaps it was just a trick of the wind. He listened longer, but heard nothing.

He quietly got ready for bed and eased himself into the sheets, flicking off his hat into the dark. Something was wrong with Ray. Either Ray was crazy, like his dad thought, or something more, like Otis thought. His uncle was planning something. He decided to find out what that was.

Rodney fell asleep to the sound of the creaking wood as the heat of the day was lost into the cool evening air and the night wind moved.

CHAPTER FOUR

ONE LITTLE WORD

odney lurched into the morning light with a gasp. He kicked the sheets off his sweaty legs. His head was heavy and his tingling arms felt dense. He must've slept on them. He dressed quickly and tiptoed downstairs.

He took a quick peek at the stair room clock embedded in the wall. It was half past the circle with horns, which made it nine thirty. He'd slept late again.

He found a note from Ray in the kitchen, mentioning that he had knocked three times to wake Rodney, but had given up and gone into town. There was cereal in the cabinet. He'd be back in time for lunch. Rodney thought it would be a good day to speak to Otis. The events of yesterday had made his mysterious warning seem more real. He could chat with him and be back before Ray came home.

He ate, grabbed his hat and slingshot (a likely alibi if Ray beat him home), and jumped on his bike. He stood as he pumped down the gravel road to the highway. Sweat streamed down his face and his shirt stuck to his back, but he didn't sit on the seat till he reached the bridge midway to the mailbox.

Once he had exited the low-grown forest and was on pavement, his trip went faster. He could see Otis's house easily. It couldn't be much more than a quarter mile away. He kept a slow pace since he didn't want to arrive huffing and drenched in sweat.

He turned up the gravel driveway and was halfway to the house when a white car, colored dirty, bounced past him. Otis parked in front of his house and stood waiting until he pulled up.

"Glad you came," Otis said. Otis wore a white short-sleeved shirt and black tie. "Go to church this morning?" He squinted at Rodney in the bright sunlight.

"No," he answered sheepishly. "I slept in. Ray tried to wake me."

"You should go to church. It's good for young people. You shouldn't miss it."

"Is that where you were?"

"For a little bit, yes. I find it calming to sit in a church. I take in some of the early service at Sacred Heart. Then I meet some friends for coffee. I'm old, talking about the world is my church." They stood before each other, staring at their shoes, pushing the dirt with their toes. Otis cleared his throat and said, "Come in and let me get you a drink."

Soon Rodney was sitting under a wobbly fan that made the ceiling creak as it rotated. He held a glass of ice tea so cold it stung his hand. Rodney took a sip. It wasn't as sweet as his mom's.

"What's your name again?"

"Rodney."

"Rodney, right, right." Otis sat in a chair across from the couch where Rodney sat. He leaned forward like he wanted to sell something quickly and quietly. "So I suppose you've noticed your uncle's weird."

It wasn't a question, but Rodney nodded anyway.

"This is going to sound strange to you, I know." He wiped his forehead with the back of his wrist. "Where to start, hm . . . I suppose you heard what happened a few years back? How he went crazy? Talking to himself and the like?"

"I thought he was being funny, but mom thinks it's 'cause he's lonely."

"It happened suddenly. I used to go to that church, White Pine Baptist. Your grandpa built it with Raymond's help way back when. It was a fine place for church until Raymond got it in his head that the building was all wrong. He went and ruined it. That was the beginning."

"Ruined it? How?"

Otis smiled and squinted. "Go look at it sometime and you'll see why. But that's not all. Raymond's preaching started getting darker. Scary stuff on demons. Temptations, powers, dominions."

"I didn't know Uncle Ray was a preacher."

Otis put a hand to his scruffy chin. "Yeah? Oh, he used to be a preacher. Good one too. At least until he went nuts. Scared people with his rantings of the unseen world." He wiggled his fingers as he said this.

"I'm full up of church," Otis continued. "But I believe, I still believe, 'specially in the spirits. I just don't think you court them. That's not our place. Leave the spirit world be, but Raymond, no, he had to stir 'em up. He'd call 'em out in church, by name!" He raised his hands beseechingly and looked to the ceiling.

"By name? You mean, demons? He knew demon names?"

Otis leaned back and crossed his legs. "That's right. You wanna know what I call someone who talks to demons?"

Rodney dropped his jaw, signaling "yes."

"Demonic."

Rodney's mind struggled back against this new picture of Ray, silly Uncle Ray. He searched his memory for confirmation to these accusations. Suddenly his father's words came into this new light. His father called Ray a "fanatic," someone who believed in "hooey" and "bugaboo."

He recalled the face of his mother at these expressions and saw not humorous denial, but quiet agreement. His mother, his father, and now Otis all saw Ray as some crazy person. His mother thought it was harmless, but his father's view was worse, and Otis's worst of all.

Rodney emitted a single response, "Whoa."

Otis glanced at the walls like he expected them to burst open. "He started letting his beard get wild and wearing all that tie-dye. Called himself a rainbow warrior. I didn't understand it, but I didn't like it."

"I don't like the tie-dye stuff, either."

Otis smiled at that and continued. "I left soon after all that started." He leaned back in his chair and stared at the ceiling. "Quite a preacher, too. I've heard plenty shake the pulpit and rattle the rafters, but no one could send a shiver up my spine like Raymond. And with just a single word."

Rodney tried to imagine Ray acting like the preachers on television, microphone in one hand, waving the other. All he could imagine at the moment was Ray singing along to Iron Maiden.

"One of the last times I heard him preach, it was on the Temptations a' Jesus, and Raymond was hollerin' about the devil when all of a sudden he stopped talking and his eyes got real big." Otis spread his rough hands beside his face to give an idea of the size. "He was silent for a long while. I just thought he forgot what he was saying. I think I always had my suspicions of Raymond. He just wasn't right. Too many long walks in the woods, bad with people. I never thought he was called to speak the Word. He just stood there looking around, not at anyone particular, but just to the side of us or right above our heads. Then he looked right at me, well not at me, but a little through me, I can't explain it, and he said . . . 'Rotsnogger.'"

Rodney was so surprised that he blurted out a single, quick laugh before he could clamp his mouth shut. He held his hand to his lips.

Otis ignored the outburst and continued. "Then he said, 'That'll be enough of your silliness, Rotsnogger,' and he came out from behind the pulpit. He had clearly lost it; everyone could see that."

"What'd he do after that?"

"Who knows? I was so offended I walked out. I only went back once more . . . " His voice trailed off, revisiting the scene in his mind.

Rodney called him back with a question, "Why'd you think he did it?"

"He cracked. All that talk of demons or talking to demons. Believe me, there's a lot of people that think he knows a bit too much about demonic activity. They think he's conjuring."

"What's conjuring?"

"Invoking demons." Otis leaned forward to search his face.

That would explain the terrifying encounter yesterday. But why would Ray be involved with demons? Rodney took the last gulp of tea. The cold liquid made his teeth ache. He set the glass down when his host stood. Otis grabbed his glass and said, "More?"

He wasn't ready to bike back to Ray's yet, so he nodded his head. Otis went back into the kitchen and Rodney stood to peruse the room. Across the tops of every table, the mantle, the piano, and hung on the wall were pictures that spanned the years from black and white into color. Rodney recognized Otis and a woman he presumed was his wife. For many years Otis had a bushy mustache, but about the time the woman disappeared from the pictures, the mustache did as well.

Rodney recalled his father's bristly chin digging into his stomach when they'd wrestle. They only wrestled when he was little. Last time he'd tried to grapple, his dad smacked away his hands and said "scat" before returning to the newspaper.

Rodney also noticed a boy, at first appearing in the woman's arms, then next just below the knees, then slowly rising until he could look down on the place where Otis was going bald. He was built just like Otis—long, copper-wire legs and arms. Otis reentered the room.

"I didn't know you had a son," he said, thumping the picture with his finger.

"I don't," Otis answered without looking up. He set both glasses on the table between them. "Not anymore."

"Oh."

"He drove him away." Otis stared at his glass.

"Who did?"

"Raymond. It was his greatest failure."

"What happened?"

"Gerald had his demons."

"Demons?" His voice came out more alarmed than he intended. Otis looked up.

"Problems. Drugs, drinking, spiritual problems." Rodney returned to his seat unsure of how to reply. Otis continued, "He was friends with your uncle. Your mother, too."

"Was she his girlfriend?" This seemed significant to ask.

"For a time."

Rodney was shocked. Such things seemed like they should be kept a secret. He didn't know why.

"Gerald went to Raymond at my suggestion. I thought it would help to talk to a man of God, but he . . . he . . . "

Otis sputtered and his face twisted. "He came back scared, no, terrified. Raymond had . . . well, I don't know what he said or did. Gerald wouldn't tell me. But what drove him off was Ray's final outburst, the thing that forced the congregation to dismiss him from the pulpit."

Otis stood and faced the wall, looking at a picture of Gerald. "I got the story from a friend who still goes to White Pines. He said Raymond was preaching the deliverance from the evil one, when Gerald got up to go. When Raymond saw him, he yelled out some nonsense word and threw his Bible at him. Hit 'em right between the eyes, then Raymond started ringing the church bell like a madman and the whole building filled with bees."

"Bees?"

"That's right, bees. Been living in the walls. Still do, I hear. They're fine unless you rile 'em up."

"Then what?"

"Well, they called me and I went to pick up Gerald. Blood streaming out his nose. Gerald ran away the next day, leaving only a note."

Otis stood and walked over to a desk. He unlocked a drawer. After shuffling through some paper he withdrew an envelope and handed it to Rodney.

Rodney didn't want to open it, but Otis stood over him waiting so he pulled out the index card inside. It was faded and yellowing, showing wear on the edges, like it was handled often. On the back, in hasty print, was written:

Dad,

I'm sorry. He has driven me away.

—G

"Who?" Rodney asked after reading it.

"Who else? Raymond."

"Why did he do that?"

Otis shook his head and stared at the floor. "No idea. Aside from a few neighborly comments we haven't talked since."

Otis slumped into his chair, but his eyes were still drilling the floor. Rodney placed the glass back on the table and backed away. "Thanks for the tea, Otis."

Otis waved his hand without speaking.

"I hope your son comes back."

Otis shook his head and rested his elbows on his knees. "He won't. He abandoned me, just like you've been abandoned here."

Rodney turned and let the screen door slap hard against the door frame. He felt his face flush. He got on his bike and stomped on the pedals. As he rode back to the street he decided to check out the church sometime. Maybe he could find someone else to tell the story of when Ray first started talking to demons. He shivered as he popped his front wheel over the potholes. He biked back to Ray's wondering what to believe.

* * *

Rodney arrived at Ray's looping driveway in a torrent of dust and huffs. His bike skidded in the gravel with each long thrust of his legs. The wind was enough to cause the branches to slap his face.

Crossing over the bridge he saw rocks perfect for his slingshot. Not quite ready to encounter Ray, he slid and slung his bike to the ground. He took the slingshot from his back pocket and marched down to the river to pick out smooth stones for slinging.

He fit five or so in each pocket and looked for targets. Bullseyes on trees from where branches had broken off, looking like swollen eyes, became his primary victims. Rocks *pinged* and *panged* into the foliage, increasing his satisfaction.

He moved his aim to a large rock in the water, just above the rapid current. His shots skittered off the dome into the black flow with deep *ploops*. The river under the forest's canopy cooled him off. A breeze caused him to shiver.

He paused to gather more ammo and in the quiet he heard a low hum. It was a soft murmuring sound that grew louder the farther he moved from the water. He walked up a slope to discover the source. As he reached the top he looked down and saw a great oak split in half, part still planted, the other prostrate on the ground. It was rotten within, and out of the hollow streamed a host of bees.

Rodney scrambled down the slope and peered into the black hole from a safe distance. He could just make out the bulbous hive hanging inside the tree. Bees flew out of it like smoke.

He reached into his back pocket where he had put a large, smooth stone and set it into the slingshot's pouch. He aimed, and for a second it seemed like the hive was pulsating, a black heart. He drew back the cords until they were taut, and released the stone missile. It sank into the throbbing mass, and everything went still before the tree erupted in bees.

The cloud expanded from the mouth of the tree like a flower in bloom. Rodney realized that a thick spear of bees was surging toward him. "Jeez!" he cried and turned to run.

He abandoned his bike and fled from the angry constellation of bees. The forest seemed to shiver with their racket. The whole way he could hear the murmuring, and he half expected to see the fist-sized black cloud following him.

He made it to the front steps and collapsed. The sun was straight above him. He looked for Ray's yellow Honda. The space beside the house where he parked it was still empty. He caught his breath and considered his options. The muffler was loud enough to announce Ray's return from afar, so he decided that if he wanted to snoop, now was the time.

If Ray really were conjuring demons, there'd have to be evidence of it somewhere. He wasn't sure how a demon would be conjured, but he thought it might involve animal sacrifice of some sort. Of all the possible places, the workshop was the most likely for Ray to cause trouble.

He walked over and lifted up the great wood bar that kept the wide doors shut. It was cool inside even though the small window unit was off. The high ceiling was cast in shadows, but he could make out the dark patches of birds' nests built atop the beams. Squeaks and chirps echoed periodically.

There were a series of worktables with a variety of saws on top or vice grips holding rocking chair parts. Wood of every cut, kind, and length was stacked or laid against the walls. He walked around, inspecting Ray's current projects. The smell of sawn wood filled his nostrils. Ray's tools were neatly laid out on the table or hanging on the wall. On one table, he saw the box of carving tools Ray used when chiseling something new on the surface of some nook in the house.

No signs of animal sacrifice, however. He laughed at his foolishness. He couldn't imagine Ray killing anything. His tenderness with the rabbits was evidence enough of that. Against the far wall he noticed the failed attempts at bat-making. Each one badly misshapen. He tripped against a table leg and sent four rockers clattering to the ground. He paused to listen for the rumble of Ray's car as if the noise would call him home. Aside from the intermittent peeps from the birds in the rafters, there was no sound. In the back, he saw a great wood cabinet. If there were something to hide, that was the only possible place to hide it.

Rodney reached the cabinet and began opening the ornate drawers. The first held woodworking magazines. Another was crammed full of receipts and pay stubs. The third was filled to the top with disposable ear plugs, orange and yellow. The final drawer held nothing more than some correspondence. The letters were haphazardly stacked, and fingering through them he noticed that they were all sent from a man in Italy.

He flipped open a yellowing page and noticed strange words. The letters were all written in what he supposed was Italian, so he tossed them back into the drawer. Digging deeper, he discovered a cardboard tube about the length of his forearm. He pulled it out. It was from the same man who had sent the letters, Filippo Campanella. He brought it over to a nearby table to open it. Inside was a rolled blueprint. He spread it out over the table, pinning the top corners with a hammer and chisel.

At the top was written *"Alvarium Maleficorum,"* and it appeared to be building plans for a little house. There were four rooms—two smaller circular rooms at the back and two oblong rooms in the front. The side view of the building showed it to be a dome, like a bulbous cathedral.

There were other words scrawled along the side. The word *"Cruentationis"* was underlined and there was a star next to the phrase *"le api sono sangue del cuore."* He read aloud, *"La porta dei demoni,*" and followed a line that indicated the central wall dividing the building vertically. He didn't know Italian, but *demoni* certainly looked like demon. Perhaps Ray was involved in conjuring after all.

Rodney heard the sputter and bang of Ray's car. He quickly rolled up the plans, grabbed the tube, and kicked the drawer shut. He ran to the door and slipped out into the bright heat of noon. Squinting his eyes, he shut the doors to the workshop and carefully stuffed the plans back into the tube. He hopped over to the tree line and tossed the tube into the brush. He'd recover it later.

Ray's yellow car slurred to a stop, a billow of dust coming over the roof. Ray opened the door and rocked himself to his feet. "Rodney? Yo, Rod? I found your bike by the bridge? Hello?"

Rodney came from around the building. Ray was wearing a blue blazer over a white button up shirt. Only his tie bore a spiral of color. "Hey, Uncle Ray," he called. "Yeah, I left it in the woods."

Ray pulled it out of the back of his car. "I thought you might've. Either that or the varlets got you. I called but didn't hear anything, so I assumed you just walked home."

"Yeah, I had a run-in with some angry bees."

Ray looked up, concerned. "Bees?" He shook his head. "Where'd you come across bees?"

"Down by the river. I don't know. They had their hive in a broken tree."

Ray seemed to consider this as though it were grave news. "Careful," he said, stroking his beard. "Bees can be mean."

"No kidding. I felt like they chased me all the way here."

Ray laughed and they went inside. "Let's get some lunch. Once the sun gets at a lesser angle we can hit some baseballs."

Rodney gave a groan in response. Ray chuckled.

Perhaps tomorrow he could bike into town to the library and find an Italian dictionary. He could check out the ruined church, too. Maybe the plans held some clue to the strange things happening around here. Until then he had to devise some plan to avoid playing baseball. Maybe he could feign sickness.

* * *

It was inevitable, once Rodney saw his uncle's high leg kick, that he would get hit. He lay in bed with a bag of frozen blackberries held to his face and cringed at each recollection of his most recent injury. The pitch, the swing, the dancing stars, the grass beneath his head, the trickle of blood down his cheek.

Ray knocked on the door. "Can I get you anything else?"

He shook his head.

"Aw, come on, Rod. You aren't mad at me, are you?"

"What else could've happened?" His voice lilted peevishly.

"That was a freak event. I've never seen something like that. The best hitter in the world couldn't do that in a thousand years."

Ray had been throwing fastballs that hissed past and ricocheted off the shop wall. He painted a white square behind his nephew and then marched off sixty feet, planting a bucket of balls beside himself. He crouched over, glaring, as if trying to make out the signs from the catcher. He shook his head, then raised and rested his glove on his paunch.

Rodney waited, cemented to the spot, bugs alighting on his nose, the grass swaying at his feet. He wanted to wiggle his bat, shift his feet like his dad told him to, but he was fixed in place, as if in stone. Ray rotated his hips and threw his leg up. Rodney's eyes bulged as Ray lunged and catapulted his arm, releasing the howling cowhide ball. Rodney fell away as the bat collapsed into a weak arc, missing the projectile. The missed ball made the entire shop thunder.

"Stay in there, head down," Ray said, choosing another ball.

Whoosh, whoosh, whoosh, was followed by *whiff, whiff, whiff* and the sound of the ball smacking the shop. On the second-to-last swing he spun around in a full circle.

"You're spinning like a pinwheel," Ray remarked, rubbing down a ball, probably just to give him time to rest and reset his feet. Rodney dug in like the batters on television.

Ray tugged his hat lower and said, "Give a big swing."

On the ensuing swing, Rodney had connected with the pitch off the inside part of the bat, deflecting the ball into his face. There was a meaty *smack* and a burst of light. Rodney keeled over and sprawled on the ground. The day flashed and spun. Rodney moaned as his uncle pulled him up and helped him to his room.

Now, Rodney stared at the beetles that were carved on the crown molding. "My nose isn't bleeding anymore."

"Nosebleeds are good for you."

"I hate baseball."

"Baseball is good for you."

"I missed every pitch except that last one."

"Oh, but it was a beautiful swing."

Rodney lifted the bag from his eye. "Is it black?"

Ray gave an appreciative whistle. "It's a nice shiner."

Rodney smiled. "Mom would kill you."

Ray laughed. "Remember that time we went canoeing, and she thought I pushed you off the dock?"

"You did push me off the dock."

"Yeah, but she thought I did it on purpose."

"That's what we all think!"

Ray knocked on the wall. "Well, life's full of mysteries." His grin made his beard bristle like a porcupine jumping. "What I remember is how preternaturally calm you were. You know," he said, letting his finger and thumb disappear into his facial hair, "I don't think I've ever seen you afraid."

"Peternaturally?"

"Preter—, preternaturally. It means beyond the natural."

"I've been afraid lots of times."

"But you never act like it. Like that time with Lucasta's dog, Mordecai. He knocked you down and chomped your finger, but you didn't even scream."

"I don't remember that. Who's Lucasta?"

"She's a friend, an angel really. Lives right down the road in fact. We went to visit her, I guess that was around five years ago. You would've been six or seven."

The memory returned to him. A big dog surprised him. He remembered being scared and then sitting on a soft couch eating ice cream. "Yeah, I kinda remember that. I guess I got ice cream afterwards. I remember blackberry ice cream. It was the best."

"Yup, ole Lucasta's full of treats. I remembered thinking how brave you were."

"Well, I was scared today. Could you tell?"

"Being brave is not the same as not being afraid. It's not bravery unless it comes with fear. Every pitch, you hung in there even though you didn't want to. That's bravery."

Rodney gave a *humph* sound and dabbed his nose with a wet rag.

* * *

That night dinner was a Lauter special, Dinner Waffles. Rodney was willing to put away his grudge for waffles.

Ray, ever the night owl, was sipping coffee. He looked up as Rodney entered the room. "Hey, slugger, how's the peeper?"

Rodney poked the purplish eye and said, "Not so bad."

Ray shut the book and stood. "Ready for waffles? I wanted to wait till you came down, because you have to eat a waffle within minutes of being cooked or else it's no good."

Rodney followed his uncle into the kitchen. Ray sighed and exclaimed, "I like my coffee like I like my chocolate cake."

"Um, black?"

"No, sweet with milk and loads of chocolate." He refilled his glass and squirted a *blop* of chocolate syrup in it. He stirred and flipped on the waffle iron. He opened the lid and waved Rodney over. "Check this out."

The waffle iron looked like a regular waffle iron. Rodney stared back at Ray and said, "What's the big deal?"

Ray smiled. "You don't see it?"

He looked again and noticed the hexagonal shapes in a flower form. "Oh, it's like your house."

"Right," Ray pointed a finger. "We're here, there's the dining room, foyer, living room, den, library, and in the center is the stair room."

"Cool."

"And if I just fill three, then I have the second floor."

"And if you want to add the attic, you just fill one."

"So how hungry are you?" Ray said with a wiggle of his eyebrows.

"I could eat a whole house."

Ray picked up the waffle batter and poured it on thick. "That's what I like to hear. First floor coming up."

Again before they ate Ray hoisted a bite of waffle and said, "I love waffles. I love waffles. I love waffles."

Rodney set out dividing his waffle into even parts. "Why do you and mom do that?" Rodney asked.

"Do what?"

"Say you love things three times."

"It was your grandpa that taught us. Told us to practice loving things. It was always easy to love waffles, but last Thursday when I did that with carrots . . . " He shook his head. "*Euchhh.* That was hard."

"You don't like carrots?"

Ray stuck his tongue out and shook his head.

"Then why even eat them if you don't like them?"

"How else will I learn to like them if I don't practice?"

Rodney ate the entire floor plan of the house with a second helping of the second floor. Ray ate three first floors and leaned back to sip on his coffee.

"So what are the plans for tomorrow, Hot Rod?"

"I kinda want to bike into town. Check out the library."

"You want books?" Ray pointed in the direction of his library. "Cause I have lots of books. Classics, new fiction, non-fiction, scientifiction . . . "

"Scientifiction?"

"Sci-fi."

"Oh. I didn't know you read that. I thought it was just, like, boring books."

Ray laughed. "I like boring books too, but I read tons of science fiction. Asimov, Burroughs, Philip K. Dick, Wolfe, Cordwainer, trust me. I could have a reading list of fifty books in ten minutes if you wanted."

Rodney stood, "That's okay, Ray. I just want to wander around the library for a bit."

"I understand. Just want to get away from the house. My monk's lifestyle isn't for everyone."

Rodney yawned, and his bones felt loose. He slouched back in his chair, tired and heavy. Ray cleaned up the dishes and waved Rodney on to bed. Somehow he was able to stumble up the stairs and go through the night rituals of brushing teeth and changing into pajamas.

He entered his room and looked out the window. It was too dark to see anything from his lighted room. A stone could've been rolled in front of the window, for all he knew. He opened it a bit so that the night sounds flowed in. It was comforting to hear the chatter of crickets and the belching of toads.

He flipped the lights off, stretched out on the mattress, and let his mind wander. He imagined himself hitting balls over the fence, the crack of his wood bat, and high fives from amazed teammates as he entered the dugout. He imagined hitting one into the gap, feeling second base under his spikes as he turned to stretch a double into a triple. He saw himself slide feet first, red dirt thrown into the sky. He heard the pop of a glove's leather and felt the slap of the tag hitting his leg too late. He imagined standing to pump his fist, but he stumbled. His foot ached like it was pierced with a nail.

Rodney's eyes snapped awake as he realized the pain in his foot was real. There was a figure the size of his backpack at the end of his bed. Rodney cried out and curled his legs up to his chest.

"Wha—what? Hello?" His spine was rigid.

The figure shifted from foot to foot. Fear rippled up Rodney's neck, his heart sputtered, and his arms contracted to his chest. He looked to the door, which was shut, but the window was wide open.

"Did Birthless wake you?" The creature's voice was screechy, like glass on glass. It was too dark in the room to see anything more than its size.

"Who are you?" Rodney's voice was raspy. There was an acrid smell in the room; it irritated his eyes and throat.

"Birthless is Birthless."

Rodney felt a lump rise in his throat like he was about to vomit. "What do you want?" he choked out.

"Torment. Birthless wants torment."

"Oh my god, oh my god."

"Someday Birthless will bite off your toes and peel your skin back."

"Oh my god." Rodney pulled the sheet to his nose.

"Birthless will grind you to dust." At this the figure rose on stubby, hairy feet; tiny wings spread out from his back, and he opened wide his long, bony arms.

"Jesus, oh Jesus." Rodney pushed himself off the bed and fell to the floor. He scrambled to the corner of the room and cowered. The creature had frozen, standing at the edge of his bed with his shoulder slumped.

Rodney breathed through his nose. It was a little runny with flecks and bubbles of mucus sputtering out. Birthless remained frozen on the bed. Rodney couldn't tell if he was breathing or not.

"Are you there?"

There was a long pause before the creature answered. "Yes."

More silence. Rodney drew another breath. "What are you doing?"

"You spoke the Name."

"Oh." They sat in the dark together. The noxious fumes decreased, and Rodney's eyes quit stinging.

Rodney slowly stood. In a quiet voice he said, "What are you waiting for?"

"You spoke the Name," it responded in a low grumble.

"So . . . what? You have to obey me?"

The demon paused again and then rasped, "You. Spoke. The NAME."

Rodney wanted the creature to go away, but more than that, he wanted the creature to stay away. He had to make sure the creature would not return. "What are you?"

"I am diabolos, a creature of darkness." The creature's voice was barely a growl.

Rodney slowly stood, keeping his back against the wall. He edged over to the light switch and flipped it. The light hurt his eyes, but the creature howled. Without thinking Rodney killed the light and crumpled back to his corner.

"Birthless HATES the light. HATES IT!"

Rodney's sight was filled with blotches of color as his eyes fought to readjust to the dark. His mind settled on a solution.

"Then I want you to run in a circle and yell . . . 'I love sunshine' every morning at sunrise until . . . until you fall over. And . . . and . . . don't come back."

He waited for another response. There was silence and Rodney wondered if the black spot he stared at was nothing at all. He was beginning to doubt the whole event when Birthless erupted in a great scream, a howl that shook the walls.

Rodney put his hands in front of him defensively. Suddenly Birthless turned and leaped out the window into the dark. Rodney squeaked in fear at the quick movement. He stood in the corner listening, but there was no other sound aside from his own heavy breathing. He ran to the window and shut it. His heart thundered in his ears. He felt alone, but not safe.

He climbed back into his bed. Surely Ray had heard the scream. It was quiet now. It hardly seemed real. He checked his foot for bite marks, but found nothing. He rubbed his toe, trying to recall the pain that woke him up.

Rodney slid under his sheets and rested his head on the pillow. It must have been a dream. It felt so real. His eyelids sank down. He felt like the entire night sky was burying his eyes in sleep. He sank lower in his bed and slept.

CHAPTER FIVE

STRIVING

Rodney woke to the sound of shouting coming from outside. He sat up and scooted to the window to press his face against the glass. There was an indistinct sound coming from the front yard. He opened the window and stuck his head out into the early morning. Definitely a voice, but he couldn't hang far enough out of his window to see what was going on in the front, nor could he hear what was being yelled. He dashed out of the room and down the stairs.

Leaping the last five steps, Rodney landed with a thud. He stumbled to the door, ripped the chain back and twisted the three deadbolts. Slinging open the door, he stared at an empty yard. He was too late or else he had imagined the whole thing.

Rodney felt a hand on his shoulder and jumped. Ray stood behind him wearing a tie-dye bathrobe, the colors spiraling like a giant lollipop.

"Morning, sunshine porcupine. Up for something hearty?"

Rodney rubbed his floppy hair, trying to make it less undignified. "Uh, yeah, sounds good."

Ray clicked his teeth and tossed his head to the side, motioning him into the dining room. On the table were two plates, one half covered in food, the other pristine. Rodney sat down before the clean plate and Ray pulled the lid off of a pan, revealing scrambled eggs and a couple of links of sausage.

"Enjoy the eggs," he said. "Those'll be the last for a while. Grover's is out."

Grover was the local grocer, notable for his big purple signage. "Out of eggs? Why?"

"Well, out of locally produced eggs. Taste better when you know the chicken." He gave a quick laugh. "Without our friendly neighborhood eggs we might have to live like regular kings for a few weeks."

Rodney tried not to imagine living here for weeks. He drew the food onto his plate with his fork and dug in.

"How's the peeper?"

Rodney lightly touched his swollen eye. "Still hurts."

"Probably be tender for a few days. How was your sleep?"

"Fine." He responded instinctively and swallowed the eggs without chewing. He was thinking through yesterday's events. What Otis said about Ray conjuring demons and then the creature he'd encountered last night. The *de-ah-blos* or some-thing. He needed to know what was going on and he couldn't ask Ray. Or maybe he could, what was there to lose?

"Actually something weird happened. Or, at least, I think it happened."

Ray cleaned his teeth with a curling of his tongue and tossed his napkin on the table. "Oh yeah? What's that?"

"I think there was a little, uh, monster in my room. Or, like, a dream maybe? He bit my toes and was making threats."

"Was it scary?"

Ray didn't seem all that disturbed or concerned. "Kinda. But . . . I don't know, he stopped being scary."

Ray went back to sawing and scooping his breakfast. "Did you use the Name?" He asked, in between swallows.

"The Name?"

"Iesous? Jesus?"

"Yea-sous?"

"That's the Greek pronunciation of Jesus' name."

Rodney looked away. "Maybe. I know mom doesn't like me to."

Ray spoke while he chewed. "Why not? That's what names are for. Anyway, demons are subject to the Name."

"Subject to the Name, like they're subject to stone?"

"Names are like stones. Yeah." Ray gazed ahead like he was doing math in his head, his head bobbing at the solution.

"What does that mean?"

"Dunno."

"Does that mean they have to do what you tell them?"

Ray shrugged. "I wouldn't know. I've never done it."

Anytime Ray was slow to spin a story or expound on an explanation, Rodney grew suspicious. The times Ray had lured him into a room for projectile pie or with a bucket of water above the door were the times Ray wouldn't elaborate on why he had wanted Rodney to enter the room. Unless he was at the edge of a nap or the end of a book, Ray was always leaping into stories, riddles, and recollections. Rodney tried to press him further. "Where do you get this stuff?"

Ray laughed and leaned back. "Books. I wouldn't worry about it."

"It was probably just a weird dream," he said and searched Ray's face for clues.

"Probably." Ray picked his plate up. "Full?"

Rodney pushed his plate to his uncle who carried it into the kitchen. "Come on," Ray called over his shoulder. "Let's get a move on the day. I thought we could practice some more baseball after we get the paper."

Rodney hollered over his eggs, "No way!"

From the kitchen he heard laughing, then there was a clatter of dishes. "No scraps for the scalawags!" Ray bellowed. "Too bad. So what time will you be off to the library?"

Rodney scooted back from the table. "Probably bike over now. They'll be open by the time I get there."

"Ya sure I can't tempt you with some of my books?" he said while hitching a thumb over his shoulder. "There's some exciting stuff back there."

"Dad makes fun of all your novels."

"Yeah," he said with contained mirth. "Why so, you think?"

Rodney shrugged. "He says they're silly, especially to reread them like you do."

Ray considered this while stroking his beard. "Hm, I dunno, Rod. Stories can contain a lot. Might miss something if you only read it once. I've learned a lot from the masters of storytelling and not just about Mars and laser guns."

"Yeah, maybe I can read some later."

Ray nodded at this, satisfied. "Well, if you go by the drugstore you can pick up the new Superman comics for me. Mr. Edison will have them saved for me."

Rodney looked at Ray in disbelief. "You read Superman?"

"Of course, don't you?"

Rodney climbed the stairs back to his room. He could never tell when Ray was serious or not, but Ray was never normal.

∗ ∗ ∗

Rodney rode out of the long looping driveway and onto the well-grooved highway into town. The heat was already wafting off the road; the air rippled, and he cut it with his bike tires.

Ray had entered his workshop just as Rodney was mounting his bike for the trek to the library. The moment he heard a saw crank up and the whine of cut wood, he dashed over to the trees where he had tossed the strange plans. He stuffed the tube into his backpack and scampered back to his bike.

The road back into town was at a slight but steady incline. Skeleton Mount loomed ahead like some low-hanging thunderhead. The first houses came into sight through the trees that hedged the highway on both sides.

Twin Rivers was a farming community built between the two rivers from which it took its name. The farms were set in the fertile plain north of Snake River, the town filling the triangle of land between the river and the curve of Skeleton Mount where the Second River descended.

It was proud of its small size. Main Street was the chief artery through the town. It carried traffic exiting the highway, showed it through the town, bent westward, and continued on until it rejoined the highway right where Snake River was swallowed up by Second River.

The post office was in the middle of Main Street, flying the state and national flags. The police department, the drugstore, the diner were nearby. To the west sat the school and hospital and other marketplace ventures; to the east, nestled against the mountain, was the library where Rodney aimed. Churches were sprinkled throughout the town.

Rodney felt a trickle of sweat down his back and his jeans stuck to his legs. He sat back on his seat and slowed his pace. He followed the curve of the road into town, looking for signs pointing to the library. Spying one, he took the right-hand turn it directed. Ahead of him was a sign for White Pine Baptist Church. Ray's church. He remembered Otis's story about Ray "ruining" the building, so he decided to take a quick detour to check it out. He turned onto Goat Horn Road, which swept north, and he saw a simple white building with a steeple on top. He slung his bike down in the parking lot and examined the church. There was nothing strange about it from the outside.

In the front of the building was a series of blooming azalea bushes. They climbed well over his head, aflame with pink blossoms. He saw the darting of bees in, above, and around the flowers. He became aware of their dull hum. He didn't see a door, but he saw a walkway off the back of the parking lot. Walking across it he thought it was odd to put the entrance at the back. He climbed up the concrete stairs and pulled on the door. To his surprise, it opened.

He entered and let his eyes adjust. The only light came from the sun shining through the windows alongside the building and from a large window above his head. He was standing on a stage; two tables were set against the walls on either side of him. In front of him were the pews, an aisle running between them, and then a small table. A rope hung down behind the table and off center to that was the pulpit.

Rodney walked down the aisle, letting his hand trail along the tops of the pews. He approached the thick rope that came down from the ceiling. He looked up into the bell tower to see the mouth of the bell and the wheel where the rope connected. He wondered how loud the bell was, and he put his hands to the rope.

"I wouldn't pull that, son."

The voice so startled Rodney that he stumbled back and fell behind the pulpit. He peeked over the table to see a broad-shouldered policeman standing in the doorway.

"I wasn't. I'm sorry, I just wanted to see." He rose to his feet as the man took a few more steps into the light. The man had short blond hair and a bulbous nose over a bushy mustache. He looked like the blond version of an Italian pizza mascot.

"Didn't mean to frighten ya. I was just driving by, saw you enter here. I tell Aaron to keep it locked, but he's careless. What's your name?"

"Rodney."

"Who's your papa?"

"I haven't, well, I'm not from here. I'm visiting my uncle." He paused before adding, "Ray Lauter."

The man's eyes seemed to bulge, he blinked three times rapidly, and then smiled. "Oh. Well. Guess that explains my next question. I was going to ask what you were doing in a church on a Monday morning."

"Yeah, I just wanted to see it."

"I'm Al Walden, sheriff 'round here." He walked down the aisle to join him. "Did your uncle tell you about the bees?"

Rodney shook his head no.

"What? No bees? Hah, I can understand." He moved to the wall and put his hand against it. "Hear that?"

Listening carefully, Rodney began to hear the dull hum of bees.

"They're in the wall. Your uncle closed up the front of this church here, wanted the congregation facing the east, he said. Bees filled it up. I think it was them azaleas out there."

"What happens if you ring the bell? Does it make them angry?"

Walden gave Rodney a slanty-eyed look. "I can't believe your uncle didn't tell you the story."

Rodney again shook his head no.

"Unbelievable," he said, brushing his hair back, setting his hat on top, then removing it again. "It's funny to me now. Your uncle was a hell-breather, always naming sins. We have differences in what we consider preaching. I do the service now. I preach on justice, being good citizens." He tapped the star on his chest. "'Swhat I know." He flashed a wide grin that made Rodney step back.

"But back then, ole Ray was doing the preaching, and he went to swinging on this rope." He paused to run his hand up the fat bell rope. Walden pointed at the wall behind them and continued, "Now bees aren't a bother unless you give 'em a big noise, something that rattles their little stingers. So a soft tug or two might rile 'em, but it won't stir 'em up too badly. However," he held up both index fingers to emphasize this, "if you give a mighty yank, you're gonna upset these critters." He tossed his head in the direction of the bees.

"But I heard from—from the mailman that bees got inside. How'd that happen?"

Walden paused with a twinkle in his eye. "Ah, Otis got to ya, did he? Yes, that's right, bees did get inside. Look here." He pointed to the center of the wall. Rodney noticed a long crack, like a bolt of lightning, filled in and painted over but still visible.

"That scar is where the old door was. This was where you used to enter and face that way, to the west. But Ray flipped it. Then, that time he lost it, pardon, the time he . . . " He lifted his eyes to find the words. "The time he prompted his resignation," he seemed pleased with this phrase and added a laugh to it. "He was just cranking on this rope. He split the wall behind him and the bees poured out. Like it was the end of days, people screaming, running."

Rodney recalled his own flight from bees yesterday. "Did anyone get stung?"

"Sure did. Scores of us, 'cept Ray. We're all waiting outside in the bright sun wondering if Ray had locked himself in the bathrooms. Finally Ray comes strutting out like nothing happened. And not one sting." He paused to let that sink in. "That ain't right. All them bees and not a single sting? Mm-mm, that's what we call, in the law and order business, fishy."

Rodney tried to draw out an explanation. "Sooo?"

Walden shrugged and brushed his mustache. "I figure he's the kinda guy that doused himself with bee repellent just in case, not that he premeditated the event. But not everyone saw it that way. Lot of folk had an even more . . . " he paused while he selected his word, "extravagant explanation of his healthy exit." He winked, "But don't let people convince you of any of that. I figure Ray's a good type. As much time as he spends around those rockers of his, I expect it ain't too surprising that he's a little off his rocker." He chortled at his turn of phrase.

Rodney excused himself soon after and made his way to the library. He found it without trouble and slid his bike into the rack out front. It was the town's single modern building; blond brick with a flat roof, columns of small rectangular windows across the front. Inside were weirdly angled walls, slant-ed wood slats dividing the different areas.

His encounter with Walden had given him another striking view of Ray. Walden didn't seem to have the dull anger that Otis held, but the picture of Ray was quite different from his own view. Otis thought he was crazy and maybe even evil, but Walden seemed to think he was more disturbed than evil.

For himself, he had always liked Ray, but had never trusted him. Ray was playful and fun, but there was something secretive about him. His motivations weren't to be trusted, and, as friend-ly as he was, there was a meanness to him, too. The baseball in-cident was only one of a string of Ray-instigated injuries. There was the time when he was seven that Ray built a giant slingshot and terrified him with water balloons the size of his head. Rodney had spent ten minutes running across the front yard of the Corleonis screaming before his mother came out to put an end to it. Another time Rodney climbed a tree behind the workshop and couldn't get down. Ray wouldn't get out the ladder to help him, but only poked and prodded him with a long stick until Rodney had fallen, branch by branch, to the ground.

He replayed these events while he wandered the rows of books in the cool air of the library. He finally found someone shelving books and asked her where the foreign language dictionaries were. She pointed him to a shelf near the wall, and soon he had claimed an empty study room bearing a couple of fat Italian dictionaries. He made sure he shut the door before he pulled out the strange plans stolen from Ray's workshop. He removed the blueprint from the tube and studied the words surrounding the bulb-like structure.

At the top were the words "*Alvarium Maleficorum*" so he looked up those first. There was no *alvarium*, all he could find was *alveare*, which meant hive, and *alveo*, which was the word for bed.

Maleficorum presented problems also. He found *mala* (underworld), *malaccorta* (unwise), *malafede* (bad faith), and *malaffare* (shady characters) before he realized that his word was spelled *male-*.

He found *maleficio* (witchcraft) and *malefico* (evil), but didn't find the exact word *maleficorum*. Still, the words were close enough to make him uneasy about this evil/witchcraft bed/hive.

He skimmed the document for another word. *Cruentatio-nis* appeared numerous times so he looked up that word next. He read:

cruccio: nm, torment

cruciale: a, crucial

cruciverba: nm inv, crossword

crudele: a, cruel

crudelmente: adv, cruelly

crudelta: nf, cruelty

crudo: a, crude

cruento: a, bloody

crumiro: nm, scab

Cruento was the closest, but regardless of meaning, the neighborhood was imposing enough for him to get the general idea. He decided to focus on some of the sentences scrawled along the edges. He chose "*Le api sono sangue del cuore*" first.

Thirty minutes of flipping through the dictionary yielded a rough draft of: "The *api sono* blood of heart". Looking up *sono* got him *sonoglio* (bell), *sonar* (sonar), *sonno* (sleep) before stumbling onto a strange little note: "*sono : vedi essere*". He didn't know what that meant, but looking up *essere* resulted in the meaning "be". The *api* be blood of heart. Seemed close.

The final puzzle was *api*. The closest words he could find were: *apiario* (apiary), *apice* (apex) and *apicoltore* (beekeeper). But there was no *api*. He stared at the bare brick wall. Through the windows in front of him he could see the librarian pass with her book cart. He frowned at the table in front of him, lost in his thoughts. It felt familiar to be isolated in a room. Rodney's life was full of solitary moments in rooms. They were his retreat, his safe-place.

Home, after a ballgame, after the jeers of his teammates and the barked corrections from his father in the stands, he'd go into his closet to hide. From there he'd imagine cheers and high-fives and his father clapping him on the back after the game. Or he'd imagine his mother coming in to tell him that baseball was stupid, that his teammates were stupid, that it didn't matter, that nothing mattered if he didn't like it.

The door opened and Rodney was startled out of his thoughts. It was the librarian.

"Doing some research?" she asked.

"Yeah, just a . . . uh . . . summer project."

"Oh, how nice. Need anything?"

"No. Oh, wait, there is something." He picked up his notes and asked, "Do you know what 'apiary' means?"

"Sure, that's a place for bees."

"Bees? Hm. How about 'apex'?"

"That's the highest point of something."

Rodney stared at his translation again. "Thanks."

"No problem. In fact, I'll go get you a dictionary so you can look up the words you don't know. I'm Lucasta, by the way."

"Thanks. I'm Rodney. I'm visiting my uncle."

"You're Ray's nephew?"

He looked up at her in surprise. "That's right, how'd you-"

"We're neighbors. I live on the same side of the road, just farther down it."

"Past Otis?"

"Past Otis." She smiled brightly. Her face was smooth and her hair was white, but she didn't look old. She looked to be about his mom's age. She turned to leave. "Be right back with that dictionary."

Rodney tried the new words into his sentence to see if they fit. "The apiary/apex be blood of heart." Both *apiario* and *apicoltore* had to do with bees, perhaps that's what *api* meant. He looked back at the Italian dictionary and his eye fell on the opposite page where he found *ape*, which meant bee. "The bees be blood of heart"? That didn't make much sense either.

Lucasta reentered the room and put down another fat book. She saw the blueprints and said, "Doing something on the human heart?"

Rodney looked at the bulbous shape on the plans again. "Why do you say that?" he asked.

She pointed at the structure. "That's a four-chambered heart." She pointed at the two circular rooms at the back. "Those are the atria, and these longer rooms here are the right and left ventricles."

"Ah, yeah," was all he could manage.

"Let me know if you need anything else," she said cheerfully as she backed out of the room. She shut the door and pushed her cart down the hall.

The last line he translated was easy. *"La porta dei demoni"* was "the door of the *demoni*." And while he didn't find demoni exactly, he did see:

> *demone*: nm, demon
> *demoniaro*: a, demonic
> *demonio*: nm, demon

demonizzare: vt, demonize

demonizzazione: nf, demonization

It was pretty clear. It was a plan for building a doorway for demons. Rodney felt the hair on his neck bristle. He heard a low buzzing coming from the light above him and shivered. He remembered the conversation he'd heard in the night between Ray and an unknown guest. Guess it wasn't a dream. Guess Otis was right.

The final definition at the bottom of the column of words was:

demoralizzante: nf, demoralizing

Rodney slumped in his chair. What should he do now?

He started to roll up the blueprints when he noticed a note written on the back. It said, "*Raimondo, Efesini 4:27. —Filippo.*" He was pretty sure the *Raimondo* was his uncle Ray. A quick flip of the dictionary told him that *Efesini* meant Ephesians, a book from the New Testament. He went back into the stacks to search for a Bible. Once he found one he returned to his study room and looked up the reference. All it said was: "Neither give place to the devil." Why would Filippo send Ray plans for a demonic doorway, but tell him not to give place to the devil?

As he considered this, the room went dark. The power had died. He could hear the ripple of surprise from outside the study room. He waited for his eyes to adjust, but nothing changed, and he remained in darkness.

He stood and reached his hand to the wall. He could follow it to the door and then down the hall out into the main area where the windows let in light. He froze as he heard the door open and shut. He felt a presence before him in the black.

A voice spoke, harsh and a bit like water sizzling in a pan. He couldn't make out the first words, but he recoiled in fear to the wall behind him. The voice spoke again, "Where is Birthless, little adam?"

A stench filled the room. Rodney put his hand before his face. "What?"

There was a loud thump and crash. He heard the books hit the wall and the papers on the table scatter. "Birthless, you bald dirt!"

"I don't know what you mean," he said, retreating into the corner. His stomach churned. He was going to be sick. As far as he could tell the figure remained on the other side of the table.

There was a horrible chuckle in the darkness. "No matter. The diaboloi will find Birthless. The new age is ending and the world will be made old again. You will see. The terms are over. The diaboloi break the boundaries. Soon the army will be amassed."

There was a clamoring on the table, and Rodney cried out as he realized the creature was moving near him. A hairy fist grabbed his neck and stood him upright against the wall. His head banged against the brick and sent him into a daze.

The creature leaned near and said, "We do not fear the Name any longer."

The hand released him and Rodney fell to the floor. The door opened and slammed shut again. Rodney sucked in air, shivering with fright. The emergency lighting snapped alive, casting a thin beam down the hallway. A minute later the lights rewoke, and he was able to see the disarray of his room.

In a panic he gathered up his paper and the blueprints, stuffing them in his backpack. He stacked the books on the table and left as quickly as he could. What were these things that kept appearing to him? Were they really demons? Was that what he had heard this morning? Or was he going as crazy as Uncle Ray?

The bright sun did nothing to calm him. He rode stiffly down the streets. He didn't stop shivering until he hit the final curve that would take him back to his uncle's house.

The only thing he could think of was *why had his mom left him here?*

CHAPTER SIX

MORTAL ILLS

Ray knocked on the door. "I'm going back to the shop. There's some sandwiches in the kitchen when you get hungry." Rodney heard him take a couple of steps toward the stairs and then stop. "Oh, and if you could check on the rabbits, that'd be great. See that they have plenty of hay."

Rodney sat up in bed. "Sure, I can do that." He heard Ray descend the stairs.

Once he returned from town, he hid in his room to formulate a plan. He wasn't sure whom to trust, and he couldn't go to his mom with crazy stories of demons and monsters. Ray was involved in something, but why would Ray bring him into this? Perhaps his mom forced Ray's hand by insisting that Rodney stay with him. Perhaps his mom was in on it, too.

He covered his face with his arms as though he were deflecting a blow. He growled, stretched, and rolled off the bed to check on the rabbits. On his way out, he grabbed a couple of carrots for them and exited into the backyard. It was just after two, and the air was as thick as a quilt. He walked to the tree line, batting bugs with his hand. *Home run, home run, home run*, he muttered as he whacked them.

The rabbit pen was a three-foot-high fence big enough for the rabbits to spring around. Like most things at Ray's house, it was made of wood. Several of the slats were carved with the names of bunnies who had passed on: Saltus, Shem, Dada, Cassidy, Houndstooth, and Rococo.

Rodney had plenty of memories with these rabbits. When he was younger, his mom would put him into the pen and the rabbits would bump and nuzzle him. He'd chase them and giggle. As he became older the rabbits lost their charm. He recalled the names of the three current rabbits: Jerome, Ebenezer, and Thundertrump.

He didn't understand the point of having pet rabbits. Ray would throw a beach ball into the pen and watch the rabbits push it around with their noses, but aside from that and petting them, there didn't seem much use in having rabbits. Ray certainly didn't eat them.

Rodney waved a carrot. "Come here boys."

Thundertrump, the great big cinnamon-colored female, made a tremendous leap and shook the fence when she landed. Rodney stumbled back. "Whoa there." The bottom of one of the slats came loose and he toed it back in place. He stuck his hand over the fence again and let Thundertrump munch. She nibbled briefly, but when Ebenezer, a much smaller, gray-furred rabbit, hopped over, Thundertrump leapt away. A cloud of dust exploded when she landed. Rodney tossed the remaining carrot in front of Ebenezer.

He looked up to find Jerome. Jerome was a much older rabbit. He'd been around longer than Rodney. His hind end was black, the front white, and his head was black with a triangle of white starting between his eyes and covering his mouth. He found him at the far side of the pen, crouching in the shade. He walked around to let him have the other carrot.

"We both have black eyes, huh?" He leaned over the fence to pet him. He dropped the carrot in front of him, but Jerome didn't even glance at it.

There was a low grunt, and Rodney looked up to see Ebenezer on his hind legs with his front paws against the fence. Ebenezer hopped back and continued to make a low grunting sound. Almost like a cough. "What's wrong, Ben? What is it?" Without another sound Ebenezer leaped over the fence like he had wings. Rodney was stunned. The rabbit paused to look back before he bolted off into the woods. "What? Wait!" Rodney chased after him.

Rodney ran to keep up with the fleeing rabbit. Every time he drew within arm's reach, Ebenezer torpedoed ahead, pausing at the top of inclines or before thick brush almost as if he were leading Rodney. Rodney ducked under branches and swatted aside the underbrush to keep up. He whistled and called, but nothing would slow the rabbit or turn him back to the house.

Finally Rodney lost him. The trail of bouncing bushes ended, and there was no bobbing ear to signal him. Rodney stumbled over a fallen log and fell flat on his chest. Looking up he saw Ebenezer crouched on a rock, one paw curled under him and his ears flat against his body. He was pointing with his nose like a bloodhound. He was so still that Rodney looked up to see what he was pointing at. He saw nothing.

Once Rodney subdued his breathing he was able to hear a strange sound, like an injured bird. He paused and realized it was coming from the direction Ebenezer was pointing. He gingerly crawled forward careful of dry twigs and underbrush. The rabbit followed.

After crawling ten feet on his belly, the noise was louder. A few feet away was a giant and gnarled oak tree with a black split down its side, like it had been struck by lightning long ago. Ebenezer was motionless except for his breathing. Its sound was a screeching that caused Rodney to shiver. He realized that it was a voice screaming.

"Hates sunshine! Hates sunshine! Hates! SUNSHINE!"

Rodney recognized that glass-scratching sound. He gathered up Ebenezer and ran back to the house, the shriek trailing behind him as he fled.

* * *

In the bathroom with his heart still motoring, Rodney splashed water on his face and picked leaves from his sticky skin and sweat-threaded hair. Perhaps he should just come out and ask Ray what was happening. He was sure Ray was involved with the strange creature.

If he was going to get out of here, he needed some way to convince his mom that he wasn't safe. Maybe he could use his dad to get out of this situation. His dad always knew exactly what to do or say to get out of trips to Uncle Ray's.

He stared in the mirror at himself. His eye was still puffy and purple. His hair flared out like brown fire.

Dinner was mostly silent aside from the clinks and scratches of forks and knives on plates, pulling apart grilled chicken and stabbing through stiff, buttery green beans. Ray offered a story or two and listened to Rodney's dry account of his trip into town. He left out the church visit, Walden, and the encounter with demons in the library.

"I met someone who knows you," he said, settling on a safe detail to mention.

"Oh yeah? Whozat?"

"Lu-, uh," his brow furrowed in thought. "Lu-something."

"Lucasta?"

"Yeah, that's it."

"Lucasta, Lucy, Lu-lu," chanted Ray, running through his nicknames. "She's an angel. She's the one with the dog, you know."

"Oh, the one that bit me? Hm, she didn't mention that."

"If your dog scars some kid for life, do you mention it every time you see the kid?"

"I'm not scarred for life, Ray."

Ray chuckled and groomed his beard with a couple of firm strokes from his large hand.

"Forgot to swing by the drugstore. Too hot and I just wanted to get home."

Ray slumped in his chair. "No Superman? Ack, and I just finished my Mars novels. What will I do?"

"Sorry for ruining your night," Rodney said with a slight grin.

Ray bolted upright. "Hey, I got an idea, let's look at Mars tonight."

"How?"

"A telescope, nitwit, up in my observatory. You remember."

"Yeah, but I didn't know you could see Mars with it."

Ray's eyes seemed filled with the night's own starlight. He grinned and leaned forward, "You wouldn't believe what you can see."

Growing up, Rodney had not been allowed in the top room of the Corleonis. He used to imagine all sorts of secrets and treasures up there.

It had long been a joke to his dad, this room with windows for looking at the stars. His father was a practical man; he managed a warehouse of building materials. He was a man of stacks and numbers, of lifting and grunting and carrying things around. He had little interest in people who stared off into space, looking at distant points of light. His father had so ridiculed the idea that, once Rodney was old enough (and brave enough) to ascend the stairs and use the telescope, he had no desire to do so.

Rodney ascended the stairs to the upper room. The top of the spiral staircase went right up to the wood ceiling. With a *humph,* Ray pushed up the trapdoor to the observatory and climbed in. Rodney followed and let the door slam shut behind him. There was some fumbling before Ray found the light and clicked it on. The room was hexagonal, as all of the rooms in the honeycomb house were, but smaller than the rooms downstairs. In the center was the fat-tubed telescope on a long-legged tripod. The roof had three large triangular windows that were roughly facing east, west, and north.

The only other things in the room were a stocky wood chair next to a table and a threadbare couch leaking its stuffing. On the table was the source of light—a lamp with a tasseled shade—and a yellow legal pad, deeply penciled with numbers and swirls and hastily written notes.

"Well, here it is," Ray said, slapping his thighs. "My fortress of solitude." Rodney fell back onto the couch as Ray pointed out the features of the telescope. He launched into how it worked and its development and would have gone on except that he noticed the mechanical regularity of Rodney's head-nods and "uh-huhs" and realized he had lost his audience.

"Sorry, floppy-top, I get lost in my own head sometimes. Let's look at some stars." He flipped the light off. "Normally I wouldn't turn on the light. It ruins your nightvision, but I wanted you to get your bearings."

"And show off your shiny toy."

He could hear the bristling of Ray's beard as a slow smile spread across his face. "You know me."

They sat in the dark waiting for their eyes to adjust to the darkness. The room shifted from black to silver as the moon-light seemed to wake up and do its job. "So what'd you name your telescope?"

Ray snorted, coughed, and chuckled. "Ah, you know me too well, Rod. Of course I named it. This here is Giacomo; that's Italian for Jacob."

"Why Jacob?"

"Don't you know your ancient Jewish astronomers?" he said in mock offense.

"Jewish Astronomer 101 is next year."

"Oh, well, here's a preview. One time ole Jake was relaxing under the night sky when he saw a vision of angels ascending and descending a ladder."

"Why would angels come down here?"

Ray stood and began adjusting the telescope. "Oh, you know, keeping an eye on things. Can't have people stirring up trouble." He aimed the tubby barrel out the easterly window. "Come here and have a peek."

The night sky was a deep and near endless yawn. Staring up at it made Rodney feel weightless, like he could be sucked into the heavens at any moment. He waved the telescope across the white dots of stars. "Wow," he said, lost amongst the million pinpricks of light. "There's so much of it."

"Got that right, kid." Ray centered the telescope. "Okay, do you know where the Big Dipper is?"

"Yeah, I know that one." Rodney hunched down to peer into the eyepiece. After five or six minutes of wild scanning and two more of micro adjustments Rodney announced, "Got it. I think."

The silently exasperated Ray bent down to check. "Good," he said. "Now go to the bowl of the dipper and jump off the edge till you see a bright star. That's going to be Polaris, the pole star. It's a star that moves very little night to night."

Rodney followed the directions. "Okay. Is that the Little Dipper?"

"That's right. It's also known as Ursa Minor."

"Is that Italian?"

"Latin for Little Bear."

"Weird."

"It was also known as Draco's wing. Some cultures thought of it as a tree that the dragon sat in."

"Where's Draco?"

"Um, below Ursa Minor, kind of looped underneath like my driveway." He scribbled a dipper on the pad of paper and drew a line humped under it.

"Ha, that is like your driveway. Did you do that on purpose so that it looked like Draco?"

"No, the workers making my driveway didn't want to go over the hill. Said it'd be easier to go around it. That was the easiest place to build a bridge over Second River." Ray took a place on the couch and put his feet up.

"So why is there a dragon in the sky?"

"The question is why aren't there more dragons in the sky. It's hard to see lions and archers in the stars, but snakes and dragons and scorpions are easy. You'd think the ancient astronomers would see more."

"There's a scorpion in the sky?"

"Oh yeah, it's really cool. It has a red star in it. Let's see," he jumped up and took over, twirling the knobs. "Ah, take a look."

Rodney pinched an eye shut and peered into the telescope. He couldn't make out a scorpion, but one star did have a rusty hue to it.

"Above the scorpion is a dude named Ophiuchus. That means snake-bearer. Cool, huh?"

"What's he doing, holding a snake?"

"Well, uh, he's squashing the scorpion. Scorpions always get stepped on. One way or another, they die under a boot." Ray seemed to be talking about something else.

Rodney sat up and looked at Ray. "Do you believe in monsters?"

Ray put a shoulder against the wall. "Yes. Especially the human kind."

"My dad says there aren't any monsters, but I never believed him."

"Well, there's the stone serpent."

"And the Warrior of Light," Rodney added.

"Seems to be a warrior for every monster."

There was a silence and from the first floor a whistle rose up. It was a high-pitched squeal that made Rodney's neck muscles tighten.

"Is that . . . ?" Rodney paused listening to his heart beat.

Ray squinted as he concentrated. "That's the tea kettle. Fibditch again. I'm gonna go turn that off." Ray threw back the trapdoor and stomped down the spiral stairs.

Rodney was left in the room with the warm light from the second floor mingling with the cool starlight. Fibditch, he thought, that's twice he's heard Ray say that. Was it a name? But what kind of name is Fibditch?

The shadows made the room wonky, and Rodney noticed for the first time carvings on the walls. Each room had a theme so he leaned closer to see what Ray had carved in this one. He followed a long looping tail to a crouched lion. Next to that one was another seated and upright like a noble king. Lions.

Ray's name for the house, Corleonis, the heart of the lion, made more sense now.

He flipped on the small lamp and surveyed the rest of the room. He jumped back when he saw the gnarled face of a lion roaring across from him. The mouth was impossibly wide and its teeth like thin daggers. It was so realistic that he could almost hear its roar.

Suddenly the trapdoor closed, snapping shut with a loud wooden *thwack*. The noise so frightened Rodney that his leap knocked the lamp from the table. It hit the floor with a crack and died. Rodney was in complete darkness.

He fell to his knees searching for the handle of the trapdoor. He thought of the angry lion behind him and scratched the wood floor frantically. His fingers caught the edge of the door as he felt a hot breath of air moisten his neck. He screamed, pulled the door open, and launched himself between the crease.

He fell forward, sliding headfirst down the stairs, cracking his shoulder against the balusters which held the rail. He flipped, rolled and rotated, landed on his feet, and pushed off again; falling, flailing, and clamoring to the second floor. His ankle turned, and he came crashing to a stop on the landing. His heart roared in his ears and he spun to see if there was any pursuit down the stairs, but there was none. His whole leg throbbed with pain from the turned ankle.

Either something was tormenting him, or he was a bigger chicken than he thought. This would have to stop. He resolved to do something, to confront whatever it was. He hobbled into his room and set his alarm clock for early morning. He'd bring his bat.

CHAPTER SEVEN

THIS WORLD WITH DEVILS FILLED

odney sat bolt upright at the cawing of the alarm clock. He slapped it silent and brushed back his hair. It was five a.m., and he had to steady himself before standing. The room was dark, for the earth had not yet rotated itself into dawn. He tugged on a shirt, slapped on his cap, and felt along the floor for his pants. After pulling his shoes on and grabbing Libra, he quietly went downstairs.

He unlocked the front door and cracked it open. There was a coolness to the predawn dark that he didn't expect. He jumped off the porch and crouched against the house behind one of the big clay jars that sat on either side of the steps. He rested the bat over his shoulder and searched the yard.

The dew had already settled across the lawn, and he realized how soggy his shoes were. He felt silly and tired, and tried to shake the sleep from his eyes. He had no idea when the sun would rise, but he knew it would be sometime after five.

He didn't have a plan. Ray said demons were subject to the Name, and he thought the voice that awoke him yesterday might be this demon. So the creature seemed to obey when he commanded it to shout out a love of sunshine each morning. If it happened again he'd be ready.

Rodney stared ahead into the darkness, squinting at any movement of the trees. His head bobbed. He felt more comfortable resting his chin on his knees. He leaned against the house. Sleep crept upon him once more.

* * *

" . . . Birthless loves sunshine! Birthless loves sunshine!"

Rodney jolted back and slammed his head against the house. Rubbing it, he sat up to see a small, black, mostly furry creature spinning in a tight circle like a pinwheel and screaming. The creature wasn't more than two feet tall, with a pointy, batlike face. He had a hairy back, forearms, and feet, and he hobbled from side to side when he ran.

The sun had just begun to peek over the horizon. Rodney's body ached and his backside was wet from sitting in the grass. He watched the demon cry out in his raspy voice his love of sunshine. When the creature fell over, he held his stomach and laughed. It was a horrible strangled sound.

The creature seemed different. Changed. It rolled over with a mirthful sigh and sprinted off toward the tree line. With a few leaps, twirls, and one crisp cartwheel, he disappeared into the woods. Rodney rose from his hiding place. He put a hand to his head, massaging the growing ache. His stomach churned with anxiety and hunger. Rodney decided that he should track down this creature. Perhaps the rabbit Ebenezer could help again. He rushed back inside.

Ray bumped cabinet doors and plates in breakfast preparation while humming some triumphal marching tune. Rodney ran up to snag his backpack, since he'd have to sneak Ebenezer into the woods without Ray noticing. He looked at his bat and decided to keep it with him for protection. Once ready he returned downstairs and walked into the kitchen.

Ray turned and let his smile break through his beard. "Rodnacious, I have made morning sandwiches." He waved his hand over the food with a flourish.

"What's that?"

Ray turned to grab two dishes behind him and showed Rodney his creation. "Behold the glory." On the plates were biscuits intersected with ham and a pale cheese sagging under heat. He placed the dishes on the island between them and reached a ladle into a steaming pot on the stove.

He stirred a thick white porridge. "Gravy, gravy, gravy. Mmm! Baby, baby, baby," and he ladled out a scoop onto the head of the biscuit. The gravy ran down like a lava flow. He looked up and asked, "Want some on yours?"

"Sure."

Ray buried the other biscuit in a lumpy pool. He snagged two forks and knives from a drawer and, handing him a pair, said, "Dig in. Literally, dig in."

They both excavated bites, cutting through the sandwich with the knives and forking the gravy-laden portions gingerly to their mouths. There was a tinge of sweetness to the gravy that cut the saltiness of the ham. Rodney chewed vigorously.

"Got a heap of work to do today," Ray said between chews.

"Thought I'd bike back into town. Pick up your comic books. Maybe get a couple for me to read."

Ray perked up. "Oh, okay. Don't let Mr. Edison talk you into that Batman trash. Get something that goes into space. Trust me." His beard was flecked full of fallen gravy.

"Batman doesn't go into space?"

Ray made an ugly face and shook his head. "No, he likes being in the dark and underground. Never trust something that spends most of its time buried in darkness."

"What about someone who has food all over his face? Can I trust him?" Rodney gestured at Ray's beard.

Ray laughed and smacked his lips. "Yeah? That's the problem with these sandwiches. I end up wearing most of it." He dabbed himself with a napkin. "There's plenty of stuff for lunch in the fridge. I'm going to work straight through, I think. No interruptions."

Ray finished his biscuit and put his plate in the sink. He slapped his belly and popped his suspenders against his chest. This is what he did before he got to work. "Okay, kiddo."

"Okay."

Ray nodded and walked out the back door. Rodney finished up his breakfast in two mighty chomps and peeked out the window to make sure Ray had entered the shop. Then he grabbed his backpack and bat and jumped out the back door. He pushed his bike out to the rabbit pen. He was going to have to catch Ebenezer and hide him in his backpack until he was down the road. He couldn't have Ray suspecting anything.

As Rodney approached the edge of the forest where the pen lay, he heard the rapid-fire chitter of the rabbits. He dropped his bike into the grass and surveyed the damage he'd done to the fence the other day when he had blindly run into it. It looked like Ray patched it up since his accident. One slat looked brighter than the others.

Rodney saw Thundertrump and Ebenezer facing each other, heads down, like they were about to fight. They yipped back and forth at each other until Jerome offered a stern bark. Both rabbits shook their heads, snorted, and backed away.

Rodney laid out his backpack, opening its mouth as wide as he could. He unlinked the gate and entered, crouching and cooing, "Come here, Ebenezer. I need to take you on a mission."

Without another word the gray rabbit skittered between Rodney's legs and plopped himself into the backpack. "Whoa. Guess you know what you want," he said and carefully zipped up the bag. He lifted his bike and threw his leg across the frame. He lodged the head of his bat into the water bottle holder, the handle bumping against his knee, and pushed off toward the gravel driveway.

He pumped hard through the thick grass, then into the slurry gravel and into the tunnel of tree limbs. The shade from the trees blunted the heat as he entered. He rode hard, careful not to sling his backpack around. He could feel Ebenezer steadying himself with his paws, balancing his weight while Rodney transported them.

At the bridge Rodney dismounted and let the rabbit out, tossing his bat down beside him. The animal waited while he walked his bike down the slope to the river bank and curled it under the bridge out of sight. He scrambled back up the ledge and cleaned his hands.

"Alright, let's go," he said, snagging the bat.

Ebenezer was already rigid, one paw up, nose pointing up-stream. The ground rose as they went eastward toward Skeleton Mount, and Rodney labored to keep up with the darting rabbit. Periodically Ebenezer would pause and sniff the earth like a bloodhound. Sometimes he'd paw a leaf before again pointing rigidly ahead.

After some time they turned from the river and headed south as if back to the house. It was hard for Rodney to tell how far east they'd gone, but soon the ground sloped away. He expected to wander out into the clearing where they'd started, but as they emerged from the tree cover he noticed three rows of shorter trees. It was the apple orchard east of the Corleonis.

He remembered picking unripe apples and tossing them at enemy trees and fighter plane birds. That stunt had gotten him banned from the orchard by his mom. His dad even withheld his night-night hug over it. Ray later snuck in a basket of apples, green and as hard as golf balls. "No big deal. Knock yourself out," he had said.

He was about to lope out into the open orchard until a rasping noise caught his ear. He hunkered down next to Ebenezer.

In the midst of the apple trees he saw a black creature sprawled in the sunlight.

The little lost demon held out a finger to a butterfly whose daft flutter mesmerized him. He lifted up an apple in his other hand and bit into it. The tartness of the young apple puckered his lips, its sour sucking the moisture from his mouth. He whistled and tempted the butterfly again with his finger.

The little thing looked harmless despite its grim features. Rodney took a breath, gripped his bat, and stepped out from his hiding place. "Who are you and what are you doing?" he asked.

The demon stopped and looked at him. He raised himself up on an elbow. "You? You see me?"

"Yes."

"But I am not visible." At that moment the butterfly landed on his outstretched finger. He gazed at it. "Not visible to you," he added.

Rodney frowned. "Yes you are. Now tell me what you're doing."

"The sunshine," he rasped. "I love the sunshine. I love it."

"Yeah," Rodney said. "It's nice."

"You helped me like sunshine." In his wide mouth Rodney couldn't help but notice the sharp, bone-white teeth.

"Oh yeah? No, uh, problem. My name is Rodney." He felt like he should move closer, shake hands, but he didn't move.

"I am . . . I am . . . " the demon turned his head to the left. "I am . . . " his voice trailed off.

"You were calling yourself Birthless earlier."

The demon looked back at Rodney. "I am not Birthless any longer," he said firmly. "I am…"

Rodney took a few steps closer. "Are you looking for a new name?"

The creature looked up at him eagerly. "Yes, do you have one? Give me a new name."

Rodney looked down at his baseball bat. He rubbed a finger along the ridges of its name. "Let's see, names . . . " He thought of baseball, he thought of Birthless running in circles, then cartwheeling, he thought of balance, he thought himself spinning around after a wild swing of the bat. A cool wind blew, and Rodney brushed his hair back.

"I got it." The demon looked up at Rodney. "Your name could be Pinwheel."

The creature's face seemed to split and crinkle into a smile. "Yes, Pinwheel. I am Pinwheel."

They stood in the grass as the sun rained down on them. He watched Pinwheel shiver in the morning light.

"Are you cold?"

Pinwheel stretched his toes out in the cool grass. "No." His eyes never stopped moving. It was as though he had never seen this place.

"Are you outside much during the day?"

"No, never. Birthless hated sunshine." He looked up at him. "But I like it."

"I can't believe I'm talking to a real live demon."

Pinwheel took two brisk steps toward him. "Pinwheel is not a demon. I am, I am, I am..." His frustration made Rodney laugh. "I am an angel!"

"An angel? I've never heard of an angel that is black, two feet tall, and hairy."

Pinwheel made a sound like a squirrel growling. "Well, I want to be an angel."

"Wanting and being are two different things." Rodney noticed a gray bullet shoot from the tree line. It leapt into the air and struck Pinwheel.

Pinwheel squealed as Ebenezer sent him toppling to the ground. Before Rodney could do anything the rabbit had pinned Pinwheel with his front paws.

"A rabbit!" he screamed. "A rabbit's got me! AHHHH!"

Rodney tried to brush Ebenezer off of Pinwheel. He wouldn't budge. It appeared that he was licking Pinwheel.

Rodney managed to drag the rabbit off the former demon. Pinwheel sputtered and stood. "Diaboloi hate rabbits," he said.

Rodney couldn't help but laugh. "What's so scary about rabbits?"

"Diaboloi hate rabbits," Pinwheel repeated quietly.

"Hold on, what's a diaboloi?"

"An accuser, a slanderer, a devil, a demon," he answered promptly as if he were answering questions in Sunday School.

"So how do 'angels' feel about rabbits?"

Pinwheel cocked his head to the right. He remembered his new status and said, "We . . . like them?"

Ebenezer was purring like a cat and nuzzling Pinwheel. He reached out tentatively and gave a hurried stroke on the rabbit's head.

"Why do demons hate rabbits?"

"Because rabbits can see them." Pinwheel gained courage and wrapped his arms around the furry beast's head and gave a hug, then a firm scratch behind Ebenezer's ears.

"Not everyone can see you . . . or them?"

"Angeloi and diaboloi choose who can see them, except rabbits; rabbits can always see."

He watched him cuddle with the rabbit. "Looks like you have a new friend, Pinwheel."

"Yes. Hi, Ebenezer. My name is Pinwheel."

"Wha? How'd you know his name?"

Pinwheel frowned at Rodney. "He told me."

Rodney heard a rapid chittering coming from the rabbit. Things had gotten weird so fast. "Come on, you should meet the others," he said. They walked through the woods, looping around the workshop where Ray labored.

"I've got so many things to ask you, I don't know where to start."

Pinwheel nodded, but was too distracted by trees and bugs and the shafts of light that pierced the canopy of leaves. They arrived at the rabbit pen. Rodney scanned the yard and house before moving.

There was a flurry of activity inside the pen as they approached. They entered, and Rodney pulled the gate closed behind them. The rabbits gathered around, leaping and nuzzling and making funny little chirping sounds. Pinwheel spoke to the animals and laughed at their responses. Rodney was anxious to get back into the cover of the woods in case Ray came out.

"Come on, Pinwheel, that's enough. Let's talk in the woods where we can't be seen."

"Bye, friends," he said waving to the rabbits.

They walked into the woods. Rodney's mind was a swirl of questions, but he couldn't work up a single one. Finally Pinwheel broke in.

"Two days ago, Birthless ran through here. The light was burning his eyes. He was scared and had hidden from the others after being made subject to the Name. He found a place to hide, a dark hole, a place to curse the sun, the Name, and the adam that enslaved him."

Rodney noticed the lightning struck tree. "Yeah, I think I came across you that day. You sounded horrible."

"Not me," he responded absently. "Birthless."

"Right, sorry." He rubbed his nose. "Quick question—why do you call humans *adams*?"

"Because adam means dirtbag." He crouched and drew squiggles in the sand.

"Oh."

Pinwheel looked up at him. "I want to be angeloi, Rodney. I don't want to serve the darkness anymore. Will you tell me how to become one of the Name's?"

"What? I don't know how to do that. I thought you knew all this sort of thing."

"Birthless was diabolos. He did not know how to become an angelos."

"Can you just say demon and angel? You're making my head hurt."

Pinwheel frowned at him, the ridge of his brow jutting outward. He nodded, but said nothing.

"Maybe we can ask Ray. I'm thinking it might be time to let him know what's going on."

"Ray, the bearded adam?"

"Bearded adam? Yeah, I guess. Ray's my uncle."

Pinwheel's eyes grew big and he took a step back. "No, no we cannot go to him. He is with the diaboloi, I mean the demons."

Rodney's center grew cold and his voice fell to a whisper. "No, I don't believe it." Rodney walked over to the twisted tree. He traced his finger down the black burnt scar.

Pinwheel spoke in a rapid voice, without halts or breaths. "I do not know the whole plan, but after the cruentation of Birthless he was summoned by the bearded adam."

"Ray," Rodney said without turning around. He looked into the pit at the foot of the tree. A root was perched above the hole, as if to cave it in, or else slipping into it.

"Yes, Ray. Birthless went to talk to Ray."

Rodney turned. "You—I mean, Birthless talked to Ray? Why?"

"Ray talks to many of the dia—the demons."

"This is too much for me." He put his hand to his face and rubbed his eyes. "And you said after Birthless was cru-something . . . "

"Cruentated."

"Yeah, right. I've seen that word on some blueprints."

"The cruentation is the way the demons enter the world."

Rodney continued, "But why do they need to enter the world? I thought they were already in it."

Pinwheel made a sound like pepper being ground. "When demons are not anchored to the physical world they must fight spiritually with angels, against whom they do not stand a chance. But to enter the world physically, to be tied to matter, would mean they can only be defeated by physical means."

"You mean, angels can't fight a cruentated demon?"

"No, only mankind."

Rodney looked at his hands and then up at Pinwheel. "Can mankind defeat demons?"

Pinwheel hesitated before replying, "The flesh is weak."

Rodney's eyes fell. "So they're building an army."

"The war in heaven has birthed a war on earth."

Despite the heat, Rodney wrapped his arms around himself. "And Ray is helping them."

CHAPTER EIGHT

DOOM IS SURE

Rodney fell against the burnt tree. He couldn't believe what he'd just learned. Despite what Otis and even Walden had said about Ray, it was hard to believe Ray would be in league with demons.

Pinwheel studied Rodney's face. "We must find angels and warn them."

"Okay, how do we find angels?"

Pinwheel looked up blankly, "What? Me? I do not know how to call angels. You are the adam."

Rodney twisted his eyebrows. "I don't know how to talk to angels either. I've never even seen a demon before this week."

Pinwheel shook his head, obviously displeased.

Rodney stood and brushed himself off. "Okay, I need to know what I'm dealing with. What does Ray want with me? Why am I here?"

Pinwheel shrugged. "Do not know. He told Birthless to keep an eye on you."

"What for?"

Pinwheel shrugged.

"Did he tell you—I mean, Birthless—to scare me?"

"No. He said to watch over you and leave you alone. But demons tempt and torment, so that is what Birthless did before you spoke the Name."

Rodney walked in the direction of the bridge. "I guess that makes sense. If he wanted me out of the way, he could do it himself. So what's his plan?"

Pinwheel shrugged for the umpteenth time.

They walked through the woods, careful to avoid the patches of sun as the heat of the day rose. After walking silently for a time, Rodney spoke again. "I suppose the only thing to do is to act normal around Ray. Maybe I can call mom and beg her to pick me up again. I can threaten to leave and go with dad. Is that mean?"

He looked out the corner of his eye and saw the shoulders of Pinwheel slump. "You would abandon me here?" His voice was a soft scraping of glass on glass.

Rodney was silent again. He hadn't thought about Pinwheel. He was a former demon in the middle of a brewing war between angels and demons. He was more alone than Rodney was.

Ahead the trees thinned, and Rodney could see the curve of the driveway as it headed toward the bridge. "Sorry, Pinwheel. I wasn't thinking. I guess I can stay and help you find an angel or something."

Pinwheel's wings perked up and even shivered.

They exited the forest and walked on the gravel until they arrived at the river. "I've got to bike into town. I told Ray I'd pick up something for him."

"I will come with you."

Rodney scrambled down the bank to retrieve his bike. Pinwheel followed. "But won't you be seen? I would definitely get in trouble if people saw me with a black furry creature."

"No one will see me unless they have the eye. You and Ray have the eye. Like rabbits."

Rodney pushed his bike up the slope, grunting. He wiped the sweat from his brow and bent low to catch his breath. "So, how did I get the eye?" He looked up, but before Pinwheel could shrug he waved him off. "Never mind, I can guess: you don't know."

Pinwheel affirmed this with his silence. Rodney climbed onto his bike and shoved off down the road. Pinwheel stretched out his wings and gave a mighty flap. He hovered behind Rodney, careful to keep beneath the tree canopy lest he collide with the branches.

Rodney wasn't quite sure how he felt about his new ally. As desperate as he was for a friend, he wasn't quite sure Pinwheel could help him. The creature didn't seem to know much and certainly didn't seem brave or strong. But Rodney had to admit that his options were limited.

Once they were out on the open road, Pinwheel increased his altitude and sailed before Rodney in the bright midday sun. Every now and then Pinwheel would circle back and whisk by him to give a slight boost of wind at his back.

When they reached the town Pinwheel kept closer. The drugstore was on the main strip. Rodney pulled up and tucked his front tire into the bike rack. He pulled back the door, and Pinwheel alighted on the sidewalk and entered. Rodney realized how strange it was to hold the door for an invisible guest. Fortunately, no one was around to see.

The drugstore was four aisles of shelves on a white linoleum floor. On the blue walls was a row of photographs, most of them black and white. As Rodney walked down the far left row he saw that they were of Skeleton Mount and a long stone wall which he recognized as the stone snake. The trees had been thicker when the pictures were taken and there had been no barrier between the path and the monument. Several pictures showed children in puffy coats standing atop the effigy and beaming.

He walked straight to the back where there was a counter that ran the length of the store. On one side were stools, and behind the bar a short-order diner. There was a pleasant looking lady in a light pink dress. She was rail thin with nut-brown skin. Her hair was up in a fat bun that dwarfed the rest of her head. She had her long nose planted in a paperback book with a floral cover and a grand, swooping title in gold.

On the other side was the pharmacy, and tucked in the corner was a spinner rack of comic books. Behind the counter was a man in spectacles with a towering wave of silver hair.

He looked up from a comic book as Rodney approached. He smiled, which signaled that Pinwheel was unseen.

"Hi there, youngster. Whatcha need?" His voice was startlingly low.

Rodney cleared his throat. "I'm, uh, here to pick up my uncle's comics. He said you keep them special for him."

"Eh?" He said, while putting down his reading material. "Yer Ray's nephew then. Otis mentioned you was in town. I'm Jack Edison."

"Oh, you know Otis, too?"

"Sure I do. Everybody knows Otis." He stooped down and retrieved a brown paper bag. It looked like it held two inches of comic books. "He'll be here for lunch in a bit."

Rodney accepted the bag and slung off his backpack. He slid the package in carefully and zipped it up. He withdrew his wallet and opened it. Inside were three crisp twenty dollar bills his mom had given him for the summer. "Uh, how much?" He held out his open wallet.

Mr. Edison looked into it and shook his head. "How about I just put it on his tab?"

"That sounds good." Rodney was tucking his wallet into his pocket when he felt a tug at his sleeve.

He turned to look at Pinwheel.

Pinwheel was pointed to the other side of the bar. "Look," he whispered. Rodney followed his finger and saw Otis climbing onto one of the stools. A moment later another figure emerged from the aisle and stood behind Otis. It was about five feet tall, black, and had long spindly fingers.

"Speak of the devil," cried Mr. Edison.

"Hey there, Jack," Otis replied without looking up.

The demon looked over and saw Pinwheel. Its eyes flashed and he walked over. His bare feet clawing the tile. "Birthless, you snake. The diaboloi seek you." His voice crackled like wood on fire.

"I am no longer with the diaboloi, Cankersoot. And my name is Pinwheel."

Cankersoot stepped back alarmed. He looked at Rodney and then back to Pinwheel.

"Did ya see your new friend?" Mr. Edison said, motioning toward Rodney. Rodney was easing backwards away from the two invisible demons.

Otis looked around and saw Rodney. "Oh, didn't see you, Rollie."

"Rodney," Rodney said, hazarding a quick glance at Otis. The old mailman was staring up at the sign above the bar, looking over the menu.

Cankersoot hunkered down to look at Pinwheel. "Have you come under the sway of this little meatsack?"

Pinwheel inserted himself between Rodney and the demon. "You are not to be inside the city. You should run back to the Old Master before angeloi snatch you up."

A long thin tongue shot from Cankersoot's mouth and tapped Pinwheel on the snout. "The diaboloi do not honor the deal any longer. We are taking the city; the bearded adam cannot stop us. If you stand against the army of Hell you will fall with this world."

Otis looked up at the lady across from him. "I'll take the grilled cheese, Ava."

The woman with the mountainous hair slapped the book shut and walked to the back to prepare the food. She raised a clamor before returning and drawing a drink from the soda fountain for Otis. She placed it on the counter and returned to the back. All wordless.

"Rodney and I will stop you." The words of Pinwheel were a lot bolder than how he spoke them.

Rodney gathered up his backpack. "I should get back." Mr. Edison had already taken up his comic book.

Otis was hunched to draw up his beverage through a straw.

Cankersoot laughed. He walked backwards and leaned toward Otis's ear. "Ray is not to be trusted," he muttered.

Otis turned and looked at Rodney as he began to leave. "Keep an eye on that uncle a' yours."

Rodney turned and ran out of the store. Pinwheel followed more slowly to ensure Cankersoot stayed put.

Rodney burst out into the rippling sunlight, gulping the moist air. He felt sweat run down his temples and he wiped both sleeves over his face before drawing out his bike.

Pinwheel exited. "It is not safe here if the demons are entering the city. They would not break the vow if they feared the hand of Heaven."

Rodney hopped onto his seat and was about to shove off when Pinwheel grabbed him by the collar. "What?" Rodney asked, "What is it?"

Pinwheel's eyes were wide. Rodney looked out into the street. Scattered about, behind pedestrians, flying over the buildings, crouched in every shadow, were demons.

"We should leave." Pinwheel gave him a little push.

Rodney stepped into his peddling, leaning as he increased speed. Pinwheel kept his hands to Rodney's shoulders, pushing him along. Rodney ramped off the sidewalk into the empty street.

"What are they doing?" he called over his shoulder.

"They are doing tempters' work. Inspiring malice and envy."

"Why did you say they weren't supposed to be here?"

"Uh-oh."

They were drawing attention. A cloud of demons had taken flight and was following them. Their jeers cut through the howling of the wind as they raced out of downtown Twin Rivers.

The buildings decreased, and slowly the multitude of demons ceased their harassing. Pinwheel kept up their speed, Rodney struggling to keep his feet to the pedals. They zipped around the long curve out of town.

They slowed. Pinwheel released his hold and sailed alongside. "The demons made a deal with Ray."

Rodney remembered the voice talking to Ray his first night here. He slammed on the brakes and pulled to the side of the road. Pinwheel landed in front of him.

"What deal?"

"Ray is well known in the Kingdom of Darkness. Many tempters would come from all over to speak to him. To cause such a one as him to stumble would win a demon much envy. But for years no demon could cause him to sway or mutter one false word toward Heaven. Until Murkpockets, that is."

Rodney scanned the road, east and west, to make sure they were still alone. No cars or creature were within sight. "Who is Murkpockets?"

Pinwheel suppressed a shiver. "Years ago he was nothing, a lowly tempter not much bigger than I. He was too insignificant to be allowed to approach and tempt someone like Ray, but he was assigned to one of Ray's friends."

"Gerald," Rodney said, thinking of the beaming boy next to Otis in so many pictures.

"I did not know his name, but Murkpockets was his tempter. He had gained his ear and burdened him with guilt and turned his heart, and Ray was stricken over it."

"So what happened?"

"Ray made a deal. If demons would stay out of the town Ray would make his home a shield from Heaven and build a gateway into the world."

"The Malaficky thing."

Pinwheel nodded. "The Alvarium Maleficorum. Murkpockets has risen in the ranks of Hell; he has grown mighty, and there is word that even the Old Master has come."

"The Old Master?"

Pinwheel looked nervously about. There was a buzzing in the cotton field next to them, but not a single leaf moved. "We should get back to the rabbits."

"Yeah, okay." Rodney walked his bike back onto the blacktop and stood atop the pedals. He coasted until Pinwheel flapped ahead of him and then pumped his legs to keep up.

Rodney slowed as they approached Ray's driveway. A pillar of warm air flowed out of the dark tunnel like a great breath exhaled. Rodney turned and pedaled hard to get through the thick gravel at the mouth of the driveway. Pinwheel angled down, but his dive was brought up short when a seven-foot demon dropped in front of them.

The great demon swatted Pinwheel aside. Rodney screamed and slammed on his brakes. The demon caught his handlebars and slung him off on the opposite side. Rodney hit gravel and slid. He coughed and scrambled to his feet. The demon was lumbering and flexing his muscles. Smoke rose off him like the sun was searing him. He lifted his great wings above him and made a canopy of shade.

He made a horrible retching sound, like he was clearing his throat. He looked at Pinwheel and spoke, "Foolish diabolos, do you think the outer darkness had not noticed your cowardice?"

Pinwheel climbed to his feet. "I am not diabolos, I am angelos."

"Your master has need of you."

"I serve the Name."

The creature's eyes flinched. "The Old Master has not allowed it."

Rodney started to say something, but as he opened his mouth the demon shrieked. It was a piercing and deafening howl. His mouth hung open as he glared at Rodney.

Rodney tried again to speak, but the demon shrieked a second time to silence him. Rodney and Pinwheel both recoiled a step at the horrible scream. The sound made Rodney's skin rattle, like glass had shattered in his veins. The creature heaved and flecks of spittle hung from his gaping maw. When the creature saw that Rodney had decided against speaking, he continued addressing Pinwheel. "Return, or be taken by force."

Pinwheel took a timid step forward. "Heaven would not allow it. The diaboloi cannot act freely."

There was another retching sound, like a chain being pulled through old nails. Apparently the demon was laughing. "What would heaven want with a worthless accuser?"

Rodney looked to Pinwheel to see his response. Pinwheel merely shivered. Finally he responded, "The adam will speak the Name, and the Old Master will be powerless again."

The monster's mouth split to show his teeth. "No ears will hear again; the diaboloi have made sure of that. But go. Go cry to heaven and see if she risks her remade world for a failed tempter." The demon turned to point at Rodney. "And you, foolish adam, your role will not be lost."

Before he could respond the demon puffed out his chest and stretched out his wings to their full length, his clawed feet dug into the earth. Rodney realized too late what the demon was doing. He shielded his eyes as the creature crouched and swung his wings with such force that the wind swept them off their feet. They were thrown to the gravel and driven back. Pebbles stung his skin, and he had to shield his face with a hand. He sputtered and brushed back the dirt from his eyes to see that the creature was gone.

Pinwheel stood and said, "That was Murkpockets, architect of the Alvarium Maleficorum." He paused, before explaining, "The beehive of wickedness."

"What was that all about?" Rodney couldn't stop the panic rising in his voice.

Pinwheel looked at him. "They will come after me, then you, and then the entire world."

CHAPTER NINE

THE PRINCE OF DARKNESS GRIM

eneath the Corleonis, deep underground in a dank web of tunnels, crawling like ants in complete darkness, were the cruentated army of Hell. The demons scurried, able to see in lightlessness more clearly than in day. They cursed as they worked, their words forming glyphs of air that their infernal eyes could decipher. At the apex of the underground edifice, suspended from the roof, was the Alvarium Maleficorum, a throbbing, bulbous structure like a warty tongue. There was a hum as a cloud of bees cycled through the Alvarium. They were black, bigger and hairier than normal bees, sticky with ichor.

A demon standing on a raised platform poured out the contents of a bucket into a trough that led into the Alvarium. This drove the bees into a frenzy, and their buzzing peaked. A signal was made, and the structure heaved and undulated as if a wave were passing through it. With a sound like a wet mouth opening, the Alvarium emitted a gory demon.

A writhing lump flopped into a tepid pool of muck. A demon standing at the wall stepped closer and grabbed a quivering wing to pull the cruentated demon to his feet. "What's your name, diabolos?"

"Smugbog," he sputtered between the spitting of goo. He wiped his face clear of the muck and flung it into the dark.

"Go to the draining station, next alcove." The demon gave Smugbog a kick to the haunches.

The bulbous hive suspended from the ceiling stopped throbbing, but thick cords of ooze continued to drain from it. The demon attending it hoisted another bucket full of black ichor and poured it in.

The disoriented Smugbog managed to stumble into the next room. He was directed to a bench and his side was pierced with a sharp claw and a tube was roughly inserted in the wound.

"Damnation," he blurted.

"Verily," replied the demon as he monitored the flow of ichor into the bucket. "The Alvarium needs ichor for the cruentation."

"How much?" Smugbog inquired while poking his belly. Ichor sputtered from the tube.

"All that is to be gotten."

Smugbog whimpered.

"The process is slow," said the demon. "The army grows but a little. Impatience is boundless."

Smugbog watched the bucket fill. "How much will come through the blood of Smugbog?"

The attendant revealed his teeth and frowned. "A half of a runt, you insipid fool! Your bleeding is nothing. From this point onward, you will not be full, not till the army of the Outer Darkness is complete." He ripped the tube from Smugbog's arm and grabbed his ears. "Begone, foul thing. Blisterteeth hopes to never smell your rot again!"

Smugbog stood, "Vengeance is mine, Blisterteeth." He hobbled to the door.

"Vengeance is mine!" Blisterteeth shouted in response.

Smugbog joined the line of demons shuffling down the slick spiral ramp deeper into the earth. Notches had been cut into the ceiling of the tunnel so that the claws at the joints of their wings could catch and prevent slipping. The cruentated demons felt slow and dense; the transition from spirits to physical beings had made them heavy and dull.

There was grumbling from all the descending demons. Indignation and complaints were blurted from the demons lined in front and behind Smugbog. He flicked the demon's head that lumbered before him. "Where do the diaboloi go?"

"To be cerated," the demon snapped back at him.

"Why must the diaboloi be cerated?"

The demon before him looked back and snarled, "To protect against the Name, blighted fool. And that Grubcough might be spared your yammer!"

Above the din of the demon's disgruntled burble was the sound of pain. It grew louder: howls, screeches, long-bellowed notes of suffering poured out of the place they were heading.

Smugbog trudged on in the black muck till they arrived at the bottom of the pit, opening into a large cavern. There were several rails before which the diaboloi knelt. Behind the rails were demons pouring molten wax into the ears of the newly cruentated.

A demon shoved him forward to a rail. He knelt and his head was wrenched to the side. The demon spoke, "Have torment, diabolos." At that he poured a dagger of scalding, dark wax into his ear.

Smugbog shrieked in pain. The demon roughly turned his head over and repeated the process in the other ear. The last thing Smugbog heard was the screams of the infernal host around him. Then the world went stone quiet.

In the grooves of the dark Smugbog saw the lips of the demon move, and black motes of sound flurried the air before him. He focused on the visual heft of language, the billow of air, and read the darkness. It was antimusic, an atonal alphabet, and he knew the command to join the ranks of the rabble outside the ceration room.

"Vengeance is mine," said the demon.

Smugbog repeated bitterly, "Vengeance is mine."

* * *

A huge, bloody lump landed in the dirt of the underground chamber. The lump stretched and its arms and legs moved to a kneeling position. The creature vomited thick black liquid.

"That was wretched." He stood in the stench and soggy mess of the room.

Another figure beside the wall drew near. "What is your name, filth?"

"Itchpot," he said and drew himself to near full height. The seven-foot ceiling was not high enough for him to stand unbent. His back and folded wings scraped dirt from the top and sides of the tunnel as he moved.

The other figure stiffened and stepped back.

Itchpot drew his lips back to reveal his daggerlike teeth. "Take me to Murkpockets."

* * *

Murkpockets surveyed the building of another hive. His aide, Yuckjoy, drew a map in the mud before them. "Here and here," he said, indicating two points at opposites and above a large X in the center. "The bearded one foils the hives along the river."

"Without the racket of water, he will hear the hum," responded Murkpockets.

"The Old Master is impatient."

"Build the new on the ashes of the old. The adam will sound an alarm if the diaboloi move too fast."

At that moment Itchpot entered behind them. "The adam will be taken care of. Do not fear him."

Murkpockets spun around to face the well fed and resplendently hairy accuser. "Itchpot? What need the diaboloi of you? Do you not rule the rat kingdom across the sea?"

"It crumbles on its own—*higauff!*" Itchpot had a habit of verbalizing every hiccup and burp he made throughout the day. He was a constant boil of rank wind and moist chirrups. The vain script of his words was particularly airy.

"Your presence here is unnecessary. Murkpockets hopes you won't be staying long."

Itchpot gave a low scoff. "Your envy is loathed, Murkpockets, but Itchpot is here to guide the attack. Your role now is to assist." Itchpot turned sideways to squeeze past the demons to appraise the hive being built.

The hive was enclosed in a wood frame. Behind a bloody veil the wax cells were made by an angry fist of bees. A demon directed it like a clay pot, running his hands down the sides to form the globular shape. The second demon inserted a wood plank, gnarled with rot, through a slit at the top of the gory veil down the center of the hive.

Itchpot continued, "The Old Master has been envious of your operation. Quite a—*hurkle!*—loophole. Far better than entry through stone." His voice was deep like the croaking of an obese toad.

Murkpockets seethed. "But you did not find the gateway. You did not broker the deal with the adam. The operation is not yours. The envy belongs to Murkpockets."

Itchpot turned to face him. "You will still be in charge of dealing with the adam and assembling the—*urgah!*—troops, but the Old Master appoints Itchpot to lead the attack. You are not qualified."

"Who is to say that Murkpockets cannot lead?"

"How many full-frontal assaults on the Name have you made?"

Murkpockets gritted his teeth. "One less than you, Itchpot."

Itchpot scoffed again and moved to leave. "Then Itchpot is infinitely more qualified. *Urgah, urgah!*" He left the cavern, speaking into the darkness, "Itchpot will check the rest of the operation. You deal with the adam. Your delays are not tolerated any longer."

Murkpockets followed the obese demon. "The delay is because the army is not yet raised. If the diaboloi move against one not given to the Outer Darkness, then Heaven will be made aware. They will discover the loophole and seek to destroy all the Alvaria before the army is full."

Itchpot snorted. "Do not worry about the army. It will be made full."

Murkpockets shoved a bony finger into Itchpot's protruding gut. "If you supplied ichor, the depths would be cruentated by dawn."

Itchpot's body heaved in a gross burp, and he chortled. "Eat your rage, Murkpockets."

Murkpockets let the waddling demon depart and muttered, "Murkpockets hates your anger, hates your sleep, hates your groveling wickedness." He returned to the room, smoldering with anger. His aide crouched over the map. Murkpockets stabbed out two locations with a claw and barked, "Build them there, sniveler." He put his foot on the face of Yuckjoy and shoved him onto the floor. He then stomped out, his wings trembling with angst and ill thoughts. Wanting to speak to the Old Master, he wormed deeper into the earth, pushing the smaller demons out of his way as he worked down the dark cavern. They grunted and cursed as he shunted them aside, descending to the lowest level where the Old Master lay.

The Old Master had lain in this belly of earth for over four years. Prior to that he had lain in a deep cavern beneath Vesuvius for nearly two thousand years. He had arrived with no pomp and only a few demons to carry him to his resting place. He had remained prostrate ever since, and rarely communicated with Murkpockets. The Old Master was forced to communicate through feebly written notes, scrawled with a single claw. He was too fragile even to speak.

Murkpockets had taken this to mean that he would lead the charge, but the arrival of Itchpot had put off his rise to power. *Murkpockets the Architect,* he fumed. *Murkpockets the Uprising.* He punched a strut as he passed, and the tunnel collapsed behind him, burying a trailing demon. The final curl to the downward tunnel brought him to the pit of the Old Master. Two short demons stood next to the small hole that led into his resting place. Before one could speak, Murkpockets thrust his bony hand to their small necks and lifted them off the ground. "How easy for Murkpockets to rip out your throats and devour you here." He threw them down. The demons knew not to rise until Murkpockets had crouched to crawl through the small hole.

He entered and rose as much as he could. The ceiling was low, and the room was empty except for the raised bed of dirt on which the Old Master lay. The stench of this room swallowed the smell of filth that filled the rest of the tunnels.

Murkpockets could make out the form of the Old Master in the dark—ashen flesh, thin bones, and twelve feet tall. He was completely bald. His wheezing was the only sound as Murkpockets entered, but the Old Master's head was elevated, and his eyes immediately seized the one who disturbed him.

Murkpockets drew near slowly and knelt next to the prone figure. "The envy is yours, Old Master."

The aged demon waved a hand dismissively.

Murkpockets leaned closer to speak into the Old Master's ear. "The adam discovers the betrayal. He resists. What does heaven hold for him?"

The Old Master raised a weary hand and crooked a jagged claw. He slowly stabbed Murkpockets in the side until a black ichor oozed out. Murkpockets hissed.

The Old Master withdrew his claw and let the fluid drain into his hand. When it was dripping with blood, Murkpockets took up a sheet of paper from a stack. Words were not trustworthy, but whether his tongue was bound or ripped out, the Old Master could communicate no other way. He was reduced to using the enemy's treasured medium.

Murkpockets placed his hand underneath to make a writing surface. His eyes, so frail in the light, could easily make out the dark and splotchy script the Old Master wrote, despite the pitch black—but reading those characters was more difficult. He strained to make out the word.

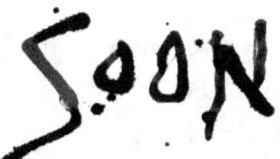

Murkpockets looked at the closed eyes of the Old Master and growled, "But if Hell delays, he will surely call on angeloi." The Old Master let his silence answer the objection.

Murkpockets moved to the next issue. "And the boy? Already he has been a thorn."

The Old Master drove his claw into him again, let the ichor fill his palm, and wrote another message beneath the first.

Through clenched teeth Murkpockets read and replied, "Isn't it all Heaven's? How long must Hell cater to her?"

The Old Master lifted a lip in a weak snarl.

Murkpockets continued, "The diaboloi run the risk of interference if we allow—."

The ancient demon cut him off with a wag of the finger. He then pointed to his first note: *soon.*

Anger boiled inside Murkpockets. He breathed out swirling black motes with the air from his nostrils. He moved on. "One last thing. A tempter has strayed from the ranks of the diaboloi. The young adam has turned him. He seeks to be angelos now."

The Old Master exposed his teeth in a grimace.

"What should the diaboloi do?"

The wavering hand of the chief demon smeared the two prior messages and began writing again, first refilling with Murkpockets's blood. He wrote with more speed and spattering. When he was finished, Murkpockets lifted the blood-message to read it. Though it was full of splatters and faint lines, he read:

NO STRAYS

Murkpockets's eyes widened in the darkness as a fierce scowl broke out across his face. He placed the sheet on top of the other hastily scrawled notes and began to leave. "Murkpockets will act immediately," he said.

The Old Master grabbed his wrist and slowly shook his head.

"But soon?"

The Old Master nodded.

"They will all fall to the teeth of Hell."

The Old Master nodded again.

Without another word Murkpockets withdrew. He hated delay, but they must not draw the ire of Heaven prematurely. Plans must be laid, traps must be set. He hurried up the narrow tunnels, again trampling smaller demons under his furious gait.

Flexing his arms in anticipation of the coming assault, he howled, "No strays!"

* * *

Far above the pit, Rodney pushed his bike from tree to tree in a panic. At each one he would crouch and peer from behind. Every shadow loomed and summoned his fear. Pinwheel trotted behind with an annoyed look on his face. Rodney shot off again, coming to a sliding stop at an embankment of ferns. He let his bike topple over and lay back to catch his breath. Pinwheel walked up and sat beside him.

"Rodney, you cannot hide from the Outer Darkness if it intends to find you."

Rodney looked wildly around. "Where do we go, then? Where is someplace we can talk secretly?"

"Demons cannot be everywhere," Pinwheel responded calmly. He cocked his ears to the side and lowered them.

Rodney's eyes bulged. "So what do we do?"

"We have to think of a plan."

Rodney's eyes spun. Lifting his cap, he put a hand to his forehead. He began to breathe quickly. "We—we need help. We can't do this. I need to call my mom. I need to talk to Ray."

Pinwheel snapped his razory white teeth in Rodney's face to get his attention. Rodney fell back with a squeak. "No need to do that," he muttered, picking the underbrush from his shirt.

"I do not know much, but . . . " Pinwheel seemed to gather himself. He took a breath and began. "For five years, Murkpockets has been cruentating demons, amassing an army. I do not know how many there are, but I know the process is slow. Even in five years they cannot have gathered many in the material world. Demons cannot move freely, and a large number of demons would attract the attention of angels, despite the hexagons."

Rodney frowned. "What are hexagons? And what do they have to do with this?"

Pinwheel glared for a second before responding, "A shape with six sides."

"Like the rooms of the Corleonis? Why is that protection from angels?"

"Hexagons are broken triangles. Angels dislike them. Being in hexagons makes them ill."

"Why would Ray build a house in hexagons?"

Pinwheel ignored him and continued, "But there are rumors that the Old Master is here."

"Who?"

"He is the serpent from the beginning. He was cast down many, many years ago. I have heard that he has been stricken mute until the end of the age."

"When is that?"

"I do not know." Pinwheel hissed and continued. "But if he is here, then the war must be at hand."

The day felt old. Its heat was stretched out thick. His hair was soggy under his cap. "So if they have this Alvarium thing that lets demons into the world, then we have to destroy it."

"We have to find it first. It will be hidden, either underground or in some dark place.

"I just don't understand what Ray is doing."

"Many men desire to be mighty in one kingdom or another."

"So Ray built the Maleficorum, and the demons are being cru—infused with blood, and they're building an army? Why don't the angels or somebody do something?"

Pinwheel stood. "I have passed through the blood. I am no longer in the realm of the angels. Only man and cruentated demon can harm me."

"But perhaps, if we can tell some angels, they can do something."

Without much emphasis Pinwheel responded with a quiet, "Perhaps. But our best hope would be to destroy the Alvarium."

"We have to find it first."

They froze as they heard Rodney's bellowed name. It was Ray. The situation finally struck Rodney. His mother had abandoned him with an uncle allied with the powers of Hell, and his only friend was a former demon.

Pinwheel clutched his elbow. "Do not trust Ray. Tell him nothing." He started to trot off into the bushes before stopping again. "I will stay with the rabbits."

Rodney ran back to the house unsure if he was running from danger or toward it.

II

CHAPTER TEN

ALL EARTHLY POWERS

When Rodney arrived at the front of the house, he saw the Honeypot loaded up, a huge blue canvas covering the contents. Ray, who wore his customary overalls with a tie-dyed shirt underneath, turned when he heard Rodney.

"Hey Rod, wasn't sure you were back or not. Sorry to holler at you. Had some lunch?"

"No, but I did pick up your comic books." He expected Ray's eyes to jump and a greedy smile to spread across his face, but Ray looked preoccupied.

"Just set 'em on the table for me. But listen, I got some other things to do today. Might be gone for a while." Ray threw some heavy boots into the passenger's side and dropped himself into the driver's seat. "Think you can fend for yourself?"

"Sure." This was his chance to snoop around the house for clues.

"There's some sandwich stuff for lunch. I should be back before dinner."

"Okay."

"Stick around the house today; I'm expecting an important call. Might need you to take a message." The Honeypot cranked and shuddered to life. Ray revved the engine, and it coughed up its dusty phlegm.

"Alright."

Ray shut the door and waved. The car rumbled down the driveway with the dust leaping around it.

Rodney waited until the car disappeared into the trees before he dashed inside the house. He ran into the kitchen and threw open the back door and called to Pinwheel. He grabbed two slices of bread and stuck a piece of ham between them. Moments later Pinwheel entered.

"Where is Ray?" he asked, looking around.

"Dunno. Said he had to do some things. Feels suspicious, but this is our chance to look for clues."

Pinwheel watched him stuff the hastily made sandwich into his mouth. "Where should we start?" he asked as Rodney swallowed.

"Let's split up. I wanna check his bedroom. It's the only place I haven't really inspected." Rodney put down the rest of his sandwich.

As he left the room, Pinwheel said, "I'll check the library. There is always trouble with books."

The squeak of Rodney's shoes was drowned out by the thunder of the wood stairs as he ran to Ray's room. He entered and flipped on the light. He couldn't help but feel a thread of guilt tugging at him. His parents' bedroom was strictly off-limits. His dad had defended it like a lion, bellowing anytime he crossed the threshold.

"Toes outside the room, Rodney," he'd roar. Rodney would inch his toes back until he was fully in the hall.

This was the first time he'd been in Ray's room. The door, every time he'd visited, had always been shut. His uncle went to bed too late and rose too early for Rodney to catch sight of him going in and out. The motif of the room was water, curling waves for crown molding and waterfalls framing the windows. The bed was enormous, built with shelves for plants that scattered tendrils up and down the bedposts, their green, heart-shaped leaves like hands claiming dibs on a baseball bat.

The sheets were a deep blue, and there was an avalanche of pillows atop them. He climbed on the bed to feel how soft it was and was surprised by how little the mattress gave. Even when he bounced up and down, the mattress remained firm. Looking at the pillows, the different shapes and variant hues of blue, he noticed a thin yellow stitching on one or two of them. A closer look revealed that the stitching was words—names— and that each pillow bore a different name. He turned them over to read each one, Virginia, Gerald, America, Lucasta, Rodney, the President, Otis, Earth, and Gil, Rodney's father's name, along with a slew of names he did not know.

He remembered a practice his mother had had when he was little. Stitched onto his pillowcase were three little bears. His mom would point at each one—Mommy, Daddy, Rodney— and they would "pray the pillow case." Usually, "Bless Mommy, bless Daddy, and give me a good sleep, in your Name, amen." He would say this with his eyes closed. Ray must have had a similar practice. The corners where you would hold the pillows were all threadbare.

Having scattered the pillows, he noticed something strange. A little paper triangle poked out of a slit in the wood of the headboard. He pressed his hand to it and slid it sideways, revealing a little cubbyhole. Inside were a battered notebook and a map, whose corner had alerted Rodney.

The map was an aerial of Twin Rivers with certain locations marked by a thick black pen. A flower shape, he realized, was the house, and connected to it was the looping driveway. A thicker line marked the bridge where it passed over Second River. There was the road that led back to town and Twin Rivers huddled against the mountains, but only Skeleton Mount was shown. On top was the stone snake wall. The rest of the mountain chain, which crawled eastward and northward, was left off.

Back to the clearing in the sea of trees, Rodney saw the rabbit pen, marked in blue, as well as three places in the woods circled in red; one was near the bridge, where Rodney had discovered the beehive. Two more places were marked with black X's.

"Found something," he yelled. He paused and soon heard the sound of Pinwheel climbing the stairs. "In here," he yelled.

Pinwheel entered. "Look," he said, spreading the map out on the bed. "Here's the house and workshop." Then he indicated the three spots, "Recognize any of these?"

Pinwheel shook his head.

Rodney pointed at the circle near the bridge. "This is where I was attacked by bees."

"A hive?"

"Yes."

"Was it black? Were the bees dark and hairy?"

"The hive was black and I didn't get a good look at the bees, but yeah, I think so. They were certainly scary."

"How big was the hive?"

Rodney thought back to the fallen tree. He saw the pulsating mass again, felt the thrum of the place in his bones. "I don't know. I mean, bigger than a beach ball."

"A beach ball?" Pinwheel looked confused.

"Oh, sorry." Rodney held out his hands giving him a rough idea of the size. "It was about this big."

"Not bigger?"

"It couldn't have been too much bigger since it was in a tree."

Pinwheel frowned.

"You think it could be the Maleficory or whatever?"

"No. Impossible. The Alvarium Maleficorum is big. It is over four Pinwheels tall and almost twice that at its widest. This must be a smaller Alvarium."

"So they've built smaller ones to bring in more help."

"Little demons like Birthless aren't valuable to the army. They are used as slaves and fodder."

"Fodder?"

"Food," Pinwheel said.

Rodney made a face.

"The smaller demons will be used primarily for ichor to bring in the big demons. The smaller Alvaria are not our concern. We must find the big one."

Rodney noticed a red circle drawn in the center of the house. Next to it were the letters A.M. He stabbed it with his finger. "Do you think this stands for Alvarium Malefi-whatever?"

Pinwheel considered it for a moment. "Could be."

"That means it's in the house." He thought for a moment. "But it can't be in the attic. I was just up there, and it's obviously not downstairs, either. Where could it be?"

"Can't hurt to check," Pinwheel suggested.

"I guess," he said as he folded the map. This might be his only chance to look at the map and notebook so he decided to take them and risk Ray's finding out. He arranged the pillows back on the bed and then shut the door behind them.

In three great leaps Rodney descended the stairs. They examined the walls looking for clues. They checked the clock set under the stairs, the sliding door that led to the library, the swinging door that led into the kitchen, and the open archway that went into the first room. There was a well-worn circular rug on the floor in front of the central pillar.

"I got it!" Rodney pushed Pinwheel back and knelt to peel up the rug. He rolled it into a fabric log to reveal the wood floor. Underneath were two lines carved into the floor. One of the lines was humped in the middle.

"Aw, man, I thought there'd be a trapdoor here."

"What is that?" Pinwheel asked, pointing at the symbol cut into the floor.

"That's the symbol for Libra. Ray just likes it," he said, running his hand over the carved lines.

"Libra? You mean, the angels of the tribe of Libra?"

Rodney spun around to look at Pinwheel. "What are you talking about?"

Pinwheel's black eyes twitched. "Libra's one of the twelve tribes of the angels . . . " He cocked his head to the side. "Correct?"

"I don't know anything about that. Ray just said it was a constellation. It means 'balance,' I think."

"What is a constellation?"

"Star patterns in the sky." Just to be sure it was nothing more, Rodney pressed on the lines hoping a door would pop up or a latch would be revealed. Nothing happened.

Rodney shivered. No telling where Ray was or when he'd return. "Where could it be?" he said aloud. He felt panic weaving themselves into his voice again. He lay down on the rug and stared at the ceiling.

They were silent. Pinwheel kept his eyes on the symbol carved into the floor. "Do all the symbols on the floor stand for constellations?"

Rodney sat up. "What do you mean, 'all the symbols on the floor'? Are there more?"

Pinwheel turned around and pointed at the foyer's floor. "There is this sign carved on the floor."

Rodney hopped up to look. He saw the large H carved into the floor. "Yeah, that stands for Honeycomb House. At least,

I think it does." He stood looking at it, and a thread from his memory tugged at him. Suddenly the symbol before him was connected to another. "Wait a minute."

Rodney stood and walked back into the stair room and searched the clock face. He put his finger on the glass. Where the seven on a regular clock would be was the H symbol in the foyer. Libra was where the number two would be.

"What if every room aligns with one of the signs of the zodiac?" he said.

Pinwheel stared at the signs. "How many rooms are in the house?"

Rodney laid out the floor plan. "The first level has the foyer, the dining room, the kitchen, the library, the living room, and the sunroom, but part of the sunroom is a bathroom."

"And this room makes seven hexagons."

"The second floor has three bedrooms, but a bathroom is built between two rooms. So four rooms, but only three hexagons."

"That is ten."

"Right," agreed Rodney. "And then there's the attic, so all together that's eleven hexagons."

"But there are twelve signs on the clock."

"There's a hidden room," he said.

Pinwheel frowned and looked around. "We must find the room."

Rodney remembered the notebook. "Wait." He opened it and flipped through its pages.

The book was filled with Ray's writing, all in blue and black ink. He read the large block letters at the top of the

pages and examined the simple sketches within. The Coat
of Colors, the Maleficorum, the Flood of Demons, squiggly
lines, hexagons, drawings of flowers. It was all too strange for
Rodney to interpret.

A page leapt out at him, a circle of symbols under which
the words *Horologium Zodiaci* were written. He recognized
the sign of Libra and the H symbol and followed the lines that
led to their names.

"Here it is!" He put his finger on the top symbol and read
out the names clockwise, moving his finger around to each:

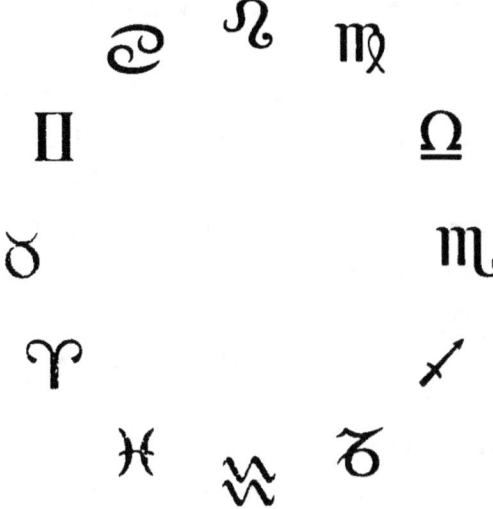

"Leo, the lion, that must be the attic. Virgo, the virgin. Libra,
balance, that's this room. Scorpio, that's easy, scorpion. Sagittarius, the archer." He paused and pointed to the library. "That's gotta be Sagittarius 'cause it's full of archers. Capricornus, the goat.
Aquarius, the water bearer. Pisces, the fish, that's the foyer. Aries,

the ram. Okay, that's the dining room. Taurus, the bull. Gemini, the twins. And Scarabaeus, the scarab. Hey, that's my room!"

"So we must find what rooms align with Virgo, Scorpio, Capricornus, Aquarius, Taurus, and Gemini."

"You check the kitchen, living room, and sunroom, and I'll check the guest bedroom and Ray's room."

They scattered. Rodney was able to identify the symbol of Gemini, Ⅱ, in the room his parents slept in and the water symbol Aquarius, ♒, in Ray's room. When he returned downstairs Pinwheel had connected Virgo, Capricornus, and Taurus to the kitchen, sunroom, and living room. Only Scorpio was unaccounted for.

Rodney slapped his head. "The workshop!"

They ran outside into the heavy air, alive with bugs, and pulled open the wide doors of the workshop. The cool air from inside pricked their skin as they entered. Unlike the house, the walls of the workshop were bare of carvings, though they bore innumerable tools, hanging from hooks and sitting on shelves.

The floor was smooth concrete. It was blank of any symbols.

"I don't get it. Where is the twelfth room?"

"The map indicates that it is inside the house." Pinwheel said, devoid of confidence.

He and Pinwheel froze at the sound of gravel and the hum of a car. It wasn't loud enough to be Ray's, but it caused them to scurry to the door and peek out. It was a white car.

"Otis!" Rodney hissed. "What's he doing here? He never comes up to the house."

They watched as the car slid to a stop in front of the Honeycomb House. The car rocked gently as Otis climbed out and frowned at the front door.

"Stay here," Rodney whispered.

"You forget, Otis does not have the eye."

"Oh, right. Okay, let's see what he wants." Rodney pushed open the door and stepped into the shaded area before the workshop. "Hi, Otis," he called.

Otis spun his head around and squinted to locate the voice. He found Rodney walking over to him. "Hello again, son. How are you?"

"Rodney," he reminded him.

"Right, yes. Is Ray here?"

"No, he's out." He watched Pinwheel creep up beside him. Perhaps he could still be heard despite being invisible.

"Thought so." Otis sounded peeved. He paused and stared up at the sky, putting his hand to his bony chin and pursing his lips. Rodney waited silently until he was ready to speak again. "Listen, tell Ray I came by. Tell him I saw the smoke and he better have the permits this time."

"Permits?"

"Fire permits," he said and ran a hand across his brow to smear the sweat into his hair. "I catch him burning things again, I'll have Al Walden write him up. You tell him that."

"Yes sir."

Otis climbed back into his car. His tires chewed gravel and kicked up dust as he turned around. They watched as the worm of dust trailing his car faded and returned to the house.

Rodney's stomach growled and he remembered his half-eaten sandwich on the kitchen counter. "Do you eat?"

Pinwheel looked surprised. He looked up at Rodney in panic. "I do not know."

"Well, are you hungry?"

Pinwheel vigorously shook his head. "No."

"So no big deal." They walked back inside. They entered the kitchen and Rodney took another bite out of his sandwich. He noticed Pinwheel fretting. "What is it, Pinwheel?"

"Demons must eat in order to stay in this world. Otherwise they fall back into their immaterial natures."

"So what do they eat?"

"Mud, mostly. But anything really. Just something to anchor their nature in matter."

Rodney made a face. "So do you want to eat mud?"

Pinwheel's eyes flashed and the snarl of his lips showed his bright teeth. "I am not a demon."

"Okay, okay," Rodney said. He turned and opened the refrigerator and pulled out a bowl of strawberries. He picked up one and tossed it to the fuming former demon. "Here, eat a strawberry."

Pinwheel caught and examined it. He ran a thumb over its dimpled skin. He looked up at Rodney and made a face. "Seeds?"

"Yeah. What's wrong with seeds? Don't angels like seeds?" His tone was playful.

Pinwheel sighed and shrugged his shoulders. He flipped the strawberry into his mouth and chewed quickly, eyes shut.

Rodney paused to see the full reaction.

Pinwheel swallowed, shuddered, and opened his eyes. "Not bad."

"You're not going to float off into the spirit world?"

Pinwheel licked his lips. "The spirit world is more solid than the material world. This world is so transient, to stay in it, a demon must be tethered to it." He made further smacking noises, greedily looking over the bowl of fruit. "So maybe I could have a couple more."

Rodney finished off his sandwich. He decided on a slice of bread with a bit of honey. When he pulled out the jar of honey, Pinwheel eyed it like it was a coiled snake.

"What? Haven't you seen honey before?" Rodney said with a short laugh.

"Yes."

He dipped in a spoon and drew it out again. "Want some?" he said, letting a long rod of honey drizzle back into the jar.

Pinwheel, wary, shook his head.

Rodney ate his honeyed bread while Pinwheel polished off the strawberries. Rodney tossed him an apple afterward and watched him carve it up with his razor-sharp teeth. Rodney pulled out the peeler and showed Pinwheel how to attach an apple and crank it skinless.

While Pinwheel stripped a pound of apples clean of their skin, Rodney pulled out Ray's notebook and paged through it, looking for more clues. Most of what he found didn't seem to help. There was a drawing of what he assumed was the stone snake effigy with *Alpha Draconis* scrawled next to it. A wavy line in blue was titled *Vino Fluvius*. It had to be the Second River since it continued down the mountain and passed in front of a circle which was presumably the Honeycomb House.

Rodney pulled open the big map and considered again the circled marks. For the first time he noticed a line that went from the edge of Ray's property through the woods to a couple of rectangles. The first was marked *Armamentarium*, and the second bore the mysterious mark £.

"Any idea what this is?" he said pointing at the area. He looked up to see Pinwheel nearly hidden behind a pile of apple peels. Nude apples were stacked on the table next to the peeler. "Pinwheel!" he snapped. "What are we going to do with all those apples?"

Pinwheel's eyes went big as he realized what he'd done. He smiled sheepishly.

Rodney shook his head, but picked the map back up. "Look at this." Rodney pointed at a thin line that went through the woods to the west and arrived at the other buildings.

"What do you think it is?" said Pinwheel.

"Maybe Armamentarium is connected to the army of demons." Rodney tapped the building with his finger. "We have to check it out."

Pinwheel looked at him. "We should bring the rabbits."

* * *

It was well into the afternoon. The sun's heat was heavy on the air, loud bugs afloat in it. Rodney had wanted to leave a note, but Pinwheel insisted they keep Ray in the dark. They easily located the path from the house to the secret location and tromped down it, the rabbits leaping with them like fuzzy guards. Ebenezer bulleted ahead, his small gray frame disappearing into the underbrush. He'd reappear later and wait before shooting off again. Jerome, the mottled black and white rabbit, traveled beside Rodney. He was the elder rabbit and hopped more slowly. The fat golden one, Thundertrump, trailed behind. Rodney could hear the great whumps she made at each landing.

The path was surprisingly wide, almost enough for a car to drive. The trail looked like it had once been more heavily traveled, but the number of low-hanging branches and abundant spiderwebs indicated that it wasn't in high use anymore. Pinwheel strode cautiously behind Ebenezer. He ducked behind each tree and peered around before going further. He was expecting trouble, but Rodney felt safer the farther they went from the old house.

It used to be a place of dull dinners and endless weekends waiting to go home. Sometimes he and his dad would sit on the couches. He would have a toy on his lap, and his dad would grip a magazine while they listened to Ray and his mom laugh in the other room. Rodney couldn't understand their mirth.

Most of their conversations went no further than a single name before the table slapping set off the collapse into guffaws. They tried'd explaining to him and his father what was so funny about Esther Osterhaus or Sam Armstrong, but invariably the explanation would fall apart at the next key phrase.

It would go like this: "Remember Michael Bunyan?" and they'd both laugh. "So precious when he gave mom that—" more laughing and some table slapping. His dad would force a tight smile, his eyes sucked dry of patience. Ray would snort and blurt out, "dried toad!" and his mom would bury her face in her hands. Ray would let his head hang back and unleash his joyous woofing.

Now the knowledge of demonic activity had warped the home. It felt dark and menacing and alive with danger. As they walked, Rodney felt better.

Ahead, he saw Pinwheel stiffen, then duck down. He waved Rodney over. "What do you see?" Rodney asked as he crawled up.

"Two buildings."

"Do you think one could have the Alvarium inside?"

Pinwheel shrugged. "It is possible."

"Lemme look." Rodney edged around the tree and surveyed the area.

The building nearest to them was a long rectangle with green metal siding, faded by the sun. In front of it was a long thin house. Rodney edged around the tree, ducking under the limbs, to get a better look. Across from the long shed was another structure, wood and chickenwire.

"Chickens," he exclaimed. He was about to take another step when Pinwheel grabbed his shoulder.

"It is curious."

"What?" Rodney scanned the area ahead for something.

"The house makes a triangle with the shed and the chicken coop."

"So?"

"A triangle." He repeated with a grimace. "Angels like triangles."

"And demons don't?"

"Like hexagons make angels ill, triangles ward off demons."

"So are you going to brave the triangle or—" he was unable to finish because Pinwheel pulled him back into the bushes, and clamped a hand over his mouth.

He followed Pinwheel's eyes to find a woman had exited the house and was walking to the coop. She wore a white sleeveless dress that touched the grass as she walked. Her silver hair was held back with a blue wrap that covered the top of her head. She looked familiar to Rodney. "Hey, wait. That's Lucasta. She knows Ray."

"Then we do not trust her."

"Ray says she's really nice."

"We cannot trust Ray."

Pinwheel was adamant that they stay hidden. If Lucasta's place was on the map, it made sense that she played some kind of role in the diabolical plot.

She checked on the chickens, made a mark on the clipboard she carried, and returned to the house. Pinwheel and Rodney stayed motionless till they were sure she wasn't returning.

"The first building must be the Armamentarium, and that weird L-looking symbol must stand for Lucasta."

Pinwheel pushed him forward. "We have to find out what's in the *Armamentarium.*"

"Alright. You keep an eye out for Lucasta." Rodney stepped out, and Pinwheel trotted to the center of the triangle. Presumably he'd made himself invisible, but since their chief threats were Ray and other demons, it mattered little.

The building radiated heat, but the bright green grass was thick and miraculously cool. He had to walk to the far end to get to the door. As he drew near, he could see a heavy padlock. He was about to wiggle it to make sure it was locked when an outburst of barking caused him to jump.

Pinwheel squealed and Rodney was pushed face first into the shed. His cap fell off as his lip split and the hot metal thundered from the force of the blow. He fell back and rolled to see his attacker. He found himself face to face with a snarling black Labrador.

The dog crouched again. Rodney cringed against the building as the dog lunged. It yelped as Pinwheel grabbed the chain connected to his collar and yanked back. "Rodney!" he yelled. "Run!" He struggled to hold the dog back.

Rodney scrambled back to the woods. He looked back over his shoulder as the beast bucked free. The chain jerked from Pinwheel's hands. He felt teeth sink into his shoe and he fell. The dog dragged him back. Rodney kicked and spun only to be pinned at the shoulders by the full weight of the dog. He screamed as the dog leaned low. The dog's hot wet breath washing over his face.

The dog paused and spoke. "Scream, pink-mud. Your days are set." His voice was low and grunting. It lilted as if holding back a cough. "No strays!" he roared.

"What?" was all he could manage before hearing another voice. *Lucasta.*

"Mordecai, Mordecai!" she called. The dog looked back silently. Rodney saw Pinwheel ease out of the way as Lucasta took up the chain. She tugged gently on the chain attached to the dog, and he obediently came off him. "Bad dog. We have a guest." She smiled, looking down at Rodney, who was pale and shaken.

"Thanks," was all he could manage. He examined his shoe, the puncture marks in the rubber sole. The teeth had missed his foot, so he rose and lifted his cap from the ground.

"Rodney, what a pleasant surprise." If it were possible, her face brightened. "Come in, come in." She turned and walked back to the house. Rodney followed, catching Pinwheel's eyes and motioning him inside.

His heart slowed, and he wiped the sweat, like thick molasses, from his forehead. He watched Mordecai trot back to his place under the shade near the chicken coop. In the dark hovel his black fur hid him. He looked like any other dog, but it felt so real that it had spoken to him.

They entered from the back porch of the house, a "shotgun house," Lucasta said. The first room was the kitchen, eggshell blue, she noted, as she pulled out a rag, put ice in it, spun it closed, and wet it under the faucet. She handed it to him. "For your lip," she said, and waved for him to follow her.

They entered the next room. The middle room was a dining room, a dark yellow color, a dull gold, with a heavy wood table and a staircase leading upstairs to her bedroom. The front room was her living room—three red couches, a fat rug, and an oval table in the center slathered with books and magazines. The white walls were hidden by paintings, three large ones with smaller pictures scattered around them like offspring.

Lucasta sat down on the billowiest couch, which looked like a deflated valentine's heart. She tossed aside pillows and flopped down on it. He sat on the smallest couch near the front door. He placed his cap on his knee.

"Sorry about Mordecai. He hasn't been the best of dogs lately. Whew, but that's twice for you, right?"

Rodney remembered Ray telling him about his first encounter with a dog. "Yeah, guess so. That's the same dog?"

"I'm afraid so. Nasty little dog now, but he used to be so sweet. Right before your first visit, he was such a cute doggy. Something's gotten into him these last five or so years."

He saw Pinwheel creep into the room. He must've been exploring. Lucasta was telling a story about Mordecai when he was a puppy. Her eyes were lost in the past. Rodney inspected the large paintings. One was a swirling blue painting of the night sky. He'd seen it before, a river of wind with stars flowing toward a moon as bright and yellow as the sun. There was a big black tree looming opposite the sun, interfering with the flow of the night sky.

Lucasta's voice hit a pitch that brought him back from the painting. "Oh, my goodness. Ice cream."

"What?"

"Would you like some?" She stood, raising her eyebrows in expectation.

"Yeah, sure. That's what I remember about last time. I got to eat ice cream."

"I've got chocolate, strawberry, and my special eggnog ice cream. Which do you want?"

"Eggnog ice cream?"

"Oh yeah, it's so good."

"I'll try that."

"Good choice," she said as she left the room. Pinwheel scooted out of the doorway to let her pass.

He crept up to him and whispered, "Sorry, Rodney. I did not see the dog in time."

"'Sokay," he whispered back. "Did you find anything?"

"I can't find a key to the building."

"Look upstairs." He looked through the doorway watching Lucasta getting the ice cream. "I'll stall her, but hurry."

Pinwheel scampered out and a few moments later Lucasta returned with two bowls of yellowish ice cream.

"Yum," she said as she handed it to him.

"You must like ice cream."

"It's all I eat," she said and giggled. She kept her eyes on her bowl and shaved off fat curls of ice cream with her spoon.

Rodney chiseled off a nugget of ice cream and placed it in his mouth. "Wow," he said as the cold pebble dissolved on his tongue. "That tastes just like eggnog."

"I know." She scrunched her nose and giggled again. "I can't get over it. It's my current favorite."

"You must like eggs."

She laughed again. "Oh, yes. I've got thirty-five chickens. I sell most of my eggs to Grover's, but I could eat omelets forever. Omelets and ice cream."

"Uncle Ray said Grover's is out of local eggs."

"Oh?" she acted surprised. "Well, yes, that's true. I'm saving them up."

"What for?"

She paused and her face cringed. She made a sound like *oop!* and clenched her fists. "Ice cream headache," she informed him.

Rodney chuckled. Out of the corner of his eye he saw Pinwheel wave at him and point to the back door. He was leaving. He heard Lucasta sigh in relief, and he pretended to look at the painting on the wall in front of him.

"You like it?" She asked.

"Yeah." It was a giant wave crashing down on some boats. He shoveled the ice cream into his mouth without looking.

"Some people think it's scary, but I think it's exhilarating. But this one," she pointed at the third large painting of two people in the air above a little town, both had wings, but one was soaring upward and the other, whose wings were frayed, was tumbling down. "This one is the scary one." Below the tumbling figure was a man plowing his fields and beyond that a large body of water. Lucasta continued, "I've always hoped he hits the water. Maybe then he'll be okay."

Rodney took the last bite and stood. "Thanks for the ice cream."

"Would you like more? I've got so much."

"No, this is plenty."

"Can you stay and let me show you my chickens?" She stood and took his bowl from him.

"I should get back." He settled his cap on his head and walked toward the back door anxious to see what, if anything, Pinwheel had found.

"I'm so glad you came for a little visit and I'm sorry about Mordecai. Next time come to the front door."

"I will." He walked off, keeping as far away from the dog as he could. Beneath the low roof of Mordecai's shelter he could see the dirt scatter at each breath of the dog. He saw Pinwheel just inside the tree line.

"Goodbye, Rodney," called Lucasta behind him. He waved without looking. "And goodbye, little friend." Pinwheel's eyes grew big. He looked at Rodney and then ducked.

Rodney heard Lucasta giggle to herself one last time and shut the door. He found Pinwheel curled beneath a bush with the rabbits nuzzling him. He sat up and said, "She looked right at me."

CHAPTER ELEVEN

Let Goods and Kindred Go

W hat is going on?" Rodney couldn't stop dismay from seeping into his tone. He and Pinwheel were jogging through the woods with the rabbits doing their best to keep up.

Pinwheel leaped and stretched out his leathery wings to glide. "She must be with them. But how could she see me? And why does she have chickens?" He'd been muttering such things since they'd left Lucasta's.

Rodney pulled up, holding his sides. "Wait, stop. Let's break a moment." He collapsed on the ground cross-legged. "Why does it matter that she has chickens?"

"Chickens attack demons if they can see them."

"And what was with that dog? Did you hear it speak?" Ebenezer clambered into Rodney's lap, while Thundertrump and Jerome confronted Pinwheel. They tittered at him, and Pinwheel leaned close. Jerome spoke in quiet chirps, then turn while Thundertrump barked his contributions. Pinwheel kept saying, "Yes, uh-huh, okay."

Rodney grew impatient. "What? What are they saying?"

Pinwheel looked up. "I couldn't see it, but Mordecai is demon-possessed."

"Why couldn't you see it?"

"Possession is different than cruentation. The spirit is hidden."

Their failures were mounting. They couldn't find the *Alvarium*, nor the twelfth room of the Honeycomb House. They had no idea what Lucasta's role in this was, what was inside the *Armamentarium*, and why her dog was demon-possessed. Rodney picked up a stick from the ground and snapped it in half.

"We've got one last option."

Pinwheel looked up from stroking Jerome's head. "What is that?"

"We have to contact an angel."

"I agree, they will advise us, but you said you do not know how."

"I got an idea. Ray's got some novels. He's always talking about how much you can learn from stories, and I saw one on angels. Maybe it'll have something about how to find them."

Pinwheel's expression sank. "I suppose since we have no other options . . . "

The rabbits followed them into the house. Rodney felt safer with them around, but if it were true that chickens attacked demons, then maybe it would be best to have a few of those too.

They went into the library and Rodney pulled worn paperbacks off the shelves. The first was *The Order of Angels*. Its cover showed a circle of bright dots on a black background. Faint outline of angels could be seen in the brightness. The cover of the second, *The Flood of Demons*, depicted a black column of smoke in a red sky, but within the smoke were demons, rushing downward. After that, anything faintly related to spiritual powers was snagged—titles like *The Fall of the Draconis, The Rainbow Warrior, Sagittarius and the Stargazer*, and the hardback book he had come across on his first day here, *The Jawbone of Heaven*. Taking it off the shelf, he saw that the author's name was Filippo Campanella, the same man who had sent the plans of the Alvarium to Uncle Ray. A quick scan revealed that Campanella was also the author of many of the other books he'd pulled down.

"There's gotta be something in one of these," he said, and tossed a book to Pinwheel. "Here, scan this for clues."

Pinwheel took up the book and turned it over. "I cannot read."

"What?"

"I do not know how to interpret your symbols. Words are a dangerous realm."

"Hm. Looks like I have a lot of work to do. Why don't you get the rabbits some food, and I'll see if I can find out anything." He picked up *The Jawbone of Heaven* and began skimming.

* * *

In the belly of the earth beneath them, Smugbog labored to dig out a place to hide. Since his cruentation, he'd been digging tunnels and alcoves for the new demons arriving daily. Whenever he wasn't digging, he was pierced and drained of ichor so that new warriors could be brought into the material world. He stuffed a few fistfuls of mud into his mouth, swallowing rocks and all, to keep himself anchored to this world. He felt the wriggle of worms in his belly. A dull ache flared up in his body. Unfit for substance, his cruentated flesh groaned to bear such weight. He gnashed his teeth and continued to dig.

The army was growing slowly. Had Smugbog's ears not been filled with wax, they would have been filled with their cries and curses. Any time he raised his eyes in the pitch black, he could see the filthy mutterings of his fellow demons careening down the tunnels.

Out of the corner of his eye, he saw the ripples of sound, someone coming, and the whirlpools of the slop and suck of the mud announced his impending arrival. Smugbog dove into his small crevice and curled up.

"Out, you simpering pile," the demon announced at the opening of his hiding place. The sound waves jostled the darkness. He stood there huffing until Smugbog exited. "Spit-thicket needs one last wastrel, and your rank carcass has been chosen."

Spit-thicket was one of the higher-ranking demons on base. He was nearly human sized and had a fang that twisted out of his mouth sideways. He'd been here for years and knew the traitor adam personally.

"What do you demand of Smugbog?" he said, once he stood.

"Spit-thicket has been given the bearded adam. The Old Master allows it, and Murkpockets roars for it. He falls to the diaboloi."

Smugbog looked up. "Heaven has abandoned him?"

Spit-thicket struck Smugbog across the brow. His head collided with the dirt wall. Spit-thicket leaned down into his ear and said, "Do you think Hell reaches for what cannot be had?" He put his foot on Smugbog's neck and pushed him into the mud. "Hell does not stretch out its hand for defeat."

"Anymore," Smugbog squeaked from beneath Spit-thicket's foot.

"Ever again," He said, before shoving Smugbog one last time. Spit-thicket spun around and marched quickly off through the darkness.

Smugbog stood up and had to hurry to keep up with him. "What of the boy?"

"He is not required of Hell."

"Then Heaven holds him dear?"

Spit-thicket growled. "Hell cares not. The Old Master says to leave the boy for now."

"And the stray?" Smugbog winced even as he said it. This had been the murmur of all since it happened. It was not a topic the leadership wished to address.

Because of this stray, all diaboloi must have their ears sealed with wax, lest they be subjected to the Name. Because of the stray, all had to peer into the black for the shape of the commands, for the whirls and eddies of sounds. It was a demanding and tedious job added to their other labors and inconveniences.

"The stray," answered Spit-thicket slowly, "will be dealt with soon. Right now, he can only cause the child panic. His fear will spawn fear in the boy. And when the time comes, vengeance will be mine."

He followed Spit-thicket up the twisting tunnels and couldn't help but envy the expansion since his arrival. The tunnels were wider and bustling with activity. They entered into a huge dome.

The drain station had been expanded, and the cavern was filled with moaning demons. Buckets of ichor were carried to a giant pulley in the center of the large room. The contents spilled out as they were hoisted upward to the *Alvarium* at the top of the underground fortress.

Down the spiral staircase that lined the cavern trudged the newly cruentated demons. They were lethargic and disgruntled as they were shuffled into the draining stations, their blood going back into the hive so that new warriors could be recruited.

"The army will soon be full," observed Smugbog still following on the heels of Spit-thicket through the crowd.

"Bah," he barked over his hairy shoulder. "There are hardly six thousand fouling the dirt."

"How many are needed?"

Spit-thicket paused. He looked up at the hundreds and hundreds of laboring demons. "Murkpockets is a fool if he thinks it will take less than the first army."

"As many as at the first uprising? But we do not battle angels, but breathing dirt."

Spit-thicket turned to face him again. Smugbog instinctively flinched. "If it were the windbags only, then you and ten other worms would be enough to bring this land to ruin, but do you not know that heaven loves these adams and eves? They are Heaven's teeth and tongue to enjoy this world."

Smugbog shrunk back as Spit-thicket warmed to his lecture. "Let me tell you what will happen the moment Hell squirms out from under the boot of the angels." Spittle began to fly from his mouth as he spoke; it was like a spiderweb fountain. He picked up a stone from the mud to make his point.

"Heaven will break open, like last time, and pour out her wrath." He split the rock with his hands and held the halves out wide. "She strikes sevenfold for the least effrontery to her precious grubs."

"But how?" asked Smugbog. "Hell is material here. The angeloi cannot touch these diaboloi."

Spit-thicket considered his answer. "Hell is shrewd, but Heaven is far more shrewd. Their wickedness upends Hell's. The Name will have something, some trick, to rescue this world. And do you know why?" Spit-thicket let his face split into a horrible grin.

Smugbog shook his head. He felt a table at his back. A demon behind him whittled a wood dagger to assist the draining.

Spit-thicket snagged a small demon from the air. The demon grunted and flailed in the larger demon's claws. "Let me show you why," he said as he held the captured demon before Smugbog's eyes.

As he watched, Spit-thicket inserted a claw from each hand into the demon's stomach. The demon kicked and cursed, and swallowed an anguished cry while slowly, horribly, Spit-thicket ripped it open, allowing the gore and dark liquid to splash and mix into the mud at their feet.

Smugbog watched with a snarl to his face, masking his fright.

When he had finished prying the demon open, now empty of innards and ichor, it ceased resisting and merely twitched in Spit-thicket's hands. He shook the dead demon and asked, "What do you see of earth here?"

"Nothing," Smugbog answered. He longed to dig another hole, far away from here, crawl inside, and never return to this slimy pit.

"That's right." He shook the carcass for emphasis. "There is nothing of earth here. The diaboloi are not of dust. But Heaven is full of its filth." He tossed the body of the demon aside. "Another may eat him. Spit-thicket was sick of his frailness, a waste of ichor."

He turned to look at Smugbog again. "Now do you see why the army will never be enough until all of Hell is here?"

"But the Old Master . . . "

Spit-thicket snapped, "The Old Master is weak. He has not moved for two thousand years." He ducked into a tunnel and continued on.

Smugbog stepped over the remains of the once cruentated demon, whose spirit was winging back to the suffering river, bereft of his material body. He wondered how long it would take him to return to the army. He shivered and followed after his cruel commander.

Following the ripples of Spit-thicket's voice, Smugbog entered a low roofed room around which eleven other demons sat. This would be the team of avengers. Spit-thicket was briefing them on their target.

"He is a saint. Many of you have encountered him before. Spit-thicket was among the first to try him as a young tempter.

Many flocked here to seek his downfall. Hell has tormented his family and neighbors with much success until he offered the diaboloi a deal: a doorway to this world if we tempted only him and withdrew from the city."

There was an outburst of scoffing and disdain from the other demons. Smugbog drew closer to the circle.

"Bribing Hell with safety did not content it." Spit-thicket coughed. He continued, "It took Hell years to reverse engineer the Alvarium Maleficorum, but now Hell has five Alvaria working at full capacity. For this, the envy belongs to Rotsnogger." He indicated a demon next to him. There were snorts and snarls in response to this. Rotsnogger could not contain his grinning malice, baring his bloodstained teeth. He did not anchor himself with dirt. Most demons were too fearful of drawing Heaven's eye over the life of a sparrow, but Rotsnogger refused to fasten himself to matter by anything dead. He argued that the life of all flesh was in the blood, so he hunted small creatures and gleefully killed them to keep himself corporeal.

"But," said Spit-thicket raising his voice above the rabble, "the adam has discovered the extra Alvaria. He has raised his hand against Hell, and Heaven does not challenge."

"Is his life to be sifted?" said Cankersoot, his long fingers flexing and his thin tongue darting.

"No," answered Spit-thicket. A brood of hisses and loud clicking of forked tongues arose.

"It is hard to take a life that does not give itself to the outer darkness," explained Rotsnogger. "The adam will be held until the outbreak. After that, his life is nothing. The ire of Heaven will come whether his breath is shed or not."

Spit-thicket stood. "Ray has brought fire to the Alvarium designated Spite. He proceeds to Alvarium Avarice. Hell strikes him there."

There was an outburst of "Vengeance is mine!" They raised their fists, flapped their wings, and gnashed their teeth. Smugbog shrunk from their rage. The demons filed out and flew up a steep tunnel heading for the surface, and he followed them.

Ahead he could see a pinprick of light between the dangling legs of the host. The sun already stung his eyes. Soon his eyes would feel the burn, and his flesh would scald. This was Smugbog's first time to exit the deep pit. Activity above ground had been scaled back recently. None but the highest ranking could leave the pit during the day. Smugbog felt envy smolder inside him.

They burst out of the hole under the canopy of the forest. They settled on the earth and let their bodies adjust to the singe and scorch. Smoke rose from their bodies until the cinder died. Smugbog tried not to writhe and whimper in his suffering. He followed the others in standing still and breathing in the cool acid of the air.

He found that the pain was less when he shut his eyes, even though the brightness of the world shone through his eyelids. He could still make out the trees with their wavering leaves. The cursed air coursed through the underbrush, causing a skittering, and Smugbog was able to see it all through closed eyes.

The clenched breathing of the demons around him slowed, and they broke the circle, Cankersoot leading the way with his delicate tongue. Smugbog watched Rotsnogger seize a sparrow from the air and stuff it fully into his mouth. He chewed, holding the dead bird on his tongue to stain his teeth, then swallowed. Smugbog shivered.

"The diaboloi will show themselves," Rotsnogger said, and the forms of the demons became slightly darker to Smugbog's veiled eyes. He made himself visible to the world around them as well and followed the group to their prey.

* * *

Rodney threw the last book on the ground and fell back in his chair. It wasn't a thorough search, but he had skimmed any section that dealt with angels and demons and found nothing about calling angels or destroying demons short of already knowing an angel and having a flaming sword. Ray said there was an abundance to learn from stories, but he was unable to learn anything to help his situation.

The rabbits sat around Pinwheel and his plate of veggies. Pinwheel was exploring the taste of celery and tomatoes and carrots. Rodney snagged a carrot nub and hid his eyes from the red glare of the low sun.

The books were all action-adventure sci-fi novels with the exception of *The Jawbone of Heaven*. Rodney spent most of his time perusing its pages. It was a scholarly book on a creature called a Basilisk, the king of snakes, which appeared in the myths and legends from one side of the earth to the other.

Rodney recognized the Thunder Snake story before turning the page and having it laid out before him just as Ray had explained. Rodney eagerly read about the method of killing a Thunder Snake, but since it involved a stone being thrown from heaven (the so-named Jawbone of Heaven), there wasn't much point in getting excited. Still no information about contacting Heaven in the event of a demonic takeover, so they were back at square one.

Pinwheel looked up from the rabbits. "Learn anything?"

"Sure did," Rodney responded in fake cheer. "Did you know that angels are actually living, breathing stones?"

Pinwheel shook his head.

"That's right. Spiritual stones, according to Filippo Campanella."

"How does that help us?"

Rodney dropped the enthusiasm. "It doesn't. Waste of time," he said, indicating the scattered books around them.

Pinwheel's shoulders slumped and the rabbits nuzzled him, which provoked a small grin.

"What time is it? Where's Ray?" asked Rodney aloud. He walked into the stair room to check the clock. The phone burst into clangs, causing Rodney to jump back. He put his hand to his heart and laughed nervously to Pinwheel. He lifted the receiver from the cradle and said, "Hello?"

"Rodney, hey sweetie. I've missed you."

"Mom!" He was surprised by his eagerness and relief at hearing the voice of his mother, but then the feeling of abandonment returned.

"What's been going on?"

"Nothing." Rodney folded his voice into as tiny a thing as he could manage. He put in the bare minimum volume in his responses to her. He realized how far away she was, how impossible to help him. While telling him about their new house, she asked several times if he was still there. Each time he responded with a low huff.

His mother realized this and switched stories midway. "Oh, hey, guess what almost happened to me?"

Rodney, ever the sucker for a story, fell into her exuberance and asked, "What?"

"A grasshopper attacked me and I almost hit a truck."

"You almost had a wreck?"

"No, I did have a wreck, but I almost hit a truck."

"What happened?" His mother was every bit the storyteller that Ray was.

"Well I was just driving down the road when my leg started to itch, like something was crawling up it. Brrr." He could sense the shivers of his mother. "I look down and there is this huge, huge black grasshopper. I screamed, of course."

"Of course," he repeated.

"And he just starts leaping like crazy. He's hitting the door and making little thump noises and I'm kicking and screaming and I didn't notice but I was drifting into the next lane. Thankfully the truck honked and I was able to swerve in time to get out of the way. Went into the ditch on the other side."

"Wow. Are you hurt?"

"No, I'm fine and the car's fine too."

"What'd ya do with the grasshopper?"

"Nothing. Darn thing just disappeared. I couldn't find it. Maybe I squished it to pieces."

Rodney laughed, "It's just a bunch 'a dirt on the car floor."

"Oh yuck."

Rodney laughed. Quick guffaws that required deep breaths afterwards to recover. He hadn't laughed like that since he'd arrived at the Honeycomb House. All his laughter was nervous or polite or shallow, but he felt a yearning reach through the phone lines and connect himself and his mother together.

They recovered from their mirth slowly and let the phone lines crackle with their huffings.

His mother finally said, "Guess my guardian angel was looking out for me."

Like a hook anchored into the back of his shirt, her comment hauled him back into his situation. Guardian angel, the idea shook him.

"So you think I have a guardian angel?" His tone changed and his mother heard it.

"What do you mean, Rodney? Of course you have a guardian angel." He could hear her concern, her motherly worry. She continued, "Are you okay? Where's Uncle Ray?"

Rodney felt the rabbits at his ankle and—in Thundertrump's case—his shins. "Uh, he's out. On a walk."

"A walk? What time is it?"

Rodney looked at the clock in front of him. He ignored the weird symbols and focused on the position of the arms. "Eight thirty."

"Oh, okay. Well, is everything else alright?"

This was Rodney's chance. He could start to unfold the mystery from the very beginning. Otis and apparitions, suspicions, rabbits, and Ray's weirdness, Pinwheel, possessed dogs, and the demonic plot against the world, but he could feel how unbelievable it would be to his mother's ears. He hardly believed it himself. He let his shoulders fall and said, "I'm fine." From there the conversation collapsed into their quiet goodbyes, and Rodney felt that he'd never see her again. He felt afraid and held back tears as he hung up.

Immediately the phone rang again.

"Hello?"

"Ray there?"

"No, he's—"

"Tell him I'll be there with Al in the morning. I've had it with him."

"Okay."

"It's Otis."

"Okay."

"Bye."

Rodney held onto the receiver, listening to the dialtone. Pinwheel entered; the rabbits patrolled the room.

"What's happening?" Pinwheel asked.

Rodney heard a rumbling and the thunderous sounds of a cannon. He dropped the receiver and ran to the front door. The sound grew louder. When he opened the door its pitch was raised to a high roar.

Outside Rodney saw Ray's car speeding down the gravel driveway, thin flags of fire waving from its roof as it swerved and skewed wildly. The rabbits leaped in front of him, their hackles up and hissing. Rodney saw why when out of the forest in pursuit was a horde of demons sprinting and flying after the burning car.

Rodney watched speechless as the car slid, turned sideways and spun, the clatter of fire, metal, and tires screamed over the groaning of gravel. The car slammed into the workshop and the door was kicked open.

A figure in a rainbow-colored bee suit climbed out to confront the charging demons. His left arm was also on fire, and he swung wildly as the crowd swallowed him up.

Rodney stumbled out onto the porch. "RAY!"

The fight did not last long, and the rainbow-clad figure was knocked down and beaten. Soon he was spread out on the ground as the demons finished. The hood was removed and Rodney saw Ray's wild beard. His head lolled back, unconscious, as they dragged him into the woods.

Rodney yelled, and the demons catcalled and taunted him in response. He was frozen to the spot. "Oh no, oh no, oh no," was all he could think to say.

Pinwheel shrunk back inside the house. "Heaven has turned her back on us."

The fire on the car slowly died, and the howls and cackles from the demons faded. The rabbits nuzzled Rodney and herded him inside the house. The house was dark and unsafe. Rodney sank into a ball. Where was his guardian angel in all of this?

♌

CHAPTER TWELVE

RAGE

Murkpockets read the returning raiders' triumphant cries skittering in the black, and he vindictively punted his way through the crowded tunnels to meet them. He licked his teeth at the cries of his underlings as he crossed the upper channel connecting the entry shafts.

Howls of envy crowded the air as he arrived at the landing. The raiding party was adding spidery bonds to their captured prey by vomiting sticky cords on his arms and legs. Black flecks spattered against the walls in his struggling.

Murkpockets leaned forward as if to spit. "How tastes the bile of Hell, Raymond Lauter?"

The blindfolded figure stiffened. "Murkpockets? Is that your stench?" The words of the saint were harder to read in the darkness, tempered with a greater fire and cooled in greater water than the demon's.

"The envy is mine," Murkpockets gloated.

"You rapscallions really stepped in it this time."

"The 'rapscallions,'" Murkpockets intoned, "are full of arrogance and do not fear the hand of Heaven in this." The demons surrounding them chortled venomously and sneered. Murkpockets raised a leathery wing to silence them. "Take the fool up to the Alvarium so that he may hear the army of Hell grow."

They began dragging Ray up the tunnel.

A chorus of taunts sprang up. "Drag him slowly!" said one. "Let the mud of the pit be ground in his bones!" said another. "Take him up the ramp so that the new may spit on him!"

Murkpockets called after them, "A traitor of Heaven is worse than a servant of Hell!" and they answered him with a wave of cackles and howls.

Murkpockets made his way to the dankest pit, where the Old Master lay prone and unspeaking. With the arrival of Itchpot, a larger and therefore higher-ranking demon, Murkpockets didn't have the access he had once had to the father of Hell. His rise in the ranks of the demons had sputtered as his work was being seized.

Murkpockets replayed his wounds, his arrival in Twin Rivers, the striking of the deal with Ray: to enter the world, to leave behind the threat of the angels forever, to grow powerful in matter, all for withdrawing from the town. He exchanged the petty successes of tempting the simpletons of Twin Rivers for a stepping-stone to the ruin of the world.

His act sent shock waves throughout the spiritual world. Demons flocked to Twin Rivers, angels drew back, and soon even the Old Master had lumbered into town from his pit in Mount Vesuvius. The trail of demons required to carry the ancient demon sent him into fits of envy. Cruentation had to stop while a place for the limp Prince of Darkness was dug. Murkpockets rehearsed his wounds to keep his anger stoked; his bid for power was stunted when the failed rebel of Heaven demanded his hovel. His hot tears made ditches in the grime of his cheeks.

Murkpockets crossed the dome wherein the demons had their newborn ichor sucked out of them so that more could come. He ducked into the tunnel that led to the rooms where the inner circle of demons bickered about plans and diversions for the bustling, rebellious horde of Hell. He passed two guards stationed outside the room which led to the Old Master's pit. Only Itchpot, like some obese cork, blocked his way.

"You are done speaking to the Old Master, Murkpockets. He does not say things twice. *Hurkle!*" He heaved at his burping; the stench in the room increased.

"He does not say things at all, Itchpot." Rumors in the lower ranks insisted that his tongue had been ripped out long ago, but Murkpockets knew better. He'd had the Old Master's tongue lacerate his face numerous times since he'd arrived in Twin Rivers.

Itchpot chortled. "Yes, and he quits his gospelling, too." He made a writing motion with his hand. "His psalms—*breep!*—have dried up. Itchpot has ceased the paper production."

Murkpockets shivered. "Foul mocker."

Itchpot burped and smiled, nodding at the honorific. "Hell will bind his forty pages and force the tempters to—*hurkle*—study it like the children of men."

Murkpockets rubbed his hands together. "Or Murkpockets can bonfire it to Heaven to let the Name puzzle over its wickedness. Now move aside so that Murkpockets can deliver the message."

"There can be nothing the Old—*urgah*—Master must hear. So leave him to his mute festering."

"Ray has been taken."

Itchpot rose from his seated position. His muscles strained under the weight and his belly swung sideways like a tired bell. "The Old Master does not need to be informed of success—*breep*—and informing him of failures garners no mercy. If Hell stretches out its hand, then Heaven has ratified it, no need to—*higauff, higauff*—preen in her allowance."

Murkpockets snarled.

"Come, Murkpockets, the Cruelties begin soon." Itchpot waddled toward him, and he was forced to back out and follow.

The pit had slowly evolved over the five years since Murkpockets and a few other demons had first started it. Initially it was just a small hole beneath the Alvarium Ray had built. As the number of cruentated demons grew, the space was expanded more and more in all directions. Finally the haphazard digging was reined in by Fibditch. He laid out what became the design of the anti-Eden. The small room beneath the Alvarium over the next few years became the hollow a four-story building could fit into. Little pockets lined the spiral ramp that hugged the cavern's walls.

At the bottom of the cavern were three tunnels. The middle one, the one Itchpot and Murkpockets emerged from, was the leadership arm. It held the abode of the Old Master and the command rooms. At least one of the top-ranking demons (Itchpot, Murkpockets, Rotsnogger, Spit-thicket, and Fibditch) could be found there, dealing out orders or punishments or whatever else needed threatening.

The other two tunnels, running east and west, were more or less catacombs where the demons recuperated after being drained or else continued the expansion of the barracks. This is where the two rivals walked now. They looked down the aisles which were pocked with alcoves for fainting, ichor-deprived demons. As they walked, smaller demons were careful to stay away from the two powerful leaders. Occasionally Murkpockets would flick out a wing to strike an unwary demon.

Draining ichor was slow, and as their number grew, there was too much time for idle demons to get into mischief. Hell would eat itself if there were idleness enough.

To solve this, Itchpot suggested that a stadium be dug out for fights and maiming, two popular pastimes in the outer darkness. It was agreed to, and another large room was begun. It was an amphitheater, a great sphere filled with smaller circles that descended to an open space in the center.

Murkpockets and Itchpot entered the great room already full of squirming, shoving underlings. The crowd flinched and fell back as the two approached. They chose seats midway down the sphere and kicked their feet up onto the backs of those in front of them.

Demons were conscripted. Great warriors were unleashed on weaker demons, or if the demons were evenly matched one demon would have his wings clipped and hands tied. Demons hate fair fights and dramatic tension. They like a clear-cut winner.

This is the lesson the Old Master insisted on. It was an insult that Heaven had mighty angelic warriors, but rarely used them. Heaven preferred the stuttering, desperate victories through the weakness of humanity. It was perverse. The mighty should always win, and if the Enemy didn't press her advantage, then Hell would show her how.

Cruentated demons were mightier than the dirtbags of flesh and were out of the reach of angels, so the lesson of strength was safe under the current conditions. The mob was already in a mudthirsty frenzy. "What is the game, Itchpot?"

Itchpot made a burping sound and scratched his paunch. "It is Sticks and Stones, *uhbaugh*. Itchpot prefers Crushing."

Sticks and Stones was a game of two demons fighting using only the bodies of smaller demons that were shackled and thrown into the arena. Crushing was more of an intellectual pleasure, one demon, the crusher, among a line of prostrate demons getting their heads crushed one by one. Both games sent ripples of envy up Murkpocket's spine.

He bristled and sneered at the two larger demons strolling onto the muddy floor of the arena. As per demonic ethics only one demon would get smaller demons to use as weapons. It was his job to make sure he kept them or broke them so his opponent couldn't use them. Fair play makes Hell sick.

"Ah," gurgled Itchpot. "That is Gag-racket, a vile deceiver," he said pointing out a lean warrior accepting a shivering demon, bound in the shape of a spear.

"Three wings on the cripple," Murkpockets said, indicating Gag-racket's limping opponent. "That he will put on a show."

Itchpot appraised the slighter demon. "Done."

They sat forward as the battle began. Gag-racket jumped and threw the demon like a bolt from the sky. His target, whose name was Garglenails, rolled sideways to avoid the assault. The thrown demon smashed into the ground, sending the muck that covered the hard stone floor into the stands. The delighted audience booed, the sound careening off the walls.

Garglenails picked up the dazed demon and slung him back at Gag-racket. Gag-racket caught two small demons tossed from the stands and slammed them both down on the sailing missile. The demon spear hit the ground and didn't move. The two fighters circled each other, Gag-racket waving the smaller demons like clubs.

Murkpockets clenched his fists and spoke between his teeth. "Now that the traitorous adam has been taken, the boy should fall soon."

Itchpot burped loudly, chewed briefly, and turned to him. "Your impatience is appreciated, Murkpockets, but the child must be taken only when the army is raised."

Murkpockets's face crumpled into a horrible scowl. He spit, the muddy glob striking the back of the demon before him. "It galls Murkpockets."

"And the stray too will fall. Hell cannot stand his weakness."

They paused to watch a particularly brutal part of the match. Gag-racket had sent Garglenails to his knees and he was making sure nothing would rise from the ground again. The arena was littered with the broken bodies of the smaller demons used as weapons.

"The army grows too slowly. The boy might seek help from Heaven if Hell delays."

"All—*higauff*—in bad time, wicked one."

Gag-racket ceased his slaughter and stood, "To the victor go the spoils!" he yelled over the boos and curses of the crowd. Gag-racket began to feast on the corpses of the slain demons. The crowd stood and began to leave, some to cram mud into their mouths to remain weighty, some to dig, some to have their ichor drained.

Murkpockets grabbed a couple of demons and ripped their wings off. He handed them to Itchpot. "It was a dull match, so here are your winnings."

Itchpot took the wings and tossed them over his shoulder. "Yes, I agree, it was a delightful fight."

Murkpockets stood and faced Itchpot. "But your delay sickens me. The Old Master said there would be no strays!"

Itchpot waved a hand. "No strays, yes, Itchpot has heard you yammer—*urgah*—about it countless times. But the Old Master has a surprise for all. Heaven overlooks it, else she would have acted."

"It is too late. Hell is moving out from under the hand of the angeloi," he said and stomped off. "Murkpockets wants the stray."

✳ ✳ ✳

Rodney awoke in bed surrounded by rabbits. He was curled around the fuzzy gray stone of Ebenezer, Jerome was at his head, and Thundertrump buried his feet. He heard the jangling snore of Pinwheel somewhere above him on the bed.

As carefully and as quietly as he could, Rodney sat up. The dresser shoved against the bedroom door was undisturbed and Libra, Rodney's bat, was leaning against the bed where he had left it.

Pinwheel argued that had demons wanted to tear down the wall they could've done so easily, but it still made Rodney feel better to barricade the way. He wasn't as confident as Pinwheel that the rabbits would keep them safe. Rodney slid off the bed, pulled his shoes on, and pushed the dresser back. As he opened the door Thundertrump sat up and barked at Pinwheel. Pinwheel stirred.

"Whazzat, Murgpoggits, huh?" Pinwheel rubbed his eyes. He saw Rodney about to slip out the door. He shook his head to get his eyes straight. "What just happened? My eyes were closed and . . . and—" he looked around. "And the sun came up all of a sudden."

Rodney gave Pinwheel a confused look. "You were asleep."

"What is 'asleep'?"

"It's . . . I don't know. It's rest. You get tired and you have to sleep."

"So that is what it is like. Wow, super weird."

Rodney shrugged. "No it isn't. It's normal."

Pinwheel looked around, checking his arms and legs for other changes. "I did not realize, but I was aching last night. I thought it was fear, but I feel better now. This is neat."

Rodney frowned. "You're weird." He moved to leave again.

"Where are you going?"

"We've got to contact my guardian angel. I have an idea."

The whole crew, three rabbits and a former demon, followed Rodney outside and into the backyard. There, right next to the kitchen window, was a ladder that led to a deck on the second story. From there, another ladder led to the third story roof.

"It's for cleaning the windows of the observatory," he explained to Pinwheel as he climbed up the ladder. Leaving the rabbits below, Pinwheel followed him.

They went straight to the top. Rodney shivered despite the early heat of the morning. He pulled himself up the ladder. He looked across the open field. The sun lit up the tree tops, and in the distance the mountain seemed smoky with fire. The air felt heavy, and a cold fright weighed down on Rodney.

Slowly, gingerly, Rodney crawled on top of the house. The roof wasn't steep and the windows of the observatory had ridges that were easy to hold, but it took him two minutes to let go of the ladder. It took another two for him to slide his knees onto the roof. He leaned against the shingles, holding the ridge of the windows on either side and hunkered down in fear. His palms ran soggy with sweat. He was forty-plus feet in the air.

Pinwheel remained on the ladder, watching him. "What are you doing?"

A wind blew, and Rodney realized he'd left his hat in his room. "I was going to—going to j-jump."

Pinwheel realized the plan. "So your guardian angel will catch you?"

"That's the plan," he said, but it was clear that he was frozen to the spot. One foot was still on the ladder, the other braced at the edge of the roof.

Pinwheel looked down. It was almost seven o'clock, and long shadows still covered the grass. "It is a good idea," he said.

"Yeah, but I don't know that I could jump far enough from the house to make it to the grass."

"You don't want to make it to the grass," replied Pinwheel. "You want to be caught."

"Yeah, but I need to give him plenty of time to catch me too."

"True."

"I don't think I can even move, though."

Pinwheel reached out to push Rodney. He jostled Rodney's leg.

"Don't!" barked Rodney. His whole body had seized up.

"Go," he said.

"I can't."

"Do it."

"No, I don't want to anymore. Back up, I'm coming down." Pinwheel dropped down the ladder and Rodney slowly scooted back. Once they were on the second floor deck Rodney's legs began to tremble. He squatted down and put his arms on his knees.

"What were you doing, Pinwheel? Trying to kill me?"

"Time is running out. The demons have taken Ray. They will come for me and you next."

Rodney hid his eyes from Pinwheel. "You said Ray was working with them."

"He was."

Rodney pulled his head up to look at the black creature in front of him. "Then why did they attack him and beat him up and drag him off?" Tears had sprung to his eyes.

Pinwheel slouched. "I do not know."

"Do guardian angels exist?"

"Yes."

"Would mine have caught me?"

Pinwheel paused and looked to the sky. "I do not know."

"But you were telling me to jump."

Pinwheel was silent a moment. "Come on, I've got a better idea." He turned his back on Rodney and descended the stairs.

Once on the ground Rodney felt better. His legs lost the jelly feeling. He followed Pinwheel into the woods, the rabbits trailing behind.

"In my first days here," Pinwheel said, as Rodney caught up with him, "since I was banned from the pit, I spent a lot of time wandering the woods at night."

They were heading in the direction of the highway, about where Rodney had tromped through his first day here. The ground grew steep as they went up the final hill of Skeleton Mount.

"That is when I found the steep place." Pinwheel said.

They trudged in silence, pausing every now and then to let the rabbits catch up. Rodney felt silly, but the rabbits did indeed give him some comfort. By the time they reached the ravine, leaves were stuck to Rodney's skin and twigs clung to Pinwheel's furry shoulders and arms. The coolness of the river cut the heavy air. Rodney took big breaths to calm himself.

The ravine was steep, and the Second River swarmed fifteen feet below.

"So you think I should jump?"

Pinwheel nodded. "It is safer than leaping off the Honeycomb House."

"There's a waterfall down that way," Rodney said, pointing westward. "I crossed it my first day here."

"I know, I followed you. Well, Birthless followed you."

"That's creepy. Glad I didn't know that at the time." He looked down at the gurgling river. The surface billowed with the speed of the current. The water was dark and quiet. "How deep do you think it is?"

Without a word Pinwheel leapt and sailed down the steep slope of the ravine with his wings outstretched. Right before hitting the water he folded them and slipped into the water with hardly a splash.

Rodney was too stunned to do anything before Pinwheel burst out of the water like a rocket, zipped up the embankment, and alighted next to him again. "It is near seven and a half lengths of me," he announced, and then shook himself, like a dog, sending the water out in all directions.

Rodney shielded himself from the spray. "Wow, that was cool. I didn't think you could fly that fast."

Pinwheel couldn't help but smile. "I can tie the front side of the east to the backside of the west."

"So seven and a half lengths, that means, what, since you're around two feet tall, something like, um, fifteen feet deep?"

"Yes, with rocks at the bottom."

"Wait, if you can fly then why don't you just fly up to Heaven? Can you go that high?"

Pinwheel shook his head. "Heaven is not up. Heaven is beside us far away."

"Beside us? Far away? Why does everything have to make no sense?"

Pinwheel shrugged again. "I have heard some adams talk about Heaven being on the other side of what we see. Nearby but impossible to reach through our own powers."

"So it's right next to us, but we can't get to it."

Pinwheel half nodded, half shrugged, half put his hands in the air.

Rodney heaved out a sigh and ran his fingers through his hair. "Great. You're such a huge help, by the way."

"We have to get your angel to show up."

Rodney looked down at the ground as it sloped into the water below. "I don't get it. If my guardian angel is here, why can't he hear us talking about him? Why won't he just show up?"

"I don't know."

Rodney crossed his arms. "But if I jump into the water and almost drown, he'll show up."

"I think so, yes."

"Think so or know so?"

"I know so," he said more firmly. "I think."

Rodney settled his feet into the soft turf, putting his weight on one leg then the other. "Okay, okay, okay." He began rocking forward. "This is so dumb. This is stupid." He took a few deep breaths. Rodney closed his eyes. "But when you're in danger your guardian angel comes to save you."

"Right."

"Stupid, stupid, stupid." Rodney took a deep breath and edged forward to scoot down the slope. He began a controlled slide on his heels with a hand on the ground to balance him.

Midway down, his speed increased and a root caught his left foot and flipped him over. He cried out and fell, bounced and rolled into the surging river with a great splash. There was a flash of light. Rodney felt a cold sting; black wet surrounded him. Bubbles tickled his face as the shock of the frigid water caused his body to clench, releasing the air in his lungs. His arms were outspread, but he couldn't move them.

A black bolt struck the water. Propelled by four limbs and two wings, something latched onto Rodney and pulled him upward. Rodney burst into the air and sucked in great drafts of it to smother the fire in his lungs. He sank down and had to be pulled back to the surface by Pinwheel's bony arm. He sputtered and kicked with his legs to stay above the rolling water.

The current was even stronger than it looked from the bank, and the rocks were too slick to cling to. They careened from one rock to another before Rodney managed to shove Pinwheel atop an outcropping. He managed to lodge himself between two other rocks until Pinwheel was able to fling the wet from his wings and draw him from the rapids.

Rodney recovered, pressed against the sides of the ravine, before they climbed out of it. Once they had moved to a safe distance from the river, Rodney collapsed to his knees. He curled up in the weeds and fallen leaves, covering his face with his arms.

They'd managed to end up on the same side of the river they'd started on, only several dozen feet from where Rodney had fallen in. He found a place where the sun angled past the tree canopy, and he let its thin heat burrow into his back. They lay motionless for some time.

Pinwheel finally spoke. "The curious thing about you and your uncle is that the demons have seen no signs of your guardian angels."

"What? We don't have guardian angels?"

"The demons seem to think that you both have been abandoned."

Abandoned. The word struck Rodney like a fist in the stomach.

Pinwheel continued, "Demons don't always see guardian angels, but typically there's some sign of heavenly protection. A bright dot of light on the forehead, a golden halo, a protective aura, something to indicate divine oversight. Demons can't touch anyone unless a person dismantles the seal of heaven themselves or the Name grants it."

Rodney wasn't listening. He curled himself into a tighter ball and focused on breathing. The leaves creaked and crackled with life, wind, and bugs. Birds pitched into the air, branches swinging with their landing or leaping, their songs scattered and clipped.

"I'm alone, Pinwheel. I've been abandoned by everyone."

Pinwheel looked at his quivering form. "Not true, Rodney."

"My dad, my mom, my uncle, I don't even have a guardian angel."

Pinwheel nudged him with his furry foot. "Not by everyone."

"Who can I trust? Who can help?"

Pinwheel kicked Rodney's soggy backside. "Not by everyone! I am here. I am your friend."

Rodney sat up, dirt and leaves stuck to him. His face slumped into a grim look. "But you didn't even tell me I had no angel. You let me jump into the river. You would've let me jump off the house too."

Pinwheel's eyes searched the ground. Rodney couldn't tell if it was embarrassment or evasiveness. "I thought I just could not see signs of your angel. I am not an experienced tempter. I was mocked. I was always afraid that I would be eaten and sent back to the outer darkness."

"I don't care what happened to you back then. It sounds like demons are horrible things, but you aren't supposed to be a demon anymore. You're supposed to be my friend." A hurt tone entered Rodney's voice. His fists were clenched. "Friends don't let their friends jump off houses and cliffs."

Pinwheel continued to plead. "We don't have much time. We had to do something."

"*We*? *We* haven't done anything. *I* just nearly killed myself! Why don't *you* do something?" Rodney stood up, his legs still wobbly with adrenaline and fear.

Pinwheel retreated a step. "I am sorry, Rodney. I did not know. I did not know."

"You're just a demon, abandoned by other demons." Rodney shoved him.

Pinwheel's eyes blinked. "Stop it, Rodney."

Rodney stood and picked up a nearby stick. "How do I know I can trust you? What if you're just using me?" He swung the stick back and forth to drive Pinwheel back.

"I pulled you from the water." Pinwheel stretched his arms out as he backpedaled.

"So?" Rodney's face was red and speckled with grit. "You told me not to trust Ray and he's gone now. He was the only one that could help us."

"I—I did not know."

"You lied to me."

"I would not lie, Rodney, you—you saved me. You pulled me from the darkness. I am subject to the Name now." He dropped to his knees to stop Rodney's advance.

"So?" Rodney looked down at the fearful demon. "I don't know the Name."

"Yes, you do," Pinwheel said.

"I don't know that Name. I am not under that Name." He raised the stick above his head. "And neither are you." He brought the stick down and smashed the crown of Pinwheel's head. The demon crumpled under the blow.

Rodney stood over the prone figure. "I thought you were tougher than that. I thought demons couldn't be hurt so easily." Pinwheel didn't respond. Rodney nudged him with his foot. Pinwheel was breathing. He threw the stick down beside the motionless demon and oriented himself to the house.

The rabbits arrived, having finally caught up to them. Thundertrump went immediately to where Pinwheel was sprawled. Rodney stumbled off into the woods with Ebenezer and Jerome following him. They chirped and tried to block him, but he stepped over them and continued. Finally they stopped and let him leave.

The ground sloped down, and Rodney leaned against the trees to keep from falling. His knees were weak, and water was still squishing out of his shoes. His eyes watered. He was alone.

He came out into the clearing, sniffling. The house looked ominous even in the morning sun. Ray's car still smoldered. His father was in Los Angeles, his mother in Nashville caring for others, Ray was lost to him, and Pinwheel was no longer to be trusted. He looked around him. Even the rabbits were gone.

♍

CHAPTER THIRTEEN

CRAFT AND POWER

Pinwheel opened his eyes. He was flat on his back, his arms and legs forming the letter X on the ground. The sunshine entered the canopy of leaves like long paddles into a dark cool lake. He listened to the morning, the whirl and clicks of bugs whose names he did not know and the beckoning chirps from birds hidden in trees.

His head throbbed where Rodney's blow had landed. The throbbing rumbled down his body (neck, chest, legs, and feet) to bounce from his toes back up. He heard its rhythm interplay with the sounds of the smaller things, both winged in air and rooted in earth. His attention expanded beyond his aches and embraced the welter of activity around him.

His body hummed with the surrounding sensations, still new to his form. Smells, once dull to his demon nose, now burst with bright spikes of floral sweetness and loamy density. His nose was overwhelmed with summer aromas.

The world, once flat to his eyes, now bristled with edges and textures. He saw the tiny grooves of petals and leaves, like fingerprints, their identities written like poems across their surfaces. He saw the slow firecrackers of pine cones, popping and stretching all summer, their stiff armor like soldiers on parade, and also the rolling softness of their sap like happy tears.

He understood the flurry of motes, which no longer looked like chaos fogging his vision as it had when he was Birthless. Now he could hear the tune of the world, the song of the wind, and the play of all things in it and he knew now that it was a dance, choreographed down to the smallest antennae thrust into the reeling.

He let his fingers pierce the dirt to feel its vigor and strength. To a demon, dust is dead and used as an anchor to maintain corporeality. But now he knew its toil and spurt, he could feel the life that trees and plants dredged out of it. He could sense the tremors of worms in their playground, their lifelong inching within it.

His eyes were opened, the sting of light was gone, the scald of living things no longer pained him; its heat fed him, flowed through and renewed him. The light presented him with endless gifts, and he wanted his eyes always to be open to receive.

He felt Jerome at his elbow and sat up. "I must have slept again."

Jerome chittered softly.

Pinwheel's shoulders slumped in response. "Yes, it is understandable that Rodney does not have faith in me."

The other rabbits joined them. They circled around Pinwheel and began to bark and titter at each other. It was a rabbit council. Thundertrump was very animated in her position, yipping loudly, with Ebenezer and Jerome quietly responding to her outbursts. Pinwheel paid attention, but remained silent.

When Thundertrump ceased, Jerome turned to address Pinwheel.

Pinwheel nodded. "I think that is the wisest counsel, Jerome. I would rather stay with Rodney anyway." Thundertrump snorted. Pinwheel noted her displeasure and continued, "I don't want to run into servants of Hell. They are mightier than I am now."

Thundertrump couldn't restrain herself any longer and burst into a smattering of rabbit talk.

"I just know, okay," said Pinwheel defensively. "I am not as strong as I once was now that I am under the Name. I can feel it. I am weak, I have to sleep now, I hunger, I thirst." The mere mention of thirsting made Pinwheel feel dizzy. He stumbled up and went over to the bank of the river. He slid down its side and put his mouth to the cool flow, pulling it in with loud slurps.

He was about to climb back when he heard the sounds of curses and the crack and clatter of demons stomping sticks and kicking leaves. He hugged the ground and climbed high enough so that he could peek over the edge of the bank.

The rabbits scattered and hid themselves, and soon Pinwheel caught sight of the gang of demons tromping through the woods. He recognized Yuckjoy, aide of Murkpockets, along with various underlings carrying something on their shoulders between two poles. Thrown over it was a mottled fur blanket made from several animals—dogs, cats, mice, and squirrels. Gore dripped from it as they walked.

Pinwheel watched them pass, the demons complaining about the brightness and the weight of their burden. He lost them in the trees, but could hear their grumbling still. Thundertrump hopped out from under a wispy plant whose yellowy filaments had hidden her. She coughed to get Pinwheel to follow.

Pinwheel reluctantly followed the rotund rabbit. Ebenezer and Jerome stayed behind.

They shadowed the demons to a place where the ground sank. In the little cleft was a charred spot with a pile of ashes and sticks in the center. One of the demons began kicking it clear, filling the air with a cloud of dust. Another demon pulled off the covering of the thing they carried.

It was a dark lump, somewhat oval, covered in dirt and hair. Pinwheel recognized it immediately. "It's a small Alvarium," he whispered to Thundertrump. The rabbit responded with a click of her tongue and then flattened her ears.

"But there are six of them," responded Pinwheel.

The blonde butterball of a rabbit emitted another harsh clicking sound.

"Do you think that will work?" asked Pinwheel. He was wringing his hands.

Thundertrump huffed and nodded her head emphatically. Without another chirp she hopped ahead, leaving Pinwheel crouching in the bushes.

Pinwheel watched the blonde rabbit bolt toward the nearest demon and cannonball into his back. The demon squealed as he hit the ground, dust and leaves exploding into billows.

Without pausing Thundertrump launched herself into the next demon, setting her paws on his chest and flipping off him into the face of the third demon. She chomped down on his ears, dragging him to the ground with her weight. And then, as quickly as it started, it was over, Thundertrump darting off into the woods. The demons gathered themselves in pursuit, all howling.

Pinwheel sat stunned at the success of Thundertrump's plan. A distant cry of anguish reminded him that time was limited, and he sprang into the clearing where the portable Alvarium sat. The sticky mass stank, and there was a dull hum from inside. He drew out a pole from the rings at the base of the Alvarium and held it in his hands like he'd seen Rodney hold his bat.

He set his feet and swung. His blow knocked a wet lump off the top of the hive and it spewed bees into the air. He jumped back, but the bees were disoriented by the light and wobbled erratically. They seemed drunk and most of them smacked into trees and fell. There they remained, dazed and crawling on the dirt.

Pinwheel approached the Alvarium again and raised the pole. He struck it like he was chopping firewood. The wood and bone frame split, wax and gore scattering. Pinwheel examined the innards of the hive. A few more sluggish bees climbed out and sputtered into the air.

He wiggled the pole to remove it. A great sucking sound as he pulled startled the birds into silence. In that momentary birdlessness Pinwheel heard heavy breathing. He spun to see two demons glaring at him.

"Ah, the little stray," the nearest demon belched out. His breath had the smell of compost on a hot August day. "The envy of taking you belongs to Damperknob."

The larger demon behind Damperknob pushed him to the side. "The envy belongs to Fibditch." Fibditch was among the higher ranking demons. He was five and a half feet tall and had tattered wings.

Pinwheel retreated so that the Alvarium was between him and the others. "I do not fear demons any longer."

The Damperknob tried to circle around Pinwheel. His hot breath cut through the smell of the crushed Alvarium, stench within stench. "What is this one's name, Fibditch?"

Fibditch answered stroking his pointed chin. "Birthless was what he was called before he was stripped of his name."

"I am Pinwheel now."

"Blown about by doctrine, no doubt," spat Fibditch.

"Damperknob heard your prattle about sunshine." The demon circled Pinwheel.

Pinwheel wondered if Thundertrump would make it back. "I am a servant of the Name." Pinwheel widened his stance and raised his arms.

The demons chortled. Damperknob's belly jostled; Fibditch's tattered wings swayed in the light breeze.

"The Outer Darkness has declared no strays from its fold." Fibditch laughed between his teeth and his chuckles turned into a prolonged hiss.

"Heaven will come to my aid." Pinwheel lowered his wings, daring them to strike.

Fibditch stepped closer and raised his claws, "Perhaps Fibditch and Damperknob can begin your dismantling." He lunged at Pinwheel.

Pinwheel slashed with his free arm, but Damperknob caught it. They lifted him into the air and Fibditch slammed his head against Pinwheel's.

Pinwheel flailed as Fibditch pinned him. He tried to lunge at Fibditch's neck, but Damperknob grabbed at his wings. Once he got a firm grip on a wing, Damperknob snapped it in half. Pinwheel howled.

Fibditch dropped Pinwheel, and Damperknob gave him a brutal kick to his chin. He crumpled and curled in the dirt before the demons, his broken wing flopping from side to side as he writhed.

"Fool, Heaven cares not for a failed demon," muttered Fibditch into Pinwheel's ear. "You should have flown."

Damperknob grabbed him by his good wing and dragged him toward the nearest tunnel. "Murkpockets will want to curse him before we send him howling back to the Lake of Fire."

Pinwheel held his mouth. His teeth had bitten through his tongue. He tried to staunch the flow of blood as he was rudely dragged. He moaned and succumbed to the helplessness growing inside him. "I am a child of darkness," he said quietly. "Spurned by darkness. I am brother to demons but brotherless. I am homeless between heaven and earth."

His captors laughed, their derision slicing the air. "Sing more songs, dark angel," scoffed Damperknob.

Pinwheel kept his eyes closed. "I am a wretch and no angel, scorned by demons and despised by God and man. Fool that I am, fool that I am, fool that I am."

"Amen," said Fibditch. "Amen."

The other demons joined them as Damperknob dragged Pinwheel by his good wing to a spot in the woods. Shielded from the harsh sun by the trees around them, the demons dug a pit to keep him in. They did not want him to see their new hell, spidering deeper under the Honeycomb House.

Once they carved out a hollow the seven of them could crouch in, they pulled him under the earth. A hole was made in the wall, deep enough to hold Pinwheel, narrow enough so that he could not move, and they brusquely shoved him in. Through all of this Pinwheel sat motionless, sunk into himself, full of woe.

Now laid flat in the earth, arms at his side, the roots of trees clawing his face and chest, he spoke to the dirt above him, whispered to it that it should fall and bury him. The demons in the hovel heard his mutterings and chuckled.

In the blackness, Pinwheel could see the six gathered demons at his feet. They were probably holding him so that Murkpockets himself could dispatch him. His failure to successfully torment Rodney was enough to end his hold on this material body, but his falling into the Name of the enemy was sure to get him eaten.

The pain of death was enough to make him tremble, but to be sent howling back to the Lake of Fire, to be thrown headlong into the turmoil of Hell and his demonic brethren made Pinwheel writhe with fear. How would a traitor be handled in Hell? How would a wannabe angel be received by the coarse and snarling fiends? He groaned and begged the earth to swallow him.

A rumbling above him shook him from his misery. Even his captors quit their blustering to listen. The rumbling grew louder. It must be Murkpockets; his end was coming. "Hide me, earth," he prayed. "Hide me."

The rumbling stopped, and the only sound was Pinwheel's own haggard breathing. Damperknob snorted a relieved laugh and was about to mock their captive again when a searing white staff shot into the pit from above.

Pinwheel heard their screams at his feet, but he couldn't maneuver to a place where he could watch. The cave was collapsing and dirt rained down. Pinwheel screamed himself as the earth closed its mouth on him and became his grave.

* * *

Rodney ran upstairs and stuffed clothes into his bag. Due to the amount of dirty laundry downstairs in the laundry room, Rodney was able to fit the rest of his clothes into his backpack. He pulled his hat from the doorknob and slapped it onto his head. He grabbed his bat, slipped his slingshot into his back pocket, and left.

With Ray gone and no rabbits, Rodney felt less inclined to be in the big empty house just waiting for demons to drag him somewhere dark. He would bike into town, go to the police, and tell them Ray had disappeared. They'd call his mom, and she'd come pick him up. He would be taken far from this place, from the freaked-out craziness. No more demons, no more looking for angels.

Rodney stopped at the front door, putting his hand to the knob. No more Ray. He hung his head. And there would be questions he couldn't answer. He dropped his bag and bat. The bat hit the floor and rolled in a circle at his feet.

He heard the crunch of gravel as a car drove down it. He remembered that Otis had said he was coming over. "Crap," he said. Ray was in big trouble, apparently, and now he'd be in trouble, too. No Ray, a burnt car, a whole bunch of unanswered questions, and a kid no one wanted to take care of.

Rodney waited until the car stopped and he heard car doors open and shut. He pulled the door back and stepped out onto the porch. Al Walden was trotting up the stairs with Otis shuffling behind him.

"Morning," he said cheerily.

Walden looked up startled and flicked his shades down a notch to eyeball him. "How do, son? Y'name's Rodney? That right?" He said 'right' like 'rat.'

"That's right, Sheriff Walden."

"Good lad, knowing your honorifics. Y'uncle in?" He latched his thumbs into his belt, weaving his belly side to side.

"No, he's out."

Otis came around from behind Walden and squatted down, putting his hands on his knees. "What? Not here? Didn't you give him my message?"

"Yes sir, Mr. Otis." He was pouring the politeness on thick. "He, um, went into town to sort it all out. I think."

"Sort it out?" Otis gestured over to the car. "Then why's his car here?"

"Oh, it, uh, caught on fire last night. That's probably the smoke you saw yesterday. I think it's toast."

Walden walked down the steps to examine the car.

Otis trained his eyes on Rodney. "That's not the smoke I saw."

"So what? He ride a bike in?" Walden said as he tentatively put a hand to the hood, to check its heat. He touched it quickly, then again longer. "Yup, still hot." He watched Rodney and Otis join him next to the Honeypot, more black and brown than yellow. "Say it's toast, too." He grinned widely.

"Yeah, Ray biked in. I guess he thought he could catch you before you left."

"We didn't see him," said Otis. He was eyeing the house, like he expected Ray to jump out at any moment and surprise them.

Rodney tried to look surprised and confused.

"So he's downtown?" Otis was suspicious.

"Any idea what happened to the rig?" Walden knocked on the scarred roof of the car.

"Um, no. I think uncle Ray said something about wires." That sounded believable.

"Uh-uh," Walden said while shaking his head. "Not wires. Guarantee."

"Come on, let's get Ray," Otis said, stomping back to the car. He shut the door before Walden even moved.

Finally, raising his hat and letting his large palm run over the thin hair underneath, Walden said, "Welp. We'll go track him down." He went to the car and opened the door. "You aight here yourself, Rodney?"

"Oh, I'm fine. I've got plenty of food here."

"Maybe you should just ride with us."

An arrow of panic went through his chest. No telling what would happen to Ray if he wasn't saved soon. "No, I can't. I'm waiting for a call. From, uh, from my mother."

Al nodded approvingly. "Hm. S'pose that's fine." He reached into his shirt pocket and shook loose a white card. He walked around the car and handed it to Rodney.

Otis crossed his arms and shouted out the window, "Let's just go, Al."

Walden looked back at him and shook his head. Then to Rodney he said, "'Smy card. Got my number on it. Need anything or ya see Ray, gimme a call. Aight?"

"Alright."

Walden put a finger to the brim and joined Otis in the car. Rodney watched them until the cruiser disappeared in the trees. He sighed in relief.

He returned inside and saw his bat sitting on the floor. He could read the crisp lettering on the bat from where he stood. *Libra*. "I hate you," he said, and gave it a solid kick. It spun into the stair room and hit the thick pillar in the middle.

Rodney picked it up and gripped it tightly. "I hate you," he repeated and swung at the pillar. He struck the pillar mightily. The bat bent a tiny divot into the side of the wood, hardly a mark. He adjusted the bat and swung again. The bat ricocheted off the pillar. The reverberations stung his hands, but the pillar stood strong, barely marred by his swings.

He turned to the clock on the wall and regripped his bat. He raised it above his head and smashed the face of the clock with a downward thrust. The gold symbols scattered and bent. The hands pointed accusingly at Rodney and did not move. The symbols for Taurus and Aries were missing, and the symbol for Gemini barely clung to the face of the clock. He swung down again and Virgo, Aquarius and Sagittarius flew off the face and skittered across the floor. Three more blows had cracked the left side of the clock, and only the symbol for Scorpio remained.

Rodney measured out his final blow. He drew back with his mouth in a furious snarl and cried, "I hate you!" and brought the bat down on the Scorpion. There was another satisfying crack, but Rodney jumped back in surprise when the whole wall moved. It was a door under the stairs.

Rodney examined the clock and he saw that Scorpio had not been dislodged, but was sunk into the face of the clock. He looked closer, putting his finger to it, and he pressed it. He heard a click and Scorpio popped above the surface again. It was a button. It must have opened the wall.

Rodney carefully pulled it back and saw a stairway. There were two steps curling down before it dead ended in a red, wax-looking wall. It appeared to be moist and sticky. He prodded it with his bat and with some effort was able to press his bat inside. He looked closer and saw tiny hexagons, some imperfect and some interlocked, but most were haphazardly pressed together. It was a barrier of bloody honeycombs.

"The Scorpio room," he said aloud.

He remembered what Ray had said that night in the upper room looking at stars: scorpions always get crushed. It made sense that the Scorpio room would be the basement, crushed by the rest of the house.

Rodney tried to bend back the barrier. He dug his fingers in feeling the wax give way as he pressed deeper. He hooked his fingers and pulled, bending the layers of honeycomb out. It was malleable and not much of a barrier, but it would be slow and difficult to get past it. The demons weren't concerned with keeping anyone out; they just wanted to stop up the stairs, to seal off the Scorpio room from the rest of the house.

He could get through, but he needed a plan. He didn't know what to expect down there. If he was going to destroy the Alvarium, assuming it was still down there, he would need to make sure he could get down and back up, preferably fast.

Rodney pushed the wall shut and opened up his backpack that was on the floor in the foyer. He pulled out his jacket and another shirt to tie around his face. He ran outside to grab the rope he'd seen in Ray's workshop. He stopped in the gravel to pick out a few larger rocks for his slingshot. He stuffed them into his jacket pocket. Once he grabbed the rope he returned to the house.

Rodney was a flurry of activity. He knew Al and Otis would be back once they realized Ray was not in town. He had maybe an hour or two. If he could just destroy the Alvarium, that might give him enough time to convince others about the demons. More likely he'd just convince them that he was as crazy as Ray.

His stomach rumbled. No breakfast, and lunchtime was coming. He went into the kitchen and rolled up some slices of turkey around a pickle and ate standing up. He drank down a glass of milk to complete his hasty meal.

Rodney spied a knife on the counter and grabbed it, sliding it into his belt. He remembered the flashlight in the drawer next to the back door and dug it out. He returned to the stair room. The ruined clock was silent. Ray wouldn't be happy about that.

He tied the rope around the center beam, double knotted and triple knotted. Then he faced the clock again. His heart ached and his breathing became thin. He felt the urge to cry out, to call his mom, to run upstairs into the observatory and hide until something happened. Anything.

Rodney realized he should leave a note just in case. He went into the library and picked up *The Jawbone of Heaven*, opened it up, and wrote on the first page: "I tried to stop them. I love you mom. Rodney Abner Niemand." It was all he could think of. He read it aloud, then added the symbol for Libra underneath.

He took the book outside and set it on the porch where it would be easy to find. Then he stood in the sun to calm the shivering that had begun to take over his body. The day was as hot as always, but Rodney shivered and hugged his arms about himself.

Rodney closed his eyes and looked up, dropping his hands to his side as he did so. "I love sunshine. I love sunshine. I love sunshine," he said quietly. He bowed his head and forced himself to stop shivering.

The whole world went silent. The chitter of birds and bugs, the rippling of the wind through trees, the clicking of grass, all silent. Rodney opened his eyes and looked around. He was startled by a loud thump off the bill of his cap. He ducked and jumped back as a fat, black lump landed in front of him.

He looked closer and saw that it was fuzzy. It was about the size of a quarter. He crouched down. "A bee," he said when he recognized it. It didn't move.

Suddenly another *spack! spack! spack!* in the gravel drew his eyes up. Three more had hit the ground. He stood and two more hit him, one off the wrist, another in the small of his back. He heard more thuds behind him, bees bouncing off the roof of the Honeycomb House. Soon bees were striking him from all sides. He raised his hands and ran back to the porch. It was a deafening storm.

Rodney fell to the rough wood of the porch as the rain of bees fell. It was a thick rainfall, louder and louder. He pressed himself against the front door, but just as quickly as it had started it was over. He scanned the clearing before him. The ground was peppered with dead bees. Hundreds of them, maybe thousands.

Rodney threw open the door. Whatever a host of dead bees meant, it couldn't be good. He ran to the beam and checked his knot. It felt solid. He tied the other end of the rope around his waist, patted the knife in his belt and the slingshot in his back pocket, and felt the small, smooth rocks in his other pocket. Last, he checked the flashlight. Its pure beam struck the clock's face.

He pushed the Scorpion with his thumb and the wall clicked open. He pulled it back and set his bat against the frame so that he could tie the extra shirt around his face. He turned his hat backwards, stuffed the flashlight under his arm, picked up his bat, holding it in the middle with two hands, and pressed forward into the bloody wax.

The wax bent back and a crease was made that was big enough for him to shoulder into. His foot pressed through the soft bloodcombs until he felt the next step. He dug his bat forward again and pushed farther.

The staircase spiraled like the stairs above him, and the light of the door was a distant sliver behind him. He estimated that the stairs were the same as the stairs above him, which meant there were twenty-four steps leading to the basement. After fifteen minutes, he'd descended six, but he'd figured out the best system for proceeding.

First, he'd bury his bat midway and then wiggle it up and down to make a hole. Next he'd dig a crease for him to get his leg into and stomp it down. The wax would fold and compress as he burrowed. Once he reached the next lower step he'd scrape it as clean as he could with the knife so that he'd have solid footing. The wax was slick and he fell more than once, banging his back and elbows against the hard wood.

About halfway down by his estimations, the stairs had curved enough that he could no longer see the light from above. The air was dense and hot, and his sweat mingled with the sticky, gory wax. The light from his flashlight was pink, and he had to unzip his jacket and slip it inside to clean it.

Rodney was burrowing his bat in, leaning against the wax wall when he felt his bat break through. He tumbled forward and slid down the remaining stairs. He landed in a hot pool of mud. There were cries and snarls in the darkness before him. He stood in the ankle-high mud and trained his light on the noise.

In front of him stood a demon about his own height. The light was stinging the demon's eyes, and he held his hands in front of his face to block it out. Rodney went stiff with fright, but managed to pick up his bat. He dropped the flashlight so that he could get a firm grip, and he swung.

His bat struck the arms of the demon. There was a crack and an explosion of dust and curses from the demon. Rodney stepped back as he noticed a yellow glow emanating from Libra. The demon stirred, and Rodney raised the bat before him again. It grew brighter, and the demon flinched and retreated a step.

"You filthy adam," the demon spat.

Rodney noticed that the demon no longer had arms. All that was left were nubs that ended at the elbows. They twitched like antennae.

There was a stirring on the ground to Rodney's right. A prone figure, wrapped in black goo, wiggled and tried to sit up. Rodney turned his bat toward the other creature.

It croaked, "Rodney, that you?"

"Uncle Ray?"

The figure fell back to the muck unable to remain upright. The demon stepped closer, snarling.

"Strike him again, Rod," Ray barked.

Rodney turned and the bat glowed brightly as he wound up to swing, bringing the bat up above his head. He stepped and turned his hips. Just as Ray had shown him he pulled his hands through, rotating them, and brought the bat around. His blow struck the demon at the shoulders. The bat skipped off and collided with the demon's head.

The force of the swing sent Rodney sprawling. He saw the demon fall.

"Home run, Rod my boy! Great wackadoo!" crowed Ray from the ground. He'd rolled sideways to watch. "Glad I treated that wood. Good call on my part."

The bat continued to glow. Rodney raised it over his head. The room was hexagonal, and on the other side of the room was a tunnel. In the center was a huge throbbing mass. The Alvarium Maleficorum was black and supported by thick wooden beams. It was shaped vaguely like a heart, bulbous and bigger at the top than at the bottom. Eight or so feet tall, as Pinwheel had guessed, and twice that in width at the top.

"Quick, Rodney. We can't hang around here. You gotta help me out of this." Ray struggled against the bonds that held him.

Rodney ran over and pulled out his knife. The material wrapped tightly around Ray from top to toe was harder than it looked. He sliced with the knife, but it didn't make a mark.

"I can't cut you loose." Rodney felt panic closing his throat. He saw his bat begin to pulse, growing brighter, then dimming. It was flashing like the warning lights of a car.

"Uh-oh, Rod. Might need to bash some more brains in."

Rodney snatched up the bat, stood, and turned. He heard a voice calling and the squeak of a pulley, the rumble of rope on wood. He looked under the looming *Alvarium* and saw a couple of steps that led down into the floor. A little lower was a platform and then a hole, which was too dark to see down, but he could see the rope leading into it was moving. Something was being hauled up. He could hear a voice calling.

"Blisterteeth, you pig, come grab the buckets. If Plugseed has to climb up there, a foot will be crammed down your maw."

Rodney whispered, "Ray, another one's coming. What do I do?"

"I suggest you hit him."

The complaining voice was drawing nearer, and Rodney climbed down and readied his next blow. The moment the fuzzy-headed demon stuck his head through the hole, he received the solid wood of Ray of Hope Bat Company's debut bat.

The demon's head exploded like a bag of flour and he fell back on the platform below. Rodney stuck the bat down the hole and saw a towerlike structure rising from the pit. The darkness was too great for the bat to fully illuminate.

The platform with the now headless demon swung side to side. He could hear the sounds of wings and the grumblings and cursings of the army of Hell laboring in the darkness. He heard a shriek from below. "The cursed adam! Get him! Get him!"

He climbed out of the pit frantically. He turned to Ray. "I think more are coming. What do I do?"

Ray jerked himself upright as best he could and said, "Hit the leg of the beehive."

Rodney looked at the wood structure that held up the *Alvarium*. It was a tree as thick as a soccer ball, lashed to the frame with rope. There was no way he could break through it, but the rope looked frayed and weak. Perhaps a good jolt to the structure would snap the rope. He opened his stance and crouched, bringing up the fiery Libra.

Just as the head of another demon popped through the hole, Rodney swung and connected with the log. The whole structure wobbled. The demon saw Rodney and yelled.

Rodney swung again, and the rope popped. Frayed cords like fingers fanned out around the single line that held it together. A moment later the line snapped loudly. The structure went sideways and collapsed on the sunken platform. Rodney heard the groan of cracking timber beneath him. There were screams and the sounds of heavy things falling. The tall structure under the room collapsed. He wondered how deep the base was.

The Alvarium leaned heavily to one side toward the tunnel. The legs on the other side had snapped off. Only the ropes from the single remaining leg kept the Alvarium from rolling off.

He could hear the clacking of talons on wood as a group of demons climbed up the ramp toward the Scorpio room. He ran back to Ray to drag him to the stairs. He barely budged an inch in the mud.

"You're too heavy."

"Keep cutting, then." Ray bucked against the restraints.

Rodney tried again to free Ray with the knife. He pried and chiseled until the knife snapped in half at the handle. The noises grew louder.

There was a roar above him, and he turned to see a demon climb over the wreckage of the Alvarium. Rodney grabbed his bat and smacked him before he could jump down. Another dust cloud scuttled the air. The glow of Libra leaped again and he knew that more demons were near.

Rodney looked up at the tunnel and saw a mass of the black creatures. Their eyes squinted at the yellow glow of the bat.

They entered the room and spread out against the wall. They were hissing and spitting and flaring their wings out.

"Uncle Ray . . . " Rodney was backing away.

The demon to Rodney's left shot forward, driving a foot into his stomach. Rodney fell back. He sat up spitting mud and trying to suck in the air he'd lost. Another demon hooked his wing's talon into Rodney's jacket and slung him to the far wall where Ray slouched.

"Get up, Rod."

Rodney groaned as his body ached for wind. He held himself up with his arms as he refilled his lungs with shallow scoops of air. He saw the honey glow of the bat on the other side of him. The demons were careful to step over it as they approached him.

One of the demons pushed him down onto his back. His feet and legs were resplendently hairy. "What did Murkpockets call this one?" he asked.

Another demon with fingers like tree roots answered, "This shineworm is called Rodney."

The hairy-legged demon crouched down by Rodney and cupped his prickly hands under Rodney's chin. "And what did Murkpockets say to do with Rodney?" He spoke his name as if it were a knife, stabbing the air with it.

"Bind them so that they can see the defeat of earth," said the crooked-fingered demon.

Rodney saw a smaller demon creep behind the others. It picked up the still glowing bat. The light revealed Pinwheel's face slanted with anger.

"Defeat this," he said and struck the nearest demon in the back.

The demons spun to see who assaulted them.

"The stray!" another cried.

Pinwheel swung, and the demons jumped back and circled. He moved to stand between Rodney and their attackers. "Go!" he yelled. "Get Ray out of here."

Pinwheel stepped forward and leveled the bat at the approaching demons. They were three times as tall as he was.

"The stray returns," rasped the hairy demon.

"He heard that Hell was coming for him and saved them the trip," spoke the other.

Pinwheel ignored them and yelled at Rodney over his shoulder. "Take off the rope and tie it to Ray."

"What are you going to do?"

Over the growls and mutterings of the demons, Pinwheel said, "I'm going to send these simpering fools back to the fire that birthed them." Without another word he lunged forward with a bone-rattling shriek, swinging madly. The demons dodged and howled, slashed and leaped about. Whenever Pinwheel struck a demon with the illuminated bat, they burst into dust.

Rodney heard more demons ascending the ramp. "Pinwheel, block the ramp with the hive!"

Pinwheel looked at the Alvarium leaning toward the tunnel's mouth. He jumped up and bit through the single rope that held it to the frame. The top-heavy beehive rolled off the slanted wood platform toward the tunnel. It reached the sloping ramp and rolled down it. They'd misjudged the size of the tunnel and it swallowed the Alvarium whole. The beehive rumbled down, boards breaking, followed by more screams and curses.

Pinwheel struck the remaining demons, each swing sending up a spume of dust. "Go!" he yelled over his shoulder.

Rodney pulled his eyes away from the fray. He tied the rope around Ray's feet, following the rope back up the steps. He felt the rope move as he climbed the slippery stairs.

He fell out of the stairway, tripping over the last step. Someone moved in front of him. He froze. It must be Otis or Al. They'd grab him, and then the demons would come bubbling up from below, and they'd all die, or at least get wrapped up in stiff black gunk till kingdom come. Whose kingdom he was too afraid to ask.

He was surprised to hear a woman's voice. "Grab the rope and help me pull."

"Lucasta?" Rodney squinted at the dark figure as his eyes adjusted. His sight lost the fuzziness and he saw silver-haired Lucasta in a long blue dress. "What are you doing here?"

"Quick, child." She had untied the rope from the beam and was winding it around her arm. She bent the rope around her waist and leaned back, using the beam as an elbow so that she could pull toward the front door.

Rodney grabbed the rope in front of Lucasta. They pulled until they were two steps out the front door. With one last heave they fell back as Ray popped out with Pinwheel helping.

"We don't have much time," he said as he hauled Ray out of the way and shut the door.

Rodney ran into the library saying, "We have to block the door with something." He grabbed Ray's chair and dragged it into the stair room and pushed it over. On its back, it could just squeeze between the center beam and the wall, its wood legs against the stair door. He looked up to see Pinwheel and

Lucasta staring down at him skeptically. "This is not going to do much is it?"

"No," said Pinwheel.

"It will give us just enough time to get Ray out of his binds and skadoodle," said Lucasta as she went into the kitchen. She came back with a knife and a bottle of honey. She knelt down by Ray, who still squirmed against the ropey goop.

"I tried a knife. It's too tough."

He watched Lucasta dip the blade in honey and then run it gently over the top of Ray's struggling form. The black ropes snapped and sprung back from the honey-drenched blade.

Ray kicked out of the cut gunk. "Whew, thanks loads, Lucy."

Pinwheel fidgeted at the door. "We should leave."

Rodney grabbed his bat and followed Ray and Lucasta out the door. They climbed into a white pickup truck that presumably belonged to Lucasta, who was at the wheel. Ray hobbled to the passenger side while Rodney and Pinwheel jumped into the truck bed.

There was a great crash behind them as the door splintered. Lucasta backed the truck out and rammed it into gear as several demons leaped out of the house. Rodney heard the engine growl and thunder as it spun gravel into the air.

Rodney lifted his bat as a demon, still cringing in the bright sunlight, tried to grab the tailgate. Rodney brought the bat down like an ax, causing the demon's hand to disintegrate.

They rattled off the driveway down the forest path that led straight to Lucasta's house. Tree limbs brushed against the truck. The truck whined and lost paint. The demons had fallen in behind them, some running, some leaping, some flying, but all screaming and cursing and smoldering in the sun.

Rodney knocked the arms off two more demons and the jaw off a third. He was nearly launched from the truck when a root sent a quake through the speeding vehicle. Pinwheel seized his jacket to keep him from flying out of the truck bed.

Another demon swooped in and Rodney stood to fend it off, but there was a heavy *thunk* sound that was driven deep into his skull. He fell forward into a black space. He heard screaming and the roar of the truck growing fainter and farther away.

CHAPTER FOURTEEN

A BULWARK

M urkpockets surveyed the wreckage of the great dome. The scaffold rising in the center to the Scorpio room had collapsed. Its fall had caused much disarray amongst the draining tables. Ichor had been spilled, and the floor was a soupy mess. The tumbling Alvarium had destroyed much of the ramp that circled the dome's walls, now crumbling and slumping to bury the demons below. Eventually, the Alvarium itself had rolled off the ramp and exploded on the floor, bees and gore slung against the walls.

Murkpockets appraised the remains of the crushed Alvarium, a useless pile of wood and viscera. The demons were too incensed to curse, and kicked themselves free from the debris. Many of them leapt into the air in pursuit of the enemies with no need of orders from Murkpockets.

The great Alvarium was finished. New ones would have to be built, but without the help of Ray, they could never build one of such size. Its dimensions and measurements, its balance of wax and gore, wood and bones, were lost.

Itchpot came waddling in. The alarm had spread rapidly through the den, and Murkpockets was expecting the gassy toad. He spread his arms out indicating the ruins. "Do you see what happens when enemies are allowed to roam?" He was going to continue his rant, but the fear on Itchpot's face stopped him cold.

"The—the—*hurkle*—the Old Master," Itchpot shivered and shook his head. "En-ki Ab-zu rises."

At the sight of the name of the Prince of Darkness coursing in the black, his demon eyes reading the cruel swirl of sounds, Murkpockets fell. He trembled on the ground. What could be the cause of his rising but this failure that he was surely to be blamed for? He swallowed a groan.

Itchpot continued through his stammering. "The . . . the . . . En-ki Ab-zu demands—*higauff*—t-to s-speak with you."

A cold tremor sliced down the core of Murkpockets's spine. He scrambled to his feet and ran, stumbling, to the pit of the newly risen Prince. Midway to the Prince's abode he passed the two guards far from their station, quivering with fear. Murkpockets' legs seized, and he collapsed. He flailed in the dirt, his stomach boiling with the mud and bugs he'd wolfed down earlier to anchor his matter. His body convulsed, and he emptied the contents of his stomach onto the ground before him. Slick mud was ejected through his nose as his body rolled again and again with the disease of terror.

Without bothering to wipe his face, he staggered to his feet and continued to the pit of the Prince. He arrived at the hole. A damp heat climbed out. He dropped down to the hovel below, but his jelly legs were unable to hold him, and he ended up as a pile of bent wings and bones.

"My servant Murkpockets, how delicious." The voice of the Prince had the look of boiling water, of cracking wind. The distant screams of the far off Lake of Fire were carried in his tremendous tone, and the air snapped at the heat of his voice.

Murkpockets covered his ears, despite being deaf to those sounds, and curled into a ball. He felt nausea roll through his body again, tears sprang to his eyes. "Yes, Prince? What is your bidding?" He was too timid to recite his master's name.

The Prince laughed, and the laughter was trembling blades cutting into Murkpockets. "What is it, Murkpockets? Do you fear me now that I speak?"

Murkpockets opened his eyes and responded as firmly as he could. "If Murkpockets may ask, what is the cause of the Prince's speaking?"

"Your Prince has rested these long years until the time came for Hell to rise again. Now is that time." The Old Master still lay on his back, but he seemed transformed into a more powerful creature than the one Murkpockets had reported to these last four years.

"But Prince, have you not seen? When the young adam and the stray found that Ray was captured, they came to free him and destroyed the Alvarium. They have set the cause of Hell back decades."

"Fool!" he roared. Murkpockets collapsed again and cowered. The Prince sat up and moved his legs to stand. Seeing him move after years of only small movements sent Murkpockets scrambling and shrieking into the farthest corner of the pit.

The Prince broke through the low roof, smashing into the room above them with his twelve-foot frame. Dirt rained down. The Prince flexed his muscles and climbed out of the pit where he'd lain.

The rooms were too small for him to stand, but the Prince of Darkness lounged back against the wall and waited for Murkpockets to dig himself out of the rubble.

"Your Prince told you to leave them alone. Their meddling would do nothing."

"No, Prince. Your message was 'no strays.' Ray, Heaven's last rogue, was taken and a plot to take the stray from Hell was laid."

Murkpockets flinched as the Prince unfolded an arm and reached into the pit to snag the half-buried stack of papers next to his pallet. He brought them up. On the top was the sheet that read "no strays."

"Whose house has Hell overrun?"

Murkpockets did not know where this was going. He answered warily, "Ray's."

The Prince of Darkness grinned, his razor sharp teeth bristling like thorns. "What would you call him if you weren't blinded by ignorance?"

Murkpockets frowned. "In the kingdom of the enemy, he would be called St. Ray . . . ?"

The Lord of Hell raised the paper.

Murkpockets' eyes bulged. Shame flooded his face.

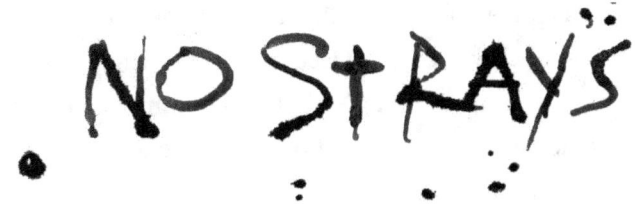

NO STRAYS

"What was the question you asked your prince?"

"Murkpockets asked if Hell should go after the straying tempter."

The Prince paused, releasing a long sigh. "Read the answer for me, Murkpockets."

"*No*," he read. "*Saint. Ray's.*"

"Does that mean you should take the lost tempter?"

Murkpockets shoulders caved in. "No."

"Does it mean you should leave insignificant vermin alone?"

"Yes," Murkpockets grunted.

"Do you really think a child, a failed tempter, and a compromised saint could stop what the Prince of Darkness has wrought? Heaven herself is ignorant, how could these three derail what Heaven tacitly allows?"

Murkpockets kept his head lowered. "The enemy has tricked the diaboloi again with words."

The Lord of Hell continued, "Heaven mocks Hell, but is petty whenever the windblown dirtbags are threatened." He reached out slowly and stabbed a finger into Murkpockets' chest. "Only that could possibly derail the plan."

Murkpockets prepared to flee. He was almost certainly to be struck down and eaten by the Old Master, whose feebleness had disappeared. There would be little chance of escape, but flight was preferable to standing like some blithe lamb. He stared at the claws that corkscrewed out of the Prince's feet.

"But your incompetence extended also to timing, and your inability to act sooner has given En-ki Ab-zu enough time to bring the plan to fruition."

Murkpockets looked up startled. "Fruition?" he said tentatively.

"Yes, Murkpockets. Enough sons of Hell are present, not in your plan, but in your Prince's plan."

The Old Master stretched out his hand and took Murkpockets about the neck. He was too petrified to move. He clutched the Old Master's hands as he was pulled nearer. The Master opened his mouth, and Murkpockets felt the singed air brush the rot of death upon his face. Murkpockets squirmed and snarled.

The Prince laughed. "That your fear is so quick to anger is worthy of envy, Murkpockets. There is loathing for you at the root of the Outer Darkness."

Murkpockets accepted the compliment with gritted teeth.

"Choose three hundred of the most vindictive to torment and kill the rebels. Send the rest back to the house above."

"A battalion? Why take thousands for an empty house, but leave a pittance for the taking of Hell's enemies?"

The Old Master slammed Murkpockets into the wall. "Do as the Prince of Darkness commands, or be eaten!" he roared. He let Murkpockets fall to the ground. At the foot of the Prince, Murkpockets groveled, not daring to rise.

He continued, "It will take time for all of Hell to muster. Do not kill the enemies until dawn. Heaven must not be roused to bloodlust till then. Let her prayers be too late."

Murkpockets let his voice sink into the dirt before him, the curl of his words in the darkness was a wispy fog. "Kill them all? St. Ray? Lucasta?"

"All!" the Prince howled in response. "The boy, the stray! Kill every beast that walks on the earth and that flies above the face of the earth. Kill anything that has breath. Be a harbinger for the coming destruction, but do not shed blood till dawn."

Murkpockets rose to his feet. "It will be done."

"Go forth and do evil."

Murkpockets raised his eyes and matched his fire with the fire of the Master's eyes. "Amen."

* * *

Lucasta's truck burst from the trees into her backyard. The branches, trapped beneath the belly of the truck, were snagged and snapped by the ground. The high whine of the engine, singing its stripped gears and loose belts, sputtered and heaved into a stony silence.

Lucasta was out before the truck was still and lifted Rodney from the bed of the truck. He was out cold; the branch to the back of his head had knocked him full of black dreams.

Pinwheel leapt out of the truck and landed in front of Ray. Ray knelt and grabbed Pinwheel around the shoulders.

"Bless ya, my fellow," he said, and finished the hug.

Pinwheel stumbled back in surprise. "What? Why?"

Ray grinned. "I don't know the plan, but I can see a good playing of it." He patted him one last time on the furry shoulder and stood. "Come on, let's get Rod to the armory. The hordes of Hell should be here soon."

Lucasta had already pulled open the shed door. Ray hopped toward it. Pinwheel paused to listen to the cursing from the forest, his former cobelligerents racing toward them. The time for outright evil had come: no more hiding from the eye of Heaven. The warriors of Hell had decided to sin boldly.

It was twilight. Already the gold sky was tarnished with dusk. Clouds knuckled up as the roar of demons drew nearer.

"Pinwheel!" Lucasta called.

He turned to go into the shed when a pain pierced his shoulder. He was pulled back. He felt the heat of a mouth, the wet of saliva mixed with ichor. He screamed and then fell to the grass. Mordecai pinned him and bared his teeth.

"The envy belongs to Toadglue," spoke the demon in the dog. He lunged again to sink his teeth into Pinwheel, but Lucasta caught him up by the chain.

"Mordecai," she called. "Down, Mordecai. Good dog." The dog struggled against the chain and unleashed deep ululations of rage. She kept pulling until they both entered the shed. Pinwheel followed at a safe distance. Once inside Ray pulled the sliding door shut.

A silver glow illuminated the shed: florescent lights from two rows of refrigerated shelves filled with eggs. Ray was kneeling over Rodney, tilting his head up. Pinwheel saw that his eyes were beginning to open.

Mordecai continued to bark as Toadglue, the demon that possessed him, mocked and taunted Pinwheel. "Little stray! Come nearer, let me grind you to the dust you want to be." Lucasta kept a firm grip on the chain.

"Shhh, Mordecai, shhh."

"It is not Mordecai," Pinwheel said. "The demon told me his name is Toadglue."

Lucasta looked at him sternly. "He is Mordecai. Toadglue is merely a spy I have played from the beginning. But it's time to send the fool back."

Mordecai craned his neck back at Lucasta, "What do you mean, you airy lump!" spoke Toadglue from inside. "You cannot draw me out, you haven't the power."

Lucasta knelt, easing her hands up Mordecai's neck, pressing him to the cool concrete floor. Mordecai growled and barked and squirmed.

"Pinwheel, could you get me something?"

Pinwheel nodded.

"Go into the back room over there," she indicated the northern wall with a tilt of her head. "There's a ladle on the wall. Dip it into one of the barrels and bring it to me."

Pinwheel dashed to the far door and pulled it open. It was a small room with three great wood barrels. He snagged the ladle from the wall and climbed atop a barrel so that he could pull off the lid of another.

With a shove the lid fell and he looked down into a dark, thick liquid. He dipped the ladle into it. It was heavy like oil and oozed into the cup of the ladle slowly. "What is it?" he called to Lucasta.

"Honey," she said while petting her dog.

Pinwheel froze holding the ladle above the mouth of the barrel, long tendrils of brown-golden goo descending. "Uh, I can't . . . uh . . . "

"It's not going to hurt you, Pinwheel, don't be silly. Everything in here has been treated with honey."

Pinwheel carefully walked into the other room holding out the honey like it was toxic.

When he reached Lucasta, she took the ladle from him and held it over Mordecai. The animal writhed and whined. "Shh," she cooed again into his ear.

"If Toadglue goes so does the beast!" shrieked the demon.

"It'll be okay, Mordecai," she said.

"The dog will be Toadglue's steed to the darkness!" Toadglue's panic came through the warped dog's howl.

"Shh," she said again and poured the rich liquid onto Mordecai starting at his head and then running a trail of the gold on his back. "In the name of the Name above all names."

Toadglue shrieked, the sound coming unhinged from the body of the dog. Mordecai convulsed and shivered at the touch of honey. A steam rose off him. The scream of the demon faded. Lucasta lowered herself over the dog and stroked him. "There's my good dog, what a good dog, a strong dog."

Pinwheel stood stunned.

Rodney sat up and looked around, his face pale in the white glare of the fridges. "Eggs? What the heck?" he said. "What happened? Where are we?"

Pinwheel looked at Lucasta. "Toadglue?"

"He's gone," she said without looking up. Mordecai gave a satisfied growl, a pleased rumble at the attention he was receiving from Lucasta.

"Why didn't the honey..." Pinwheel cast a quick look at Ray and Rodney. He lowered his voice. "Why didn't it hurt me?"

Lucasta looked up at him. "Because honey doesn't hurt angels."

Pinwheel stumbled back and slouched against the wall.

Rodney raised his voice. "Hello? What's happening? Where are we?"

"Easy there, bucko." Ray answered and walked over to Mordecai. He went down on his knees and scratched the dog's jaw. "Feel better, Mordy? Yes, yes you do."

Rodney gingerly felt the back of his head. He cringed as his fingers brushed the welt. "Will somebody please say something?"

At that moment the roof thundered like an avalanche was falling on it. It was followed by howls of anger. The commotion continued for several seconds before it fell silent again.

"Testing the roof," Ray said while looking up. He looked back at Rodney. "You took a nasty blow to the head. A low-hanging branch nabbed ya and shuffled you off to lala."

"Where are we?"

Ray stood and walked over to a sink set in the back wall. "Lucasta's shed. This is our armory." He began washing his hands, getting the honey off.

"It's full of eggs." Rodney motioned at the row of refrigerators and the cartons upon cartons beyond the glass.

"That's right. And honey."

"Where are the demons that were chasing us?"

"Outside, trying to figure out the best way to get us."

Rodney turned to look at the heavy wood sliding door. "So why haven't they burst through?"

Lucasta rose as Mordecai leapt to his feet and shook. Globs of honey were flung to all parts of the room. Lucasta laughed. "Mordecai, sweetie, come here. I'll rub the honey in. It'll protect you." Mordecai obeyed. Lucasta spread the honey evenly across Mordecai.

"Alright, Rodnesia," said Ray, wringing his hands dry. "It's time to flesh things out for ya. Lucasta, as I mentioned earlier, is an angel." Lucasta bowed her head and smiled. She ran her hand down Mordecai's tail, stripping off a handful of honey. She redistributed it down a leg. The dog was energetic, wagging his tail and woofing, but was otherwise well behaved.

Rodney held his hands up. "Wait, wait, wait. You didn't tell me that."

"Sure I did."

"Well, I mean, not like an *angel* angel. Like a real one. Like an actual, real angel." He saw the look he was getting from Ray and Lucasta and decided to let it drop. "Keep going."

"So she's been in charge of amassing our weapons, and I was in charge of laying the trap."

Pinwheel rose from his spot on the floor and drew nearer to listen.

Ray stood and wiped his hands across the front of his tie-dyed bee suit. "Oh, and hey," he said as he spun around and grabbed a wood bucket from beneath the sink. "Fill this with honey, would you?" He handed it to Rodney.

Rodney took it, but stood confused. Ray was about to turn away when Rodney threw the bucket down, it clattered loudly on the concrete floor. "No. I'm not doing anything until you tell me what the hell is going on."

"Rodney," he said in a calm tone. "We need to act fast because Hell, indeed, is going on."

"Seriously, Ray. Tell me what's happening. If this is a trap where are the weapons? What kind of trap is this? What have you gotten me into?" He clenched his fists and stared down the man in the multi-colored bee suit.

Ray picked up the bucket and walked into the back room where the three barrels sat. He dipped the bucket into a barrel and let the honey seep in. Ray returned with the laden bucket and dipped his hands into it. "I admit the plan is a bit thrown together. But I had to do something. The town was being ripped apart." He lifted his hands and began spreading the honey up his arms. "So I came up with something."

"You used me as bait."

"What?" Ray said in disbelief. "That's not true. I wasn't planning on you being here, but I didn't think it was a problem since you're under the Name."

"And that makes me safe?"

Ray stopped coating himself in honey and looked at Rodney. "No, it doesn't make you safe. Just the opposite in fact."

"It puts me in danger?" Frustration and anger rang hot in his ears and he balled his fists. Rodney stepped forward and threw a punch at Ray, the blow landing against his paunch, sticky with honey. He threw two more blows before Ray scuttled back, wincing, his hands raised defensively.

"Hey, whoa, stop. That's not what I meant." Rodney stopped, but he kept his fists up and his jaw set. With a smile Ray added, "Being under the Name doesn't put you in danger, it makes you the danger."

Pinwheel intervened. "There's no time for this."

"Pinwheel's right." Ray said. "We need to prepare for battle. Here, put this on." He handed Rodney the bucket of honey.

Rodney looked at it and then up at his uncle. "We're in so much trouble right now and all we're doing is getting sticky!"

"I admit that I'm winging this plan as we go. It's hard to outsmart Hell, but I've got Heaven at my back."

"At some point," Lucasta said, joining Ray at the sink.

"At some point, Heaven's got my back." Ray added. "But as it turns out, everything has worked like a peach. We're all here and we've got the means to dismantle the little rapscallions outside."

Rodney's eyes bulged. "With what? Eggs? Really?"

"Yes," said Lucasta, beaming with pride. "Plus, I've put a honey glaze on all the eggs."

"This is crazy," Rodney said. "Like, really. Totally, totally crazy." He looked around for agreement.

Ray grew serious. "What do you know about the Easter Bunny?" He dabbed some honey on his face like he was applying camo face paint.

The tone of Rodney's voice sharpened. "Why? Is he going to help us? Are you the Easter Bunny?"

Ray smirked. "Ever wonder why bunnies and eggs are the symbols of Easter?"

"Yeah, that never made sense."

Ray smiled. "Make sense now?"

Before Rodney could answer there was a loud roar from outside followed by a thunderous bang on the wood door. Rodney jumped in fright and backed away. The door held firm.

Ray scratched his beard. "Ah, a battering ram. So they've figured out how to attack a honey protected building." Ray pointed to the barrels. "Rodney, Pinny, y'all should honey up."

Pinwheel took a step back, but Lucasta rushed over. "It's okay, Pinwheel. You'll be fine." She turned Pinwheel around and began applying honey to the rough skin of the former demon. Pinwheel flinched as the first threads of honey rolled down, but was soon smiling and chuckling under Lucasta's touch.

Rodney watched with slanted eyes. "Great," he said. "The demons are coming, and all we're doing is making ourselves tasty."

Once Ray finished anointing himself with honey, he started unloading a pallet of eggs from the fridge. "Roddy, if you're not going to slather yourself in honey you could at least dip that broom in it." He gestured to a broom leaning in the corner. The door sounded again with another blow from the outside.

Ray talked over his shoulder while unloading more eggs. "The reason an egg-laying bunny is the symbol of Easter is because rabbits are like bloodhounds for demons, and eggs are, essentially, demon bombs."

Rodney dipped the broom in a barrel of honey. "Demon bombs and bloodhounds? Sounds superstitious."

"Naw, just the opposite. Salt makes slugs melt, metal is wiggled by magnets, Mentos can make Diet Coke jump." He gave Rodney another wompy-sided smile. "It's science."

"I thought it was just, like, a symbol."

Ray held up three fingers like he was taking the scout's oath. "Symbols are real, and reality is symbolic."

Rodney turned, shaking his head. "Demon bombs, huh?"

While Rodney had his back turned Ray grabbed the bucket and snuck up behind him. "Yup, eggs make demons blow up. S'what I hear, at least." He raised the bucket over Rodney and doused him in honey.

"What the!" he sputtered under the outpour. "Jeez, Ray." He wiped it from his eyes, and Ray helped guide the excess down his shoulders and back.

"Trust me, Rod. You'll want to have some armor." The door rang again with a blow from outside.

Rodney gave in and scooped more with his hands and spread it across his chest and legs. "This is so dumb."

The door rumbled and shook. "Ray," Lucasta called. "The door is about to break. We need to act soon."

"Grab your bat, Rod." Ray nabbed the broom and took a position in front of the door.

Pinwheel dipped a couple of rags into the honey and wrapped them around his hands. Lucasta tied a rope around the bucket and approached the door as well.

Rodney noticed a faint glow all about them. The honey emitted a warning of demons.

Ray appraised their little troop. "It'll do," he said with a tight smile. "Alright, Pinwheel, I want you to yank back the door on my say so."

"Got it." Pinwheel put his hands to the handle and waited for the word.

"Rodney?"

"Wait, wait. This is happening too fast. Those demons can bust rocks and rip up trees. We have a broom, a bucket, and a baseball bat."

"Don't worry about it. Just throw eggs until they get close. Then whap 'em with your bat."

He turned to the angel. "Lucasta, I want you to go out first. Show 'em your flame and the big sword."

"But I can't hit them with that. They're out of the realm of my angelic weapons."

Ray smiled again. "Yeah, I know. But you think they'll remember that when a charging angel in full fire appears before them?"

Lucasta chuckled. "I suppose you're right, St. Raymond."

Mordecai moved next to Lucasta and crouched, ready to spring forward. A low growl rolled in his throat.

"Lucy will drive them away from the door. Take positions just outside the shed. We'll take out as many as we can and then retreat. Don't get grabbed, and, above all, remember," he caught Rodney's eye, "have fun."

Lucasta placed herself at the mouth of the door. Her blue dress seemed to move in wind. "I'm ready."

Rodney shook his head. "No, no, I'm not ready."

"Too bad." Ray said and gripped the broom with two hands like a broadsword, its straw head near the ceiling. "Pinwheel?" he said.

Pinwheel nodded.

"Now."

Ω

CHAPTER FIFTEEN

TREMBLE NOT

Smugbog was shoved to the ground by Cankersoot, a senior demon with a frighteningly long tongue and thin fingers. He stood outside the shed where the traitors of Heaven and Hell had fled. The horde congregated around the brick building.

The biggest demons fought over who should lead the charge. Spit-thicket, with the long, twisted fang cutting into his face, grappled with Rotsnogger, the demon with blood-stained teeth.

Cankersoot leapt into the fray with a frightening cry. Daylight lessened, and the pain of light faded. The chill of darkness, its numbness, was the envy of the demons after they'd endured the long hot needles of the sun. The demons watched the three great ones fight. It was a vicious match of biting, striking, and tearing with teeth and claws. Rotsnogger was in the center of the melee, punishing the challengers. He carved a deep X into Cankersoot's chest, and Spit-thicket lost an eye to the vengeance of the conqueror.

Before the gore had stopped dripping from Rotsnogger's fingers he issued orders. A thousand demons to all sides and another thousand on the roof. A wall of demons shot up into the air. Smugbog was thrown back by the gust from their wings.

As the demons alighted on the roof, they began screaming and cursing and leapt again into the air.

"It burns!" one demon called.

"Damnation!" howled another. Others echoed it. The vain script of their curses clouded the dusk.

"Poisoned with honey," commented Yuckjoy to Rotsnogger.

The demons hovered over the roof in the dying light still sputtering their curses. Rotsnogger snarled at the building. "What of its walls?"

Yuckjoy turned to the horde, "Rotsnogger commands that one of you touch the walls." The group of demons shuffled back, muttering.

Rotsnogger seized Yuckjoy by his fuzzy forehead and dragged him to the building. "Rotsnogger asked you, Yuckjoy." With that he ground Yuckjoy's face into the brick. The smaller demon howled and struggled against Rotsnogger. His face smoked where it scraped against the brick. Finally, he dropped Yuckjoy and turned to the others. "The building where the traitors hide is tarnished with honey, therefore the diaboloi must build siege engines. Break down their walls!"

The host of demons broke out in jeers and anguished hoopla. Rotsnogger appointed his chiefs and broke down their duties. Smugbog was listed among the group to stand guard at the shed's single door. Fibditch, the demon above them, marched along, riling them up, striking the demons that looked weak, driving the others to wrath.

Smugbog watched the demons rip down trees in order to build siege engines. Others set out on tasks kept secret from the peons. All were careful to avoid the chicken coop.

"Slimestub cares not for waiting," said the demon next to him. The one-eyed Spit-thicket, still aching over his recent shame, picked up the complaining demon and hurled him headlong into the shed. Slimestub rocketed into the brick wall and splattered messily. Spit-thicket murmured and limped away.

Smugbog turned to the demon next to him and recognized Damperknob, a tempter just senior to him. His evil was the envy of the lower hordes. "What happens when a diabolos leaves its husk?"

Damperknob appraised the lifeless pulp of Slimestub at the foot of the shed then said, "They wing back to the Outer Darkness. To the Lake where the diaboloi fan the flames of their own hatred."

The bustle around them increased as a large tree was felled behind the shed. It was slowly dragged to the door. They watched the battering ram get stripped of its branches. Smugbog let his malice pull his face into a wicked grin. "Pity the adams; the arm of Heaven cannot touch us now."

Damperknob shivered. He glanced around, then whispered to Smugbog, "But there is an angelos loose."

A bolt of terror shot through the grinning tempter as he deciphered that terrible word. "What? Here? Smugbog thought this forsaken Gomorrah was bereft of angeloi?"

Damperknob shook his head with frenzy. "No, Damperknob saw it. The stray was caught. Damperknob was guarding it with six others when a flaming sword caused the pit to collapse. The stray was taken."

"If Heaven is involved, then where is the army of Heaven?" Smugbog cried incredulously.

"Fibditch says it must be a stray angelos, like the saint has strayed from the path and dealt with diaboloi."

"Is it the eve inside?"

Damperknob shook his head. "She was not resplendent. Cannot be."

"But can angeloi hide their glory like diaboloi can be rendered unseen?"

Damperknob shoved Smugbog to the ground and sneered. "Accuse Damperknob of knowing orthodoxy? Accuse Damperknob of supplications to the Name?" He gave Smugbog a harsh kick to the ribs.

Smugbog sniveled and held up his hands. "Heretic, you are heretic!"

Damperknob accepted his apology without a word and turned to watch a group lift the battering ram. "It begins," he muttered.

Rotsnogger stood on a newly erected platform and held up his hands. "Vanguard of Hell! Prepare to defy Heaven!" The demons roared as the battering ram surged forward and struck the door. It held firm.

Smugbog rose to his feet. He noticed another tower being erected behind the shed. Trees were being filed to points by a group of demons. Fibditch went down the rows of demons, preparing them to charge once the door broke. The ram was hauled back and thrust forward again. Yells and curses were intermixed with the crash and clatter of the siege.

He felt a rage boil up inside him. He set his eyes on the door and snarled. The door rattled again. A crack in the wood was revealed when the battering ram was withdrawn. If the demons could touch the door, it could easily be ripped off and the slaughter could begin.

Smugbog found himself shoving aside the demons in front of him. "A chain!" he crowed. "A chain to rip down the doors!"

Rotsnogger roared a command and a rapid search for a chain began. Demons were already tearing apart the nearby house, and a flurry of activity was sparked by the order. Other demons dug through the clutter already piled up in the yard. Glass shattered, walls fell, howls rang out when a demon touched something glazed in honey.

One demon pulled out a garden hose from under the great pile. He was gleeful until he backed into the chicken pen. The watchful chickens flew into the wire barrier and clawed the demon mercilessly. He howled and jumped back as the surrounding horde mocked his pain. The chickens shrieked and pawed at the earth like bulls about to charge.

Rotsnogger pointed to Smugbog, "You, tie the hose to the door." He was handed the hose. Smugbog cursed his words. He snatched the hose and bolstered his fear with hate. He slowly approached the door.

A row of demons lined up behind him, taking up the rest of the hose and preparing to rip the door off its hinges. Smugbog looped the hose through the wood handle and began to tie it. His hands trembled. Without warning the door was pulled back. A bright light flashed and seared his eyes. He screamed as the whole world went blindingly white. A roar of terror ripped through the army of darkness.

Smugbog stumbled back. He then felt his head disintegrate, and his spirit was sucked back to the Outer Darkness.

* * *

Rodney fell back. Lucasta had disappeared in a white light. Screams erupted from the demons outside the door. Ray rushed forward and struck a demon with his broom, wielding it like an axe. The demon burst into a cloud of darkness and dirt. Mordecai rushed forward and sank his teeth into the arm of another demon.

Rodney looked again into the light where Lucasta was and gasped. Lucasta had six wings and an enormous flaming sword. She spun and slashed air, driving back the demons. The night, too, was driven back in her shine. She was a bold spotlight in her backyard. The demons were fleeing to the trees.

"Rodney! Boyo! Get out here!" called Ray as he beat back the hordes with his broom. He laughed as he smacked demonic heads. Mordecai frolicked in their midst, sending the demons he struck into black puffs. Armless and legless demons were the lucky ones, screaming and cursing.

He moved forward and brought up his bat. He chose an immobile demon sputtering his hatred unintelligibly. He brought his bat down upon his head, ending his complaint mid-howl. He looked up at the scattering horde and saw Ray open the chicken pen. The chickens rushed out, chanting their bok-bok-boks over the din.

Rodney felt emboldened with a demon brought to dust at his feet and leaped upon another wounded enemy nearby. He heard Ray call Mordecai. Rodney just happened to look backwards and saw a hovering cloud of demons descending behind them.

Rodney struck another lame demon. "They're behind us!"

"Whoops!" called Lucasta. "They figured out that my sword can't hurt them."

"Fall back," Ray cried, whirling his broom.

The demons had indeed grown wise to Lucasta's bluff. Rodney took position at Ray's side. Lucasta hovered above them, a beacon of light, but unable to harm the demons physically.

Sweat streamed from Rodney's forehead. "What do we do?"

Ray looked over his shoulder toward the shed and yelled, "Anytime now, Pinwheel!"

At that, Pinwheel rushed out of the shed, throwing eggs into the demons barring their way. The demons, caught by surprise from behind, turned to face their new attacker.

"Charge!" Ray bellowed. Mordecai shot into the wall of demons. Rodney followed his uncle into the fray.

Eggs spattered, and demons exploded. Rodney took an egg to the face and fell. Ray grabbed him and helped him into the shed, then dropped to the floor. "Grab some eggs, Rodster."

Ray took a handful from the stacks and began lobbing them into the oncoming crowd. "Lu!" he screamed above the battle roar. Mordecai entered the shed and skidded into Rodney, who fell into a stack of egg crates.

Lucasta, with a mighty thrust of her six wings, flew through the demons and into the shed. Pinwheel rushed to the door handle and pulled it shut.

Rodney wiped egg yolk from his face and spat. "That'll make 'em think before busting in here again."

They all sighed in relief, but they could still hear the army of Hell outside the shed.

* * *

Rotsnogger snarled and barked. "Cowards! Do you not know that Heaven is powerless against us now?"

"But eggs!" a nearby demon screamed in disbelief. "Eggs harm the diaboloi? First honey, now eggs!" It had been hundreds of years since the last fight between mankind and cruentated demons.

Rotsnogger thrust a hand through the panicked demon. He twisted and wrenched out the guts. The demon fell. Rotsnogger roared. "Of course Heaven cannot play fair. The Name is full of trickery and games! But their delays will give the sons of Hell the victory." He clenched his fist then raised it. "Ready the second wave!"

The night air deadened the command. No hoopla or cursing from the demons, only cold determination. Silent envy ate at the horde.

Screaming erupted from the trees. Demons scattered into the air; some stumbled out of the woods. "Chickens!" some screamed. "Rabbits!" screamed others.

Rotsnogger snarled. He saw Fibditch approaching him. The smaller demon was trembling. Rotsnogger smiled to see his inferior's dread. "Speak, worm."

"You are to send back the army to Saint Ray's house."

Rotsnogger scoffed and snorted and blew air angrily out of his mouth. "At the edge of victory? Nay, send back the wounded. Let the limping drag back the lame."

Fibditch hesitated. He bent down to stuff his mouth with dirt. Once weighty enough to speak again he rose. "The command comes," he swallowed, "from En-ki Ab-zu."

Rotsnogger wavered and nearly knelt down in fear at the name. "His envy?"

Fibditch nodded, unable to say the word again.

"Speak!"

His words tumbled out, a confluence of fear and sibilants. "The Prince demands that you send back all but three hundred. You are not to shed blood until dawn. Then, once the strays are overrun, return immediately to the Honeycomb House."

"Choose them, and send back the rest." Rotsnogger barked. Fibditch scuttled off. The demon shivered. "En-ki Ab-zu has risen," he said to himself. He flicked his wings and shot into the air. "The strays will be brought to their knees before dawn, and Rotsnogger will arrive in the blood of the Prince's enemies."

* * *

Al Walden leaned back in his chair and hung up the phone. "Marianne Marleena Holstrum?" His voice was a great thundering in the small office. There was a stirring outside his door. Through the frosted glass he could see the wide form of his secretary, Marianne, whose full name he sang throughout the day.

Marianne peeked into his office, "Yes, Al?"

"Made a mess a' things."

Marianne's face stayed the same. "How's that now?"

"Called the boy's momma. Might've let slip that Ray hadn't been seen in a couple days."

Marianne winced. "Didja say that the boy's gone, too, or that he was home alone?"

Al made a painful grin, his eyes retreating into slits. "Said I seen him, but not Ray."

She entered enough to lean against the door frame. "Either way I suppose it'd rile up the momma."

"More'n a tad," he said and scratched behind the badge on his chest. "She comin' down to get the boy, I gather."

"Tonight?"

"First thing tomorrow."

"Ya gonna arrest Ray now that he won't have to watch the kid?"

Al smiled. "I haven't checked the books yet, but I don't think arresting comes from being Inconvenient to Fine." He kicked back from his desk and stood. He reached for his broad hat hanging on the rack behind him. "I'm gonna see if I can find that kid."

"Want me to call Neddie, tell her you'll be a tad late?"

"Marianne Marleena Holstrum, would you call my beloved and tell her I'll be driving the whole of my district from one end to the other?"

"Yes sir, I will," she said primly.

"It'll give me time to think up a sermon for Sunday."

Marianne followed Al into the main room of the police station. "Whatcha talkin' on this week, Al?"

Al turned and rested his hand on the butt of his gun. "I was thinking same as last week. Justice."

Marianne shook her head and gave a gentle laugh. "And the week before."

Al stood at the threshold of the outside world and hitched up his pants. "Marianne Marleena Holstrum," he said without looking at her, "when you got a message that needs hearin', you don't stop until every last cell in every last soul has heard it three times slowly." He looked back and smiled as he saddled his sunglasses on his nose, and, for dramatic effect, eased them up with a finger.

Al followed the bend to Ray's strange house as darkness fully fell on Twin Rivers. He looked at his watch and saw that it was just after eight. Worst case scenario, Ray is gone, and the boy needs to be taken to the shelter. No, worst case would be both Ray and the kid are gone. He should call Ms. Katie at child services just in case.

He thumbed up the number of Ms. Katie and called. "I hope I'm wasting your time, Ms. Katie, but I need to ask if you got an extra bed available tonight. Uh-huh. Okay. Well, I'll call you if I'm bringing someone in. Alright, goodnight."

He slid the phone into his shirt pocket and slowed as he reached Ray's gravel driveway. He followed the loop, crossed over the Second River, and descended into the clearing. He pulled up to the stairs and opened the door. The hot night was cut by a crisp wind. A slow wind that hardly moved the trees. He stood squinting into the darkness. The car hummed.

Now the kid was gone or else hiding in this dark old house alone. Looking at the quiet house, not a single light on, Al realized that the boy wouldn't be here. Ray must've swooped back in and split with him. Visit his sister or something while the heat was on.

Al slapped the roof of his car. "Dang."

He felt movement behind him. He saw nothing but darkness and farther back the trees. He felt movement on both sides. Al ducked in fright and turned, first left then right, finding no one and nothing.

"Hello?" His voice was high and wavy. "Ray? That you?" He felt watched on all sides. He spun around, keeping a hand on the door of his car. His other hand went to his belt to touch the Glock 9mm holstered there. He had secretly named his gun Shadow, but it failed to comfort him.

He felt a blast of warm air on the skin of his neck, a breath blown from somewhere soggy. The hairs went stiff and his shoulders hunched and tightened. He jumped into his car and slammed the door. Something pounced onto the roof. The car shook.

Al started the car and screamed as the wheels spit rock. He accelerated wildly into the grass and dug a shallow ridge in Ray's front yard as he cut back onto the gravel. He pressed the gas down and the engine roared. The front of the car dipped and the hood dented, like some invisible boulder had been dropped on it.

The patrol car shot into the woods, and limbs smacked the light bar on the roof. From behind him he heard glass shatter, and there was a howling from somewhere.

The car lurched around the long curve and fishtailed as it approached the bridge over the river. It leapt across, bouncing hard into the gravel on the other side. Al braked wildly, spun, banged into a tree, and mashed the gas pedal again.

He couldn't keep from screaming, and he couldn't tell if the car was being clawed by some invisible attacker or if it were the low hanging tree limbs.

His car jumped from Ray's driveway across the road and into the ditch on the other side of the highway. The airbag deployed, and the world went dark.

CHAPTER SIXTEEN

ARMED WITH CRUEL HATE

Rodney looked up from his pillow of empty egg cartons. Lucasta and Ray were setting up caches of eggs as barriers. The war was on; no need for further refrigeration. Pinwheel was in a deep sleep nearby, his mouth hanging open, emitting soft whiffs of breath. The demons had been quiet since the retreat back into the armory. The door was not tried, the roof was not assaulted, even the howls and cursing had ceased. The silence was unnerving.

Rodney was too wired to sleep. He could still feel the weight of his bat in his hand. His fingers tingled, his hair pricked up in chills. Ray seemed every bit as fiery, but without the fear that had contracted his own muscles. He huffed and rose, stiffly, to his feet.

"Not able to nab some shut-eye?" asked Ray.

"No." He joined them in shifting crates of eggs for easy access.

Ray had outlined a strategy for the next attack. A high and perilous wall of stacked egg crates was built against the bricks nearest the door. Eggs for throwing were arranged concentrically opposite the wall of crates. Once the door was breached, they were to take out the first wave with the nearest row of eggs, then retreat and pull down the wall of eggs on the second wave. Lastly they were to throw eggs from the stacks they now prepared.

"What happens after we use up all of these?" Rodney asked, while reaching into a fridge for another flat of eggs.

"Well, then I think at that point the demons will surrender."

"Really?" Rodney said, surprised by the hope in his voice. He noticed Lucasta frowning at Ray.

Ray clenched one eye shut like he was wincing in pain. "Probably not."

"Definitely not," added Lucasta. "Hell doesn't stop. They either think they win or get crushed trying."

"So what happens when we've thrown all these and they're still coming?"

"We retreat to the Honey Hold," she said.

Rodney looked at the back room. The wood door looked solid. Another door built by Ray, no doubt. "And then what? Starve?"

Lucasta looked at Ray. Ray's lip muscled into his left cheek. He shrugged. "Don't you worry, Roddy, there's more to the plan. Just haven't figured it out yet."

Lucasta walked to the back fridge. "And we won't starve, at least not today. Look." Ray and Rodney walked to the back row where Lucasta had gone. She began pulling out items at the bottom of the last fridge. "Bread, butter, jam. Even ice cream. I brought it out here just yesterday."

"You knew this was going to happen?" asked Rodney.

"I've known something like this was going to happen. Yes. I just wasn't sure of the timing."

They went back to their mini fort and had a midnight snack. Rodney buttered up a thick slice of bread and then drizzled honey on it. The honey was dark and slow-moving, but seemed to grow bright once it touched his bread. He let it drip onto his shirt and hands.

Lucasta and Ray were chatting about the town. He heard them mention Otis.

"Oh," he blurted through a full mouth. They turned to him. "Something on your mind, Roddo?"

"Otis and Sheriff Al were looking for you. Are you in trouble?"

Ray laughed. "Oh yeah. I'm definitely going to get a fine. Been burning Alvariums. Otis thinks I burn piles of leaves recreationally. Probably thinks I burn other things recreationally too." He gave Lucasta a wink.

"Otis seemed mad when he stopped by this morning."

"Me and Otis, well, he's had some struggles. He puts some of his difficulties on me, and that's fine too. Me and Otis'll get along someday, I think."

"Otis is a fine man," added Lucasta. "Misguided sometimes." Lucasta picked up a pint of ice cream, chocolate, and pried it open.

"I will say this," Ray said, holding a finger in the air. "The man hates the tie-dye."

They all laughed.

Rodney cleared his throat. "Yeah, what's the deal with you and tie-dye?"

Ray was picking the strawberries out of the jam. He licked his fingers. "I always fancied myself a Rainbow Warrior."

Lucasta snorted in mirth.

Rodney shook his head. "What's that?"

"Well, angels are white light, and if you refract light, you get the full spectrum. A rainbow. So I thought that I could be the counterpart to the Warrior of Light."

"The Warrior of Light that fought the Thunder Snake?"

"Yup. I figure the Warrior of Light and the Rainbow Warrior would make a pretty good team. What do you think, Rod?"

"He'd probably hate your rainbow bee suit. Warriors are supposed to have cool armor."

Lucasta emitted a snooty *hmph*!

Rodney couldn't stop a smile. "What, Lucasta? What'd I say?"

"*He* happens to like wild colors, but you're right, Rodney, *he* doesn't think much of Ray's posturing." She pronounced the *he*s as though she were inflating a balloon.

"Come on, Lu," Ray said in a waxy low voice. "I know where I stand in the Kingdom."

"In the play pen?"

"In the trenches."

"In the pig sty, you pigheaded ninny."

"I'll do the name calling 'round here."

Lucasta scoffed again, then muttered, "Rainbow Warrior."

Ray leaned against the crates. "You call yourself a warrior. When was the last time you fought back something aside from the urge to eat more ice cream?"

Lucasta shot to her feet, dropping the pint of ice cream. Her spoon clattered on the floor. Her blue dress rippled. Her skin started to glow. "You know what I gave up. How dare you? You ignorant lump! You foolish thing!"

Ray looked over to Rodney, who sat in wide-eyed amazement. "Starting to sound like the little rascals outside." He gestured with his thumb.

Lucasta's light faded, and she sat back down. She picked up both the ice cream and the spoon, cleaning the spoon on the hem of her dress. "Anyway, *he* thinks you've overstepped your boundaries, as *he* told you back when you first started this harebrained plan." She spat out the *he*s as if they were sour.

"Well, that is . . . your, like, personal opinion." Ray's voice was a soft, backpedaling *hrumph*.

Rodney blinked and shook his head at Lucasta. Her biting tone cracked his confusion, he finally understood. "Wait, you're the Warrior of Light? You fought the Thunder Snake?"

Lucasta stabbed at the ice cream carton with a spoon. "We didn't call it the Thunder Snake."

"Whadja call it?"

Her eyes brightened. "Liv-ya-than."

"Leviathan," Ray muttered, clearly pouting.

"Whoa."

Lucasta leaned forward. "'Whoa' is right. Did you see how big he was?"

"Yeah."

Her eyes leapt with light. "We battled for a million million miles straight down."

"In space?" Rodney felt his heartbeat lift and fly.

"Yup. Just me. I couldn't deflect the sorry beast. Tried to knock him into Jupiter. That's a fun place."

Ray yawned. Lucasta ignored him.

"Once we hit earth, I knew that I had to do something desperate. That's when I sealed him in stone."

"Ray says demons are subject to stone."

"Yes, it's a wonder he hasn't tried building a cathedral in his backyard."

Ray grumbled under his breath. Rodney suppressed a laugh, then asked, "So did that kill him?"

Lucasta stabbed at her ice cream. "No. Subjecting them to stone doesn't kill them. Just traps them."

"Puts them in corporeal form though. Like cruentation." Ray smirked.

"Not like cruentation," Lucasta said firmly.

Ray looked at Rodney. "Pretty much exactly like cruentation."

"They're trapped in stone. They can't move."

"Unless they escape."

"That's why you protect it."

Rodney realized that this had been an ongoing argument between Ray and Lucasta. Both their voices were getting testy and stern. They glared at each other, continuing their feud in silence.

Rodney looked at the two warriors, each with their mission, pursued with passion. Then he looked over at Pinwheel, whose head was lolled back and tongue hanging out. A newborn angel in flight from all he'd known.

"Who am I?" Rodney asked, breaking the staredown between Ray and Lucasta.

"What do you mean?" Lucasta asked.

"I don't know who I am or where I stand in this fight," Rodney said. "Well, I mean, Pinwheel is escaping the demons, you're guarding the Thunder Snake, Ray is—actually I don't know who Ray is either."

Ray put on a hurt expression. "What do you mean? I'm one of the good guys."

"Yeah, but you built a way for demons to enter the world."

"I built them a noose to put their necks in."

Lucasta shot Ray a look, but drew near to Rodney. "Ray is on the side of the angels, even if his plan is foolish."

"Bold," Ray said under his breath.

"Foolishly bold," Lucasta amended, but then, kneeling, she said, "And as for you, Rodney, have you strayed?"

"I—I . . ." Rodney looked to his sneakers. "I guess. I mean, yes." He blinked back tears.

"Do you stray now?"

Rodney looked up at Lucasta. Her face radiated peace, but her look was severe. "No," Rodney said firmly. "I want to be here. I want to fight with you."

"Rodney Abner Niemand, do not stray from this path." She waited until he nodded, then said, "Peace be with you."

Swallowing the heaviness that had settled in the back of his throat, Rodney inhaled the honey-fumed air.

"Anyway," Ray said, drawing the attention back to himself, "whether I'm a Rainbow Warrior or not, I still think this is what they'd wear." He crossed his arms. "Plus, it's pretty."

Rodney rolled his eyes. "I think it looks silly," he said, and stuffed the final bite of bread into his mouth. His cheeks bulged as he chewed.

Ray chuckled. "You saving that bit a bread for later, Rodney?" Ray brushed at his own chin to indicate something on Rodney's face.

Rodney felt a chunk of bread stuck to his chin with honey. He scooped it into his mouth, shyly smiling. His dad would frown at him while he ate. Critique every stray fleck of food or miseaten noodle that loudly slurped into his mouth. "What are you doing over there?" he'd say. "Eat it, don't throw it all over your face."

His mom loved it, though. She had a whole binder of milk-mustache photos, both of him and of her. His dad would quietly push himself from the table whenever the camera came out, but mom would clown for half an hour in the middle of dinner with him. Noodle scars, she'd call the stripes on his cheeks from slurping up a noodle too fast. Her favorite things to photograph were corn teeth and asparagus tusks.

Rodney's eyes went glassy. He felt his head droop and slide.

"Why don't you get some sleep, Rodney. We just might have a long day tomorrow."

Rodney rubbed his eyes and stood. "Yeah, okay. 'Night, Ray. 'Night, Lucasta."

"Goodnight, little saint," said Lucasta as he entered the Honey Hold, where it was darker.

He chose a corner and nudged the door closed with his shoe. He placed his bat next to him. In the dark the bat emitted its gold light, warning of demons. His eyelids fell, and a great heaviness covered him and pulled him into rest.

* * *

Rodney was standing atop the Corleonis in the bright morning light. The sun moved through the sky like a swift turtle through a pond, ripples of heat washing over him. He looked far below him, to the thick green grass, and saw his mother waving. He had just raised his hand to wave back when he saw Ray and Pinwheel running out of the forest. The roof buckled beneath him, wood cracked and glass shattered and metal groaned, and he felt himself begin to topple.

He fell, and the lights went out. His cheek struck the ground of the Honey Hold and shouts of alarm woke him. He sat up. Another clash and clatter caused him to leap to his feet, out of his stupor. He pulled back the door, and his spine went cold, paralyzed at the sight of a tree driven through the roof. Ray stood on the smashed spearhead of the tree and swung his broom at the demons entering through the pierced ceiling. Pinwheel and Lucasta were behind a barrier of crates tossing eggs at the charging demons.

Rodney saw that the tree had knocked over a couple of the fridges, crushing the stacks of eggs they'd laid out earlier as well as spilling their clutch of eggs. Yolk oozed to the ground. Lights flickered and died. Demons roared as they rushed down the tree to meet Ray's honey-soaked broom. At its touch they burst into dust and howls.

There was a boom and the door behind Lucasta and Pinwheel buckled.

"They're coming through!" Rodney yelled. His honey-glazed bat flared as he approached the fray. There was another thunder from the wood door and a great crack as its middle shattered from the outside blow. A third heave sent the head of the battering ram through. Demons poured in.

Rodney saw the furry blur of Mordecai savaging a hapless demon who had fallen from the ceiling. Lucasta and Pinwheel retreated to stand by Rodney as the door was knocked clear of its hinges. Ray jumped down from his perch on the tree and swung wildly to keep the horde back. He slipped on the slimy, yolk-covered floor. The demons surged to bury him, clawing and biting the air.

"Ray!" Rodney yelled, but was frozen to the spot.

"Back!" was all he could reply. But before he was crushed under the wave of demons, a gray stone shot through the cleft in the door and bulleted into the backs of Ray's attackers. It was Ebenezer, ears flat and claws out. He mauled two demons, sending them writhing and flailing in fear.

Ray was able to get to his knees and take out a couple of demons still on him with a couple of looping swings. A third attacker dodged Ray's backswing and struck him with a black fist. The demon roared and crouched to lunge until the fuzzy girth of Thundertrump barreled through the door and undercut him.

Together the two rabbits scattered the demons at the door. Thundertrump followed them out into the night. Ebenezer joined Ray in retreat. Ray grabbed Rodney by the shoulders and pulled him into the Honey Hold as the demonic horde flooded the main room.

Once inside, Pinwheel and Lucasta pushed the doors shut and Ray dropped a thick wood crossbar locking the doors from the inside.

"Everybody got their fingers?" Ray was breathing hard, but kept an easy grin in place.

"What happened?" ask Rodney.

"Little beggars dropped a tree through the roof. How's that for thinking?"

Lucasta knelt down next to Mordecai and was checking him for wounds. Mordecai began to lick the honey off her face, and she sputtered laughter with her lips shut tight.

"What do we do now?"

Ray cocked his chin and began brushing down the porcupine of his beard. "Hrrm," he muttered. "Well, don't think they can get a battering ram in there. Least not one that can take down this door." He pat it. "White oak. I planned—"

"Ray!" Rodney barked.

He frowned.

"Listen!"

They put their ears to the door to hear the hoots and hollers of the demons. Ebenezer blurted out a scoff.

"Heh, they weren't making any omelets, but they managed to break a whole slew of eggs."

Rodney backed up against the barrels of honey. "That's not going to get rid of all of them."

"Oh no, but they won't be getting in here, either."

"So? We got three barrels of honey, a bat, a broom, and that's it. We're trapped. Outnumbered and hopelessly surrounded."

Ray's eyes grew big as he turned and put his back to the door. He looked at each person, angel, nephew, demon, dog, rabbit, letting his smile draw them up into his mad joy. "They can't escape us now."

CHAPTER SEVENTEEN

AMID THE FLOOD

The door erupted into thundering, kicks, and Al's hollering. Otis woke and wiggled out from under his book and onto his feet.

"Whazzat?" he called. "Al? That you?"

"'Sme, Otis!"

Otis cracked open the door and saw Al slumped over, hands on his knees. He was dragging breath into his lungs from some deep faraway place.

"Al, what's wrong? What're you doing? It's, it's . . . " He looked around to find a clock, gave up, and opened the door fully for Al to enter.

"Dang fool," he gasped and stumbled in. "One dang fool thing after another."

Otis directed him to the couch and went to get him some water. When he returned, the sheriff downed the water, chuckled as he wiped the sweat from his brow, and began to explain his late-night venture. "Went out to check on the boy, Danny."

"Ronny."

"Ronny, right. Place was dark. Nobody there, so I was driving back out when a coon crossed the road." He pulled his pink lips into his mouth and made a slashing motion with his hand. "Wrecked the cruiser. Right in the ditch." He stroked his mustache.

"So why are you out of breath? He chase you down the road?"

Al laughed. "No, I thought I could run here." He looked up into Otis's eyes. "I'm not a young man anymore."

Otis frowned and looked at his friend. Al did not have the look of a man accustomed to running, nor of a man who thought he could. What would send Al scurrying a quarter mile at night to his house?

"Well, we can call a guy, help him get your cruiser back on the road."

Al stood and ran a hand through his hair. "Naw. I'm beat. I'll do it in the morning. If you can just drop me off at my house, that'd be great."

"You're going to leave your cruiser in the ditch?"

"It'll be fine."

Otis tried to dismiss the strange behavior. Perhaps a strange day turns everybody strange. He grabbed his robe and put it on over his T-shirt and flannel pants. He kept his slippers on and jangled the keys to signal to Al he was ready.

In the car, Otis felt Al grow tense. As they neared, he could see the patrol car tilted nose–first into the ditch across from Ray's driveway. The front door was still open. Otis slowed down and stopped in the road.

"What are you doing? We don't need to stop." Al's voice was clipped like he was holding his breath.

"Your door's wide open, Al. I'll close it. You got your keys, right?"

Al made a show of patting his pockets. "Left 'em in the car, I suppose. Good call, Otis."

Otis got out and climbed down into the ditch. There was a deep gash in the roadside. The front end of the car was smashed. He looked into the dark interior of the car and noticed that the airbag had been deployed. He reached inside and withdrew the keys, still in the ignition. He climbed up the four-foot embankment with his hands before him.

"Al, I need to take you to a hospital."

Al jumped at Otis's voice. He was pressed up against his window staring into the dark trees. "What's that? Oh, I'm fine. I just need to get home."

"Your airbag went off. Did you know that?" Otis got in the car and handed over his keys. Once the car was moving, he noticed Al visibly sigh.

"Yeah, airbags are so touchy. A mighty sneeze would send those things off."

"Front end of your car was pretty banged up. Were you trying to avoid the coon or trying to run it over?" He looked over at Al to gauge his response.

Al's eyes shrank into anger. "What're you saying, Otis?"

Otis returned his eyes to the road. "Nothing, Al. I'll take you home." They drove the rest of the way in silence.

He dropped Al off and wheeled around to return home. He wondered if Al was mildly concussed from his wreck or if something more had happened. Did Ray have anything to do with it? He began to consider the possibility that Ray had kidnapped the boy or in some way terrorized him. Perhaps he should stop by the house. If someone was hiding up there, they wouldn't be expecting anyone more after Al had gone.

Otis let his head rest on the steering wheel as he waited for the last traffic light out of town to turn green. He felt hot in his robe and loosened the belt. He drove slowly, letting his eyes find stars between the cloud gaps. As the light of the city was left behind the stars were uncovered.

He pulled into Ray's driveway and followed it to the bridge. As he drove he noticed the slide and gravel-slurry of a vehicle in great haste. *Al's car, I bet.*

He drove into the clearing, but the darkness did not lessen in the open air. Clouds must have bundled up the sky. He exited the car, wrapping his robe more tightly around himself despite the heat of the night. He crooked a finger down the heel of each slipper to affix them more firmly to his feet. He felt silly trudging down the gravel driveway to spy on his neighbor. *Ray is so unstable. It's only a matter of time until he snaps.*

In the darkness the house could be a Mayan pyramid. There was something ancient about its design, something pagan about its build. It had always been a concern of his to have such a structure nearby.

The lights were still out, and as he approached, the smell of smoke and char filled his nose. Ray's burnt out car must still be smoldering. Otis crept up the stairs to the porch, shivering after every creak and complaint of the wood. Softly he touched the front door and paused to listen. He heard nothing.

He tried the door latch, and it clicked loudly as the bolt withdrew. It opened smoothly. He marveled over the craftsmanship of the door, heavy but well balanced, silent on its hinges. Otis stepped inside. The dim light of the cloud-obscured moon and stars made little difference to the black interior.

His next step was sticky, like stepping into a puddle of syrup. He looked down, but the light got lost in the layer of whatever covered the floor. He moved deeper into the house, through the foyer and into the middle room, the slime still an inch thick on the ground. The stairs to the second floor spiraled up the wall around a central beam.

In the few times he'd been inside, he'd never gone beyond the foyer and living room. He was annoyed at the hexagonal rooms, the wasted space, the odd slant of all the furniture. He went to the foot of the stairs to climb. He put his hand on the rail and jumped back in fright. The ooze ran down the rails as well.

He tentatively sniffed what covered his hand. The smell of old meat and mud slurry turned his stomach, and he slung the gunk off as best he could, wiping the rest on his robe.

Otis started up the stairs again, putting his hand against the wall to guide him in the dark. His hand again hit a slow flow of sludge on the wall. As he backed away, disgusted, his eyes caught movement before him.

A dark figure descended the stairs, twelve feet tall, ducking to avoid the ceiling. Otis could make out the glinting of the slits of his eyes. He scrambled back and screamed. His slippers slid, and his legs flew up. There was a loud crack as his head struck the floor, and the black was swallowed into a deeper black.

* * *

Pinwheel bolted up in the darkness of the honey hold. "Ray," he hissed. Ray snored, hunkered against the barrels of honey.

Perched atop the barrels, Lucasta emanated a glow, "What is it, Pinwheel?"

He checked the walls, listening intently. "I hear something."

"Wake Rodney," she commanded, and leaned down to slap Ray's face. A couple of firm strikes to the cheek called the bearded saint back to wakefulness.

Lucasta leaned down over Ray's head. "Pinwheel hears something."

Ray's eyes searched the room, and his face broke out in a grin. "Good. I couldn't think of a good way to get at them. Better they come at us."

Rodney was nudged from sleep by Pinwheel. He settled his hat back on his head, wincing still at the knot from the tree limb. As he lifted his bat he saw that it was emitting a dim yellow light. "Look!" he said.

"They're close," squeaked Pinwheel.

Mordecai trotted over from the door where he was standing guard. Rodney reached out a hand and stroked his gooey coat.

Ray was looking at the ceiling and picking kinks out of his beard. "Maybe we should move the barrels in case they come through the ceiling again."

"Good idea," said Lucasta.

They set about shifting the heavy barrels of honey. They slid, slung, and wheeled them to the sides, one barrel at each brick wall. Rodney and Pinwheel, who was holding Ebenezer, stood with one, and Lucasta and Mordecai took the second. Ray hopped onto the last one and sat, kicking his legs out. "Guess we wait, now."

Rodney held his bat up. Its glow was brighter. "Closer."

They held their breath. They could hear noises, tapping, a muffled curse every now and then. The bat brightened. Rodney turned and backed toward the center of the room. "Closer," he repeated.

There was a loud crack and they all spun to face the walls. Ray leaped from his barrel and grabbed his honey-charged broom.

Rodney took a few steps forward to determine the direction of the sounds. Without warning the floor fell away, and he tumbled down.

"Rodney!" Pinwheel howled. "They're coming through the floor!" He snagged Rodney's wrist before he was pulled under.

"They got me!" Rodney yelled, his eyes white with panic. His bat rolled to the wall.

Ray jabbed his broom handle down the pit to strike a climbing demon. "Take that, ya little beggars!"

Lucasta rushed to Pinwheel. Mordecai growled, his sticky hackles spiked.

Rodney screamed again. "They're biting! They're biting me!"

"More honey!" Ray yelled and threw down his barrel. The whole barrel cracked open, and a flood of honey poured slowly down the hole.

The pit erupted in screams and curses and a spume of black smoke. Lucasta and Pinwheel fell back as Rodney was released. His shirt was torn, and they could see bleeding bite marks in his side.

Before anyone else could act, Mordecai shot down the hole. His snarling and barking sent shivers down their spines. There was a loud scrum in the pit, yelps, howls, thumps, and snarls.

Lucasta bent over the hole and called, "Mordecai, come back!" She picked up Rodney's bat and looked up at Ray. "I can't fit."

Pinwheel pushed her aside. "I'll go."

"Wait!" Ray cried. "Let's drop some more honey down the hole." He turned and grabbed a second barrel and tipped it over. Honey oozed out. They heard Mordecai's yips become more frantic.

"Hurry!" urged Pinwheel.

"That's good enough," Lucasta said.

Pinwheel dropped down the hole. Ebenezer followed. There was a flurry of sounds.

"Rodney!" Pinwheel called from below. It was an anguished cry.

Rodney groaned. Screams of anger and fright clattered out of the pit. Rodney took Ray's hand and allowed himself to be lowered into the dark hole. It was filled with a coppery smell and smoke. He crouched at the bottom in the honey-drenched mud. He steeled himself and pushed forward.

Above him in the Honey Hold, Rodney heard a loud roar. The door behind Lucasta rocked and bulged, a thunder of wood on wood sounded.

Ray looked to the door. "They're attacking from all sides!"

Lucasta slumped to the floor, her eyes lost in the pit. The door cracked and buckled again.

"Get ready, Lu."

A third assault, and the wood groaned and the hinges strained to keep their hold. Ray looked to Lucasta one last time. Her face was blank, the light from her eyes gone.

In the dark tunnel, Rodney heard movement before him. It was a small passageway; the sides pressed against his shoulders as he crawled. He pushed forward, feeling the fine dust of dead demons and their brittle bones and severed limbs. He crawled past the struts and columns, suppressing his panic. The tunnel curved upward, and soon the sludge became dry dirt that caked his hands and knees. He couldn't hear Ray behind him. He tried to turn, but there wasn't enough light to see.

Finally, Rodney could make out the hobbling form of Pinwheel in a pool of light ahead. The tunnel abruptly bent upward. Rodney shifted and climbed out of the hole.

Morning was already lumbering over the horizon. They surveyed the wreckage of Lucasta's yard, stunned to silence. The grass was uprooted and trampled, the house was blasted out and leaning to one side, the chicken coop was a twisted wreck, felled trees and branches of all sizes covered the ground.

Rodney noticed Pinwheel crouched over something. He walked over to see him cradling the body of Mordecai. There was a sound behind him. The crack and roar of battle. "Ray and Lucasta can't get out through the tunnel. We've got to help them!"

Ray's battle cry reverberated from inside the shed, a bellow that shivered the rafters. Rodney grabbed his bat and rushed through the door with a whoop of his own. He rounded the turn to find thirty or so demons pressing forward to get at Ray. He struck a demon in the back and saw Ray go under the mob.

A demon turned and struck Rodney in the stomach, claws tearing skin. He fell and dropped the bat. The demon snatched his hand back and hissed. It smoldered with honey, but not enough to disintegrate his fist. He raised his arms to deliver the killing blow.

At that moment Lucasta soared out of the Honey Hold. She took up Rodney's bat and in one seamless motion slashed the demon into smoke and screams.

The demons turned at the commotion behind them. Lucasta unleashed her full light. Rodney went blind. There was a shriek as Lucasta attacked.

One demon cried out, "She cannot tou—," but was silenced with a blow from Rodney's bat. Rodney's eyesight began to return.

The demons atop Ray were thrown back as Ray rose up like a swimmer coming out of the ocean. Lucasta twirled and dodged, spun, stabbed, kicked, and dismantled shrieking demons with airy elegance and calm. Some tried to flee, but Ray charged and pushed what was left of the horde into the teeth of Lucasta's attack. Soon, clouds of dust were all that remained of the demons in the Honey Hold.

Once the onslaught was over, Lucasta dropped Rodney's bat and went out into the morning light. They followed her.

She collapsed beside Pinwheel and held Mordecai, wrapping both her arms around him. She closed her eyes and bowed to the earth. Ray and Rodney hung back until she rose. Her face was soft with fatigue and sadness, but remained silent. Ebenezer hopped over and snuggled her elbow, and Lucasta ran her hand down his soft furry back.

Ray checked his torn bee suit, poking his wounds. They surveyed the yard, empty of any other demons. "Where's the rest of the little beggars, I wonder?"

Pinwheel stumbled back. He collided with Rodney and pointed into the sky. "*Look!*"

They lifted their eyes to the west and saw a black column. Not a cloud, but a dark and swirling pillar. Neither was it a tornado, for it went up many miles into the sky, and the air was silent.

Rodney was about to ask what it was when a shaft of fear took his breath away. Pinwheel dropped to his knees. Even Ray's wide shoulders slumped at the sight of a tower of demons rising over the continent.

CHAPTER EIGHTEEN

THE BATTLE

Al Walden walked out on his porch, its green paint curling off the gray wood. He stretched, arms out like an airplane. His uniform was as crisp and new as the morning light. The sun etched the crest of Skeleton Mount in stark blues and grays. A slight wind rattled through the trees slung westward by the curve of the mountain. It felt unseasonably cool, a break in the heat perhaps, a sign of a mild summer.

A good sleep and a mug of stiff coffee had knocked the silly fear from his memory. He had been tired last night, and there was something that had caused him to swerve into the ditch.

He could hear Fred's rig turn onto his road. The powerful churning of the tow truck faded behind the whoosh of the air compression brakes. Al affixed his hat, downed the last puddle of coffee, and placed the mug on the porch rail.

He greeted the tow truck with a raised hand and climbed in. "Morning, Fred." Fred nodded and shifted the vehicle into gear.

Fred wore coveralls stained from yesterday and every day prior. His orange ball cap was grimy, frayed, and pulled low on his brow. Beneath the heavily folded bill, his brown eyes scanned the road for obstacles and dangers. Fred cast over a quick look. "Had an accident?" his voice was soft and ill-fitted to the scruffy face.

Al forced a laugh. "Darn coon. Just scooted across the road."

"Car won't drive?" Fred was well known for his clipped and stingy talk. Language was a luxury he couldn't afford, it seemed.

"Oh, I'm sure it'll go. Just need it pulled out is all." Al watched the Second River pull away from the road and disappear into the trees. He knew he'd see it again when he checked in on Ray.

In the distance he could see his cruiser, looking too large for the tiny ditch it was protruding from. Fred maneuvered the truck so that it was end to end with the police car.

Al got out and scanned the sky. Clear blue as far as the end of the earth. "Nice day," he said, as Fred fiddled with chains.

"It'll heat," he replied.

"Cooler than it's been in a couple months."

"It'll heat," Fred repeated as he descended the ditch. Fred examined the car. "Airbag's deployed."

"Touchy sonuvagun. Don't worry, I can drive it." He started recounting the last time his airbag had deployed, hoping to rile up Fred over the potholes along South Washington Street, but Fred just grunted while he worked.

Very soon his car was back on the road. The front end was banged up, but he was not vain about his vehicle. Might decide to preach on vanity this Sunday. Fred waved and drove back into town without a word.

Al stood in the road facing Ray's driveway. The sunlight didn't penetrate the thick woods and even the gravel path looked dark and foreboding. He forced out a scoff, but delayed getting in his car.

He should check on the boy; his mother would be in by lunch. Ray was about to find himself under a heap of fines. He planned on handing down as many as he could think of. He was about to settle into his seat when a sound rang out in the silence: a loud crack, like a tree splitting, followed by the crash of limbs and leaves and the heavy thump of the earth.

Al held his breath. He thought he could hear shouts and screams. Perhaps it was the wind or birds. He exhaled loudly. He opened the door and flopped into his seat. Birds, he thought.

It struck him that he had not heard any birds today. None. The sky was a blank blueness. He got out of his car again and stared into the woods. No movement, no sound, no squirrel or bird.

There was another distant crash. He sat, cranked the engine, and reversed the car so that he could turn into Ray's driveway. He took a deep breath, blew it out between firm lips, and pressed the gas.

The gravel sounded like war in his ears, tank treads and cannon fire, jet roar and bomb blast. He could see the ridges his hasty flight had made yesterday. He came to the bridge and paused. The Second River spoke over the hum of the engine, but nothing else moved.

He felt the hair on his neck prick up and his chest tightened. "Don't be a fool, Al," he said to himself. He gritted his teeth and accelerated over the bridge. It was probably nothing. His face broke out in sweat, bee stings of nervousness, and he forced himself to smile.

He was still smiling when the tree speared the front end of his car. The cab shook and windows shattered. Al was running away before the smoke settled.

$$* * *$$

The great swath of demons had nearly negated the sky. The black pillar swayed as it bulged and rose higher. Rodney had to fight the urge to hide.

"What do we do? What do we do?" Pinwheel cried.

Lucasta turned her back on the dark tower and walked eastward into the sun's new light.

Ray spun around. His eyes found the truck. It was dented and heavily scratched, having been shoved aside by the pursuing demons. There was a single gash along its side, the metal torn like paper, but it still looked roadworthy. He ran to it and reached in to turn the key. It cranked; the engine caught life and grumbled. Ray hopped in, careless of the glass. "We have to get back to the house!"

Rodney ran inside the shed to retrieve his bat. When he exited, Pinwheel was in the back of the truck, beckoning him to hurry.

He climbed in and saw that Lucasta wasn't in the cab. "Where's Lucasta?"

Pinwheel pointed toward the trees. He looked and saw the angel, with her arms outstretched, looking upward. Ray turned the truck around.

Rodney yelled, "Are we leaving her?"

Ray leaned out of the window. "She's doing more than we'll be able to accomplish. Trust me."

The truck entered the woods and the sky, with its swerving horde, disappeared. Rodney clung to the truck as it rattled over the roots and ruts. "Why isn't the Air Force attacking the demons? That column is huge. It goes for miles into the air. They gotta know it's dangerous. Why don't they do anything?"

Pinwheel spoke without turning his head. "They cannot see it. Those demons are not cruentated."

Rodney swallowed, but the panic remained high in his chest. Their best warrior left behind, one former demon, one boy with a bat, one man, limping and grinning, versus ten thousand *thousand* demons.

The truck roared out into the clearing. Ray saw Otis's car and slid in behind it. He jumped out. "Otis?" he called. "Otis, are you here?"

Pinwheel and Rodney leapt over the side of the truck. They formed a triangle behind Ray as he crept up the stairs. Rodney held his bat aloft.

The door was open. Ray called in, but no one answered. They entered slowly. Ray clenched his teeth and sucked in a breath at the sight of the interior.

Otis lay sprawled on the floor, but the thing they noticed first was the dark red goo that covered every surface. "Ichor," Ray said.

Pinwheel caught Rodney's eye. "Demon blood," he explained.

It was thicker than syrup and clung to their shoes. They walked slowly, careful not to slip and fall.

Ray knelt by Otis, checking his pulse. "He's alive." Ray stood and lifted Otis by his arms. He began dragging him outside. Pinwheel and Rodney let him pass, but they did not follow him out.

There was a creaking noise upstairs. Pinwheel walked into the stair room and ascended. Rodney approached the stairs and looked up. "Pinwheel, what are you doing?"

Pinwheel spoke without stopping. "It is time I confront Murkpockets."

"Wait," he said, and returned to the door. He slammed it shut, then carefully crossed the slickened, ichor-covered floor and joined Pinwheel on the steps.

Pinwheel turned to face him. He was two steps ahead, which negated their height difference. Pinwheel's eyes were watery.

Rodney held him by the shoulders. "You can't do that. Murkpockets is, like, four times your size. He'll kill you."

"Rodney," he said. His voice was soft and fluttering with fear. "This is it. The horde in the sky . . . we cannot . . . " His voice sank, his eyes fell.

"But they aren't cruentated, they're spirits. The Alvarium is destroyed! We don't *have* to fight them. Lucasta can—."

Pinwheel shrugged off his hands and backed away. "No, you do not see!" He gestured with his hands, spreading them out to indicate the ichor-covered walls. "*This* is the Alvarium.

Every demon will take on substance. They will enter this world and destroy it. We can do nothing."

"But Lucasta can call in the angels before they get here."

Pinwheel shook his head. "It is too late. The horde is above us now and help is too far away."

"But Lucasta—."

Pinwheel's eyes sharpened and his lips snarled. The breath of his words was shredded against his daggered teeth. "She is through with fighting. Did you not see her? And Ray is a fool. The world is lost. I am a fool, and I am lost." He turned, his shoulders fell.

Rodney remained silent. He could hear a howling high above the house, a distant scream from the sky with devils filled.

"I am a stray from demons and abandoned by heaven. I am nothing, and to nothing I will return. I would rather die fighting Murkpockets than be tormented by the coming Hell on earth."

He took another step before Rodney grabbed his hand. "You're not alone in this. I'm going with you." As he spoke his voice wavered, but stayed the course of his words. "I'm in the same situation, and I'm not leaving you."

Pinwheel raised their hands, clenched, and shook them. "Let us send Murkpockets to the fire."

They climbed the stairs, careful not to slip in the crimson sludge. They reached the second floor and saw that ichor had been sprayed and spread across every surface here as well. It rained from the ceiling like water from a dank cave. They heard a scuffle above them, from the observatory.

They exchanged glances and silent nods as Pinwheel advanced to the spiral staircase and ascended. Ichor dripped from the stairs and floor above. Rodney followed, clinging to his glowing bat.

Pinwheel reached the trap door, pushed it open, and let it fall back. Ichor flowed down on them both. They climbed into the room to see that it was empty and a huge hole had been torn into the roof and wall.

"Where is—" Before Rodney could finish, a spindly arm reached down from above and grabbed him by the shirt collar. He screamed as he was lifted through the roof and found himself face to face with Murkpockets, who was stained and sticky with ichor.

"Hello, foolish adam."

From below Pinwheel screamed and shot through the rift in the roof. His claws out and his teeth flashed.

Murkpockets caught him mid-leap with a twisted claw in Pinwheel's gut. There was the wet pop of flesh tearing and ichor gushed out of his side. The little demon doubled over and bled at the foot of his former commander.

"Nice of the stray to donate his gore to the cruentation of the army of darkness."

Rodney, still clutched by Murkpockets, swung the bat in an arc aimed at the demon's head, but the demon caught it with his free hand.

The bat sizzled in the demon's hand as the honey ate through his skin. He wrenched the bat from Rodney and dropped it to the roof. It clattered and fell down the three levels of the house, roof to roof to earth. The sound of it hitting the ground was lost among the swirl of wind and the distant howling from the pillar of demons.

"Murkpockets is no mere tempter. Your weapons are weak." He set Rodney down and turned his attention to Pinwheel, setting his foot on him. "Little lost demon, what do you say to this?" Murkpockets held his hands up to the swirling maelstrom. "You chose the wrong side. In a few moments, the gathering from all corners will be complete, and they will rush through this house and enter the world, where nothing will be held back from their hand."

Pinwheel writhed in pain. Rodney looked up at the cloud of demons. It was a throbbing mass that blocked off the sun. The day was smothered under a gray blanket, and the wind ravaged the trees.

Murkpockets sneered and nudged Pinwheel off the roof. Rodney heard the thump and scramble as Pinwheel clung to the roof below to keep from falling all the way down. Murkpockets focused on Rodney. Rodney shivered and tried to step back, but there was something behind him.

He looked down and saw a huge demon carcass, ripped open and hollowed out. Rodney jumped and nearly fell off the roof. He felt dizzy and crouched until he regained his balance.

Murkpockets scoffed. "Itchpot, a loathsome diabolos that Murkpockets reviled. His gore was saved for last. En-ki Abzu gives the envy to Murkpockets and sent this weakling to the gnashing."

Rodney looked off the edge. It was well over ten feet down to the next level where Pinwheel writhed. He could jump from one roof to the next to escape, but one slip and he would tumble forty feet to the ground.

Murkpockets continued. "Little dirtbag, have you heard? Murkpockets has a new name." His grin shivered and slumped into a snarl. "Murkpockets the Architect and Ba'al Zebub."

Rodney was too frightened to respond. He could see Pinwheel pull himself into a crouch, trying to stand. He couldn't help but look northward at the approaching column of demons. He could still see dots and pockets flying across the sky to join the writhing host.

Murkpockets glanced over his shoulder to see the final members amassing. "Yes, the time is almost here." Then back to Rodney. "It is time to choose your fate." He took a step.

Rodney edged away, hoping to get Murkpockets' back to Pinwheel. "What do you mean?"

"You do not yet have a name." His voice sizzled and snapped in the cool air. "St. Ray the Traitor, Birthless the Stray—their fates are sealed, their names are given. But you . . . " His voice trailed off, carried away by the wind.

"I'm Rodney."

"Rodney Who? Rodney What?" Murkpockets spit a thick globule of muck. "Your name won't last. Your flesh is weak. You will be blown into nothing in minutes. When the mustering is complete, the army of Hell will rush down through this house of honeycombs and take on a rough substance that your earth will tremble and fall before." Spit and ichor flew from his mouth as he spoke. He seemed to shiver with rage.

Rodney felt his fire dampen. His arms fell limp to his sides.

The towering demon took another step toward him, and Rodney edged away. Pinwheel watched from below. He clung to his wounded side, but stood and steadied himself.

Murkpockets now stood by the fallen Itchpot. He reached down and snatched off the wide head of the dead demon. The remaining ichor oozed down in spinning threads, trebled by wind. He held it out to Rodney. "Take and drink."

"What?"

"Take and drink, you fool. Do you want your name to go on? Drink of this ichor and take on immortality. You will have the strength of demons."

"No."

"You will survive this Armageddon if you are made immortal. You will be made a son of Hell."

Rodney saw Pinwheel nod and widened his stance. "No, I stand with angels."

"The side of fools," the demon snapped.

At that moment Pinwheel lunged at Murkpockets. Rodney braced himself, but Murkpockets caught Pinwheel with one hand. He spun and threw him down, down through the roof and two floors of the house. Wood snapped, glass shattered, and the whole house reverberated with the blow.

"Noooooooo!" Rodney screamed. He fell to his hands and knees and looked down the hole. Pinwheel was crumpled and broken at the bottom. His eyes fluttered and closed.

"His fate is sealed."

Rodney stood and set his face in stone.

"You have rejected immortality. Now you must beg for the life that you have. Kneel, and Murkpockets will let you live. You will be the last of the adams on earth."

"No."

"Submit as a conquered foe, or be the first to die."

Rodney's eyes filled with tears as he thought of his mother. He wanted to speak to her, even if it was for the last time. He felt a heavy regret well up for ignoring her before she left. He just wanted to say goodbye.

Murkpockets knelt over the hole and inhaled deeply, his chest expanding. He exhaled loudly, filling the structure with a thick stream of hairy, black bees. He arched his back and vomited more bees into the house, again and again, until a low thrum rattled the wood.

"Ba'al Zebub," the great demon said. "Lord of Bees." He smiled, baring his teeth. "It is time now to cast yourself down before me or endure all the terrors of my heart."

Rodney looked down through the scree of insects and saw Pinwheel rise. Pinwheel looked up and held his fists up, putting them together and then pulling them apart like he was snapping something. Rodney realized what Pinwheel was going to do as he backed away to get a running start.

Rodney looked up at Murkpockets. "You're very proud, aren't you?"

Murkpockets sneered, and his eyes widened. "Yes," he hissed.

"Do you know what pride comes before?"

Murkpockets cocked his head quizzically.

"NOW, PINWHEEL!" Rodney yelled.

Murkpockets flexed his wings and scanned for the attack. Below them there was a loud crack as Pinwheel threw himself against the central column, and the roof trembled. As the beam snapped the entire house began to sag and crumble.

Rodney stumbled away from the center. The second and third floor curled in and fell. He heard a voice cry, "Jump!"

Rodney turned and jumped into the open air as the Honeycomb House sank away into itself. He closed his eyes and fell to the advancing earth.

♌

CHAPTER NINETEEN

ON EARTH IS NOT HIS EQUAL

Ten minutes before, Ray had dragged Otis to the far side of the truck and laid him down. "Rodney, you and Pinwheel stay here with Otis while I check out the house." He stood and looked around for them.

"Rodney?" He heard the front door slam shut. He ran back to it and tried the handle. It was locked. He threw his shoulder into it, but the thump shifted his bones. "Rodney! Pinwheel!" Ray called, rubbing his shoulder and grumbling at the solidity of his own carpentry. No one answered.

He trotted around the house to the back door, but it was locked as well, and as sturdy as the front. He continued around

the house, trying windows, but they were sealed with con-
gealed ichor.

The sky was darkening as the great pillar of demons positioned itself above the Corleonis. "What are they doing?" he
asked himself as he stared at the miles high column.

He returned to the truck. Otis was still out cold. "What are
they—." It struck him like a shaft of ice up his spine. "Oh no,"
he gasped.

The house, a matrix of honeycomb to ward off angels, had
been transformed into a giant Alvarium by the ichor. All that
was missing would be the bees, but any demon Throne class or
above would be able to exhale all the bees necessary for cruentation. Ray wondered if there was any way to drive the truck
through the door and pull out Rodney and Pinwheel in time.
Or maybe he could get Lucasta and she could . . .

Rodney's bat struck the earth like a bolt from heaven. Ray
jumped in fright and looked up to see where it had come from,
but all he could see above the roof of the house was the swirling cloud of demons.

He ran to pick up the bat, then hustled up the front stairs.
He shattered the window next to the front door and pressed
the honey-treated bat to the ichor-sludge. It smoldered and
melted the stiff black goo like a blowtorch through metal.

He made an opening and slowly widened it, working the
bat up and down. "I'm coming, Rod!" he yelled. He stuck his
top half through and tried to worm inside.

Then, the walls bubbled and the floor rippled. Black bulbs
emerged from every surface and flew into the air. The bees,

shaggy and evil-looking, soon filled the space inside. Ray sputtered and guarded his face from the skittering insects.

He placed a foot inside the house when a thunderous crash knocked him backward onto the porch. He forced himself through the window, slipping in the sticky muck, and saw Pinwheel in a crater of wood.

"Pinwheel!" he called. Bees swarmed. They were thickest farther into the house. Ray couldn't get any closer. "Pinwheel!" he called again.

Pinwheel stirred. "Where is Rodney?"

The former demon looked stunned. There was a long gash in his side that ran thick with his own fluids.

"Pinwheel, there's no time. You have to bring down the house. Take down the shaft!"

Pinwheel struggled to his feet. He nodded and looked up, bringing his fists together. He pulled his fists apart and moved back for a running start. Ray pushed himself through the window again. Bees followed him out.

He jumped off the porch and stumbled forward as he heard a great crack. The entire frame of the house shifted and groaned as beams and load-bearing walls crumbled and fell— as if they were built to fall.

Ray looked up and saw Rodney at the edge of the third roof. The house was falling. "Jump!" he cried, and Rodney, fearful and instinctive, jumped.

Ray's breath caught in his throat, his heart leapt. Everything seemed to go silent as Rodney hurtled to the ground, the house toppling, the black finger of demons descending.

Suddenly, there was a streak of light and Ray was thrown into the tall grass. There followed a deafening crack, like thunder. Ray stood up to see his home descend into the pit beneath it, as though swallowed by the earth. Smoke and dust erupted.

The pillar of demons touched down on the wreckage and scattered. The air was scribbled with demons. Ray cringed amidst the chaos.

He felt a hand on his shoulder and he turned. There stood Lucasta in full angel regalia with Rodney standing beside her.

"Lucy," he stammered.

"Fear not."

Another ear-splitting crack seemed to tear the sky in two. Rodney and Ray both ducked and looked around. The sky had erupted with angels, each with four wings and a sword eight feet in length and flaming. The demons with one voice shrieked.

The two armies fell into each other, claws and teeth, swords and fists. Trees were uprooted and swung or thrown like javelins. It was a horrific clash that extended hundreds of feet above the smoking ruins of the Corleonis.

Lucasta shouted over the din, "Try to get out of the way. I'm going in." She stepped back and seemed to grow six feet taller. Four wings flared out from her back, and her hair grew bright and wild like the sun.

Rodney covered his eyes and drew back. He heard a snort like an ox as Lucasta stamped her foot. Tremors surged through the ground, making him stumble. Next, he heard a roar like a lion and a screech like an eagle, and then the voice of a waterfall.

"Fear not," she repeated.

Rodney watched as Lucasta moved her hand before her blinding face to draw down the visor of a helmet. She shot up into the air.

Ray caught Rodney's eyes and said, "Whoa. Intense." He picked up Otis and began dragging him away from the center of the action.

Rodney saw his bat and grabbed it. "Where's Pinwheel?"

Ray's face tightened. "We need to get out of here."

As if to punctuate Ray's words, a demon was struck from the air and entered the earth in front of them, passing into it as if a cloud. A moment later the demon raised himself from the ground. He looked at Rodney and screeched. Rodney positioned himself and brought around his bat with as much power as he could muster, but his bat passed through the demon and the force of his swing pulled him off his feet. The demon hissed at him.

"Easy, Rod. These demons are in the realm of the angels. We can't get at them." Ray faced the demon. "Which means you're in a world of trouble."

The demon bared his teeth and spoke through them, "Ray!"

Ray peered at the demon and recognized him. "Ah, lookit you. Gerald drove you off, eh?"

"It won't matter; the world will worsen for him again." The demon spat and leapt back into the fray raging above them.

Rodney turned and shouted, "I'm going back for Pinwheel." Ray called after him, but Rodney was already running to where the house had stood.

Rodney reached the lip of the hole and looked down, careful of the edge. It was deep, and Rodney felt dizzy looking into it. There were beams and boards strewn and stabbed into the sides of the pit all the way down. At the base there was a mound of debris where the cavern once was. A portion of roof was near enough for Rodney to drop down on. He slid down the side and picked his way to the bottom of the pit.

"Pinwheel!" he called. He paused to listen, but he could only hear the sounds of battle above him. Shifting aside some debris, he found a crevice and climbed down, squeezing through ichor-drenched wood. He called again.

There was a shifting below him and a cough. "Pinwheel!"

He pushed some boards with his feet and reached into the gap with his bat. Something grabbed it. Rodney set himself and pulled. "Hold on, Pinwheel."

Rodney pulled, but the place where he stood shifted, boards cracked and complained. He scrambled back to keep from sliding deeper. A hand emerged and Rodney grabbed it and hauled Pinwheel into his arms.

"Rodney," he said weakly.

"Let's get you outta here," Rodney said and lifted him. Rodney climbed out of the rubble. He found a place to lay Pinwheel down and looked over his injuries. Pinwheel was so covered in ichor that it was hard to discover how much of it was from him and how much from the ruined Alvarium.

Pinwheel's eyes fluttered and opened. "What happened?"

"You did it, Pinwheel. You knocked down the house before the demons could be cruentated. Lucasta showed up with a bunch of angels once the house went down. They're cleaning up the demons now."

Pinwheel's mouth slivered into a smile. "Least I'll have plenty of company when I go back to the outer darkness."

"No way. You're sticking with us, buddy. I'm just going to get Ray and we'll get you out of here."

The shingles and splintered boards where Rodney stood trembled and slid. Pain erupted from his foot, causing him to stumble, and Pinwheel fell back. Rodney saw a twisted talon piercing his foot, and, as it corkscrewed back out of his sneaker, the pile bulged and fell away, revealing Murkpockets rising to his full height.

"You dirt," he spat. "You will be my food. Truly, Murkpockets will go to the gnashing with you in my teeth." He lunged for Rodney.

Rodney swung with his bat, striking Murkpockets's right forearm. There was a sickening crack, but Rodney kept swinging. While the great demon cradled one arm, Rodney switched his grip and swung at the other. Dust was flying as the honey-coated bat ate away at the body of the demon. Rodney took out the knees, causing his opponent to buckle and bow at his feet. He dismantled the demon swing by swing until Murkpockets looked into Rodney's eyes with cold hate and roared.

"Go to Hell," Rodney said. He struck the final blow like he was swinging an ax, bringing down the full weight of Libra on Murkpockets's head. With a thunderous crack the head of the Architect exploded and the demon fell down dead, fading to dust at the boy's feet. Rodney brought up his bat to see that it was cracked, splintered at the barrel. He tossed it aside.

There was a squeak behind him where he'd left Pinwheel. Rodney turned to see the biggest demon he had ever seen. Bigger than Murkpockets by far. He was hairy, with two forked and twisted horns on his head, and his midsection was pimpled with fleshy gnarls and bony thorns, as if he were some monstrous she-wolf.

The giant demon held Pinwheel like a broken thing. He placed his hand on Pinwheel. Dragging his fingers across his prone form, carving tiny furrows in his flesh. Pinwheel grimaced, but was too weak to move.

"Put him down!"

"So, you are Rodney." The demon's voice was roaring fire and twisting metal. The tumult of battle was drowned out when he spoke.

Rodney looked around for his bat. He saw it near the remains of Murkpockets. "Your leader is dead. I killed him."

"Leader? Murkpockets was no master of mine."

"Who are you?"

The creature paused before answering. "En-ki Ab-zu."

Rodney wasted no time in responding. "Never heard of you."

"The earth is mine and all the fullness thereof."

"I don't care. I said, put him down." Rodney bent down to retrieve his bat, holding it at his leg, barrel down, hiding its damage.

"Ray is quite the deceiver, a liar like his Lord. You are no boy. You are another headcrusher."

Rodney felt hot breath stick to him and sting his skin. He ran a hand across his brow, mopping away the sweat and grime. "You'll find out what kind of headcrusher I am if you don't put Pinwheel down."

The Old Master sent a long, forked tongue through his teeth. "You care for this stray, the forlorn lump of stink and ichor?"

"He's my friend."

En-ki Ab-zu spoke without taking his eyes off Rodney. "Will you die for him?"

"Yes."

The Old Master snarled. He placed his hand over Pinwheel's mouth and gripped his head. There was a muffled cry and Pinwheel's hands went weakly to the greater demon's fingers. "Put your weapon down, deceiver."

Rodney lifted the bat. He felt the barrel shift where the crack had weakened it, but it stayed erect. It had one more good blow left in it. Maybe.

There was a tumble of dirt from above and Ray's voice rang down. "Don't listen to him, Rod. He's a snake."

En-ki Ab-zu closed his fist tighter around his captive. Pinwheel's weak struggle ceased.

"Wait!" Rodney held out a hand. He was out of options, no more stalling, no way to attack him without Pinwheel dying. He tossed the bat away and it tumbled down the pile.

"No!" Ray howled.

The Old Master immediately dropped Pinwheel and in a flash he closed the gap between them. His claws closed around Rodney, pushing the air out of his lungs. The Old Master unfurled his wings, digging the claws of his wings into the walls of the pit, and with a mighty heave they shot into the air.

The Old Master cut through the fray like a branch among leaves. Demons drew back and angels watched as the cruentated demon flew higher into the air.

Rodney felt the blood rush from his head. The sounds of war receded. He gasped and lost consciousness.

* * *

Ray fell back as the Old Master shot out of the pit. Rodney's arms and legs dangled from the great demon's fist as he passed through the airborne battle.

"Lucasta," he yelled over his shoulder. "We've got a problem!" Ray slid down into the crater and scrambled to the place where Pinwheel lay.

He got down on his knees and lifted Pinwheel's limp body from the rubble. Ray sat him upright and gently slapped his face to wake him. The little former demon had been beat up pretty good over the last few days. Innumerable scrapes and scratches, a broken wing, and a gaping wound in his side.

Ray ripped off a sleeve from his bee suit and used it as a bandage. The multicolored sleeve looked like a cummerbund on a shaggy tuxedo.

"Pinwheel, buddy, ya gotta quit napping, man."

Pinwheel's eyes lolled. His pupils circled before juddering and locking onto Ray. "Rodney," he muttered.

"Yeah, we'll get to him, but we need to get you going." He stood and helped Pinwheel rise to his feet.

The sounds of battle had fallen off. Ray inspected the sky above them, finding it empty of combatants. There was a far off clatter, but the cries of anguish and anger had ceased. While he was looking, an angel descended into the crater and alighted in front of him.

The cherub's armor was scored with blows and bite marks. The sword smoldered like a decanted volcano. A bright hand went to the helmet and pushed up the visor. The cherub diminished in size and its light lessened, and Lucasta stood before them in her human form.

"Lu!"

"Where's Rodney?"

"We gotta go get him. That big bugger carried him off." Ray could hear the panic in his own voice.

Pinwheel made a great effort to stand on his own. "We have to go now, the Old Master is sure to rally the forces of Hell. We have—we . . . " He slumped back, and Ray put out a hand to steady him.

Lucasta sheathed her sword. "His army has been routed. We fell upon them like lions."

"Then what?" asked Ray. "He's using Rodney as a hostage? To escape?"

"Impossible. He knows he can't escape."

Pinwheel grabbed Ray's wrist. "He wants revenge. That is his only instinct."

Ray bit his lip and exchanged a look with Lucasta. "We need to move fast."

"The Legions can be organized for a search. We can scour the continent in mere hours."

"That is too much time." Pinwheel said. "We will never make it!" He scrambled to the wall of the crater and began climbing out.

Ray grabbed him by his good wing. "I know where he's going."

Lucasta reached the same answer. "The Liv-ya-than."

"We gotta get to Skeleton Mount."

At that moment the ground shook as a second angel touched down. Dust took flight, and debris shook and reset-tled. The tremors caused Pinwheel to slide back. He turned to face the angel.

Unlike Lucasta in her angelic form, this angel had six wings—four enormous wings were located on his upper back and two smaller wings at his lower back that he arched forward, the forward feathers curling inward over his feet. Pinwheel had never seen a seraph before, and trembled.

The seraph raised a finger to Pinwheel. "Birthless the demon, now called Pinwheel," he paused, making sure Pinwheel was listening.

Pinwheel saw the seraph was aflame, white fire writhing from his armor and robes. He pressed himself against the dirt wall, cringing but unable to look away.

The seraph's voice rumbled. "You will come to me."

Ray started to intercede. "Wait, no. We have to—. " He held his tongue as Lucasta leveled her sword at his throat.

"Ray," she said calmly. "Barachiel has spoken."

Ray had never seen Lucasta reply with such conviction. He dropped his shoulders and cast his eyes toward the little creature, who knelt down with a sunken face.

Barachiel unsheathed his sword and approached Pinwheel.

II

CHAPTER TWENTY

THE BODY THEY MAY KILL

R odney awoke, still in the grip of the Old Master, five thousand feet in the air. A cold wind battered his head and limbs. They dropped through the clouds, moisture stinging his eyes. He felt dizzy and sick; their rapid descent made his stomach knot and churn. There was a loud snapping sound that Rodney realized was the demon's leathery wings unfurling to slow their fall.

The attempted demonic coup had dragged dark clouds from every direction. The early afternoon sky had stayed gray, clouds knuckling up as if to pound the earth itself.

They broke through the cloud covering and he could see a mountain beneath them. They were about a thousand feet above its highest point, but racing closer every moment. Within seconds Rodney could see a lake and the thin, squiggly line of the river that descended from it. He was jolted with fear as he realized they were drawing nearer to a large stone zigzag—the stone snake or, as he now knew, the Leviathan.

Rodney gathered his thoughts. Pinwheel was seriously injured, maybe dead; the angels were in pitched battle with every demon within a day's flight of Twin Rivers. How many that made he wasn't sure. Rodney had no idea how long he was out, but the flight couldn't have been more than a few minutes, maybe even seconds.

He knew he didn't have much time. Even if Ray could gather help before he was killed, how would the angelic force combat a cruentated demon?

The Old Master flapped with greater and greater strength until they were hovering twelve feet from the stone effigy.

Rodney was dropped unceremoniously. His feet struck the head of the stone snake and his legs buckled. His right ankle turned as his full weight fell on it. He skidded off the head and fell another six feet into the moist dirt. The wind rushed from his lungs, and he bit his tongue.

Rodney sucked in air, while the Old Master settled behind him. His ankle and punctured foot throbbed. Both were beginning to swell. He scooted backwards against the mouth of the stone snake as the Old Master turned.

"Here is where you will die." The heat from En-ki Ab-zu's mouth cut through the air, making it stifling.

"Your army's been defeated." Rodney didn't know this for sure, but it seemed unlikely that the leader would flee the scene of a victory. He gingerly applied pressure to his foot to see if it would bear his weight, but the slightest effort induced flashes of white pain.

"You are under the misapprehension that Hell wishes to rule this world." The Old Master placed a hand on the stone snake as if petting it. "You are wrong."

He turned and walked to the river a few feet away. "The diaboloi do not want this world for their own; the diaboloi want this world for the fire."

Rodney pushed with his good leg, bracing his back against the stone, and rose to his feet. He wobbled but stood firm, careful to keep the weight off his injured ankle.

"All that will remain of this world will be death and the rebels." He turned to face Rodney once again. "And the rebels will be kings of this world."

"You say that like I'd want to be a king of a burnt world."

"Better to rule in ruin than to serve in paradise."

"I'll take the paradise, thank you very much." Rodney saw the demon flinch at his sarcastic gratitude.

"Sadly for you, it is not a choice."

Rodney thought about making a run for it, but even if he'd had two healthy legs, the idea that he could escape a twelve-foot demon was preposterous.

En-ki Ab-zu continued, "Behind you is the Liv-ya-than. A greater destructive force has never yet been matched.

"Ever heard of nukes?"

"Bombs are a hazy fear, and they kill too quickly. But to be hunted by the Liv-ya-than, to live in the world where the Liv-ya-than roams to and fro across the face of the earth, that is true terror."

Rodney snorted, "Too bad it's trapped in stone."

En-ki Ab-zu bared his teeth in a horrifying smile. "No, foolish adam. It is trapped in the physical world—but not yet released. All that is required is blood." The Old Master curled his talons, flexing his tendons.

"The plan was destined to succeed. The Name isn't nearly as shrewd as he thinks. This isn't the first time he's been outwitted."

"Your plan was to have all of the demons be destroyed? You're a bigger idiot than I thought."

"With the activity of the angeloi there could be no release for the Liv-ya-than, but when the straying saint offered his home as a hell away from Hell and the Alvarium Maleficorum as a door into this world, the plan began to fester. Either unleash the army of Hell into the world or create a distraction to release the Liv-ya-than. Whatever the end, Heaven loses its most treasured jewel." The Old Master opened his mouth, revealing yellow teeth as thin as nails. A tongue flicked out, and his eyes widened while he gauged Rodney's response.

Rodney felt a burning lump in his throat. His breath was constricted. It had been hopeless for so long, but now that his adventure was drawing toward its fatal end, he felt a deep yearning for more.

He put a hand to his head and pushed the hair down. Somewhere in the melee he had lost his cap. His hair was still sticky, mottled with dirt and twigs. His mom would paw and pick at it if she could see him now.

The Old Master watched emotions boil over Rodney's face. A smile crept over the great deceiver. Rodney was caught up in a net of love, laid long ago by his mother, then increasingly by the family and friends tangled in his life.

Hot tears cut paths down Rodney's grimy cheeks. He balled his fists as a fierce jealousy for the world coursed through his veins. He was about to lose the world, and it stung even though the world would follow him in destruction.

The Old Master judged the moment ripe for his offer. "But you could be a king of this world. I will take your blood, but the Name isn't the only one who wields death." The Old Master drew near and knelt before Rodney. "Death is mine."

Rodney stood his ground despite the urge to crinkle like paper on fire. "What are you saying?"

The Old Master snatched Rodney, holding him about the waist, and shot into the air. Rodney clung to the coarse fingers of the demon. There was a slight smoldering where remnant honey stung.

The Old Master dragged them two thousand feet into the air and slowly spun so that Rodney could survey the country. The day was dying early. Having seen enough horrors, the sky had piled high the clouds, and the sun had sunk beneath them. Rodney searched for shafts of angels surging from the direction of Ray's house, but he saw no help.

"Consider the kingdoms of earth, Rodney. As far as the eye can see and farther can be yours." His wings went stiff and vertical and they dropped like a bolt to the earth. Before impact, however, the Old Master stretched out his wings bringing them to an abrupt hover and a smooth landing.

He dropped Rodney much more softly this time, who was able to keep upright, holding his wounded ankle off the ground.

The Old Master remained in the air to tower over Rodney. His voice became louder, and its heat singed the air. "You can be a prince to this world if you will kneel and worship me."

"What do you mean 'prince'?"

"Not all adams must die. Worship me, and I will shed your blood to release the Liv-ya-than and raise you up after to be a chief in the army of Hell."

"You'll kill me and raise me up again?"

"Death is a door, and the key is mine."

"What about Ray and Pinwheel?"

"You may do with them as you please." The demon waved his hand dismissively.

"What about my mother?"

The Old Master's eyes flashed. "An eve?" He managed to hide his sneer. "Yes, you may spare an eve."

"What about Lucasta the Angel?"

"Angeloi will have no place on the last earth."

"So if I worship, you'll let me live and I can spare Ray, Pinwheel, and my mom?"

"And live forever," he hissed. "And ride the Liv-ya-than into destruction. And have the entire human race cower beneath your might." He lowered himself to the ground. "If you just kneel down before me and worship."

Rodney searched the sky. It was a gray blankness, a gravestone set over the sky. His voice fell into soft wind. "No."

The Old Master's lip quivered in disdain. "Then you will die and never be more than dirt. Enjoy the rot."

Rodney looked up into the eyes of the great demon. Above his head, but just beneath the veil of clouds, Rodney spied a single pinprick of light. It was streaking downward and directly at them. Light curled off the bolt.

"You're wrong. Pinwheel is coming for me."

"The stray will die as shamefully as you." En-ki Ab-zu raised back a hand, his claws extended, to strike Rodney down where he stood.

Rodney threw his hands before his face. The temperature of the air spiked. He could feel his face brighten and he heard a low-pitched whoosh like thrown fire. He didn't know what was happening, but his instincts told him to move. He dove sideways.

Peering through his fingers he saw the Lord of Hell turn and the bolt of light pass through his head, incinerating it. The headless trunk of the Old Master fell to its knees and toppled over.

The bolt traveled into the head of the stone serpent and smashed it, sending fragments everywhere. Rodney felt his skin sting as he was peppered with rock shards.

"Wow," was all he could manage as smoke and dust surrounded the area. The head of the stone serpent was crushed, reduced to rubble by the explosion. He stood and approached the smoldering crater.

In it stood a strange boy about Rodney's height. He had dark hair but pale skin, and he wore a simple white robe belted with a yellow rope. The boy was bewildered, looking at his hands, turning them over and flexing his fingers.

Rodney staggered over some rubble, and the boy looked up. His eyes were slate gray.

Rodney cleared his throat and asked, "Who are you?"

The boy's eyes widened, and he said, "Rodney!"

CHAPTER TWENTY-ONE

FROM AGE TO AGE

Out of the hills in early evening, where the foot of Skeleton Mount comes to a rest, a white truck rolled into Twin Rivers carrying a man, his nephew, and a guardian angel. Rodney looked at Pinwheel, squished between himself and Uncle Ray. Pinwheel was fiddling with his hands, no longer three talons and a thumb, but soft, pink, articulate, wigglesticks of endless fascination. He was splaying them before his face, then slapping them to his cheeks, causing a rosy flush. Rodney laughed at Pinwheel's antics and introduced the former demon to pinching and tickling, pokes and tousled hair.

Ray also had a hard time keeping his eyes on the road. Lucasta's truck had gone through a lot the last couple of days, and it almost went through a mailbox before Ray corrected their course with a jerk of the wheel. There'd been enough destruction for the day, and he didn't want to add Lucasta's truck to the list.

Ray explained to Rodney what had happened after En-ki Ab-zu had flown off with him. A high-ranking Seraph named Barachiel had taken Pinwheel to be transformed into an angel through a process called calcation. Flying into the head of the Prince of Darkness isn't part of the process, but it seemed an expedient use of it.

While the angels were dispensing with the last of the demons, Ray had jumped into the truck and had taken the back road up the mountain, avoiding the firetrucks and police that were speeding to his house. The cover story was to be as vague as possible—mention having to pick up Lucasta's "nephew" who was flying in, and then imply engine trouble.

"There's one last problem," Ray said.

Pinwheel was jolted out of his playfulness, and Rodney's face fell quickly into concern.

Ray grimaced. "We can't call you Pinwheel."

Pinwheel seemed crestfallen. "But that's who I am."

Rodney patted him on the shoulder. "Don't worry, Pinwheel, we can just give you a first name. Like," he paused, gathering names, "Tommy or Billy Pinwheel. That sounds good."

Pinwheel made a sour face.

"No, no," chimed Ray. "His name is Peter. Peter Pinwheel, the Stone from Heaven."

Pinwheel nodded his agreement and practiced a wide-toothed grin.

Rodney tried it on his tongue. "Peter Pinwheel. Peter. I like it."

"Me, too," said the newly christened Peter.

"Petey, Pete-ster, Petunia." Ray spitballed.

Rodney slapped his forehead. "Get used to it, Pete. Ray won't ever call you by your real name again."

* * *

They picked up Lucasta and drove to the remains of the Corleonis. Al was still there in conference with the fire chief. Ray only had to mention that he was picking up Peter before Al launched into the minor earthquake and sinkhole explanation. He went into great detail about the tree that had speared his cruiser and that Otis had visited at the moment of the earthquake, but had been thrown to safety. There was even talk of a pocket of natural gas that might've been the cause of some powerfully real hallucinations. Ray admitted that he'd had more than a few strange visions lately.

Rodney's mom arrived looking haggard and bewildered. She rushed out and hugged Rodney and punched Ray's arm. Once she surveyed the wreckage of the Corleonis, Rodney had to endure another round of suffocating hugs, but Ray got off with a couple of shoulder squeezes. Both winced over their nicks and scrapes and bruises.

They all piled into the van and drove to the hospital to visit Otis. He was awake and bandaged, with his arm in a sling. Ray launched into the official explanation, describing the sinkhole and even pantomiming the collapse of his house while Otis nodded in wide-eyed relief. Otis was especially convinced about the pocket of natural gas causing hallucinations. He insisted that Ray was far more affected by it than he knew and forgave him for his oddity over the years. Ray stayed with him that night, and as the others left the two, they were in deep and jolly conversation.

* * *

By the end of summer, Ray had already made plans for a new house, something boatlike with a circular dome and some sort of lighthouse tower on top. They were clearing out a space for it in front of the sinkhole, which was slowly filling up with water. At the rate it was going, it would be a pond before the end of the year.

Ray had quickly converted the shed into a loft where he showered and slept. For his meals he hiked down to Lucasta's.

The rabbits returned, as well. Jerome and Ebenezer first, then Thundertrump with a brood of eight—and a sleek, light-gray cottontail soon named Skylight. Peter was hard at work naming the eight babies.

Virginia decided to quit her job in Tennessee and move back to Twin Rivers. She found a nice house around the corner from White Pine Baptist church and began constructing a website to expand Ray's woodworking business. Rodney rode out to Ray's every day to help him clear land or construct rocking chairs.

As August was drawing to a close, when the hemisphere had gone as far into heat as it could and was beginning to slip into cooler weeks, Ray had everyone over for a groundbreaking ceremony. Lucasta and Peter, Virginia and Rodney, Al and his wife, and even Otis. They'd become close again now that Ray was done talking about demons. Plus, Gerald had called his father to let him know he was doing better and that he'd visit sometime soon.

Ray stood up from the newly constructed picnic table and raised a glass of crisp apple cider, crooking a thumb into his denim overalls. He wore a bright new tie-dyed shirt underneath. "Friends, family," he paused as though aligning a constellation of words. "We gather here today to break bread and break ground on a new home."

He paused and gestured toward the pond where his house had once sat. "We bid goodbye to the Corleonis, the Heart of the Lion, also known as the Honeycomb House. It was a worthy home." He bowed his head, but couldn't suppress a smile. "I name the pond in its place my own Little Galilee."

He lifted his eyes and gave a wink to Rodney. Rodney hopped off his chair and grabbed the shovel leaning against the shed. He handed it to Ray, who placed a foot upon it and set its edge to the earth.

"Today is the beginning of my new home. Of course this means it must have a new name. You've all seen the plans, you've seen the point like a prow cutting the sea, you've seen the dome rising like a forecastle of a ship and the marvelous lighthouse on top. Therefore I name her," here he stuck the shovel into the ground and eased up a wedge of earth, "the Argonautica. May she sail atop this planet for many years. I look forward to riddling her walls with my ancient glyphs and symbols."

Rodney rolled his eyes, his mother shook her head, Otis frowned, and Al looked over to his wife and shrugged. Lucasta and Peter, however, gleefully clapped their hands. He tossed the dirt to the side and then held out the shovel to Rodney. "Rowdy Roddy, wanna dig a hole?"

Rodney made two quick thrusts into the dirt. He held out the shovel, but Peter erupted in a high pitched "wheeeee!" and dove into the hole hands first to add his own efforts to the project, throwing scoops of earth between his legs. They all laughed at his exuberance.

"Peter, honey, try not to get every speck of dirt on yourself," cautioned Lucasta. In her lap she petted a puppy, his skin like a pile of fuzzy laundry. He was a black lab named Darius who had learned to hop like a rabbit.

Otis took the shovel from Rodney and took three furious stabs at the earth. Otis passed the shovel to Al who jostled his broad shoulders and set his jaw.

Suddenly it had become a competition. He hefted four loads of soil and flung them wide. He held the shovel up to the three ladies who each in turn declined. Otis snatched it back and stood on the foot rests, causing the blade to sink into the ground. Roots popped and cracked as he leaned back and wiggled up the dirt edge. Al sucked his teeth and flexed his hands.

As the digging duel continued, Ginny came up behind her son and draped her arms around him. She put her lips near his ear and whispered, "How are you, Rodney?"

He leaned back into her embrace and replied, "I love sunshine, I love sunshine, I love sunshine."

Ray motioned him to follow with a tick of his head. They walked around the shed, where they'd dragged the remains of Ray's car, a burnt-out metal husk.

"When're you gonna get a new car, uncle Ray?"

"I don't need one, really. Lucasta lets me use Eggy whenever I need."

"Eggy?" Rodney scrunched his nose.

"Yeah, 'swhat I call her truck." Ray squinted and scratched his beard. "Or maybe I should call it Embryota, like embryo and Toyota."

"Lucasta's truck is a Ram, though."

Ray frowned. "Like I said, Eggy. Anyway, my point is, can you believe she didn't name her truck?" He chuckled to himself, then added, "But that's not what I brought you back here for." He walked behind the wreck, the tall grass shushing against his work boots, and lifted a wooden bat that was leaning against the shed. He patted the barrel against his palm then held it out to Rodney.

"Made you a gift. Ray of Hope bat company is back in production for a limited time only."

Rodney accepted the shaft. The weight caused his arms to dip before he adjusted to it. "Cool." It was smoother than Libra and weighted more perfectly up and down the shaft.

"It's a bit heavier," Ray said as Rodney appraised the wood. "You might not realize, but you've gotten stronger."

Rodney rolled it over in his hand to read the inscription. Written in a swerving font was the word *Ophiuchus* followed by ♉.

"O-few-choos?"

"O-fee-yu-kiss, I think," Ray said. "Means, snake-wrangler."

Rodney sighed, running his fingers over the groove of the letters. "Everyone has a special name . . . " His voice trailed off without finishing. His mother had told him that she was going back to Lauter, stranding him with Niemand. His father had put off seeing him until Christmas. He still felt like he was a burden, burdened with a name nobody wanted.

Ray seemed to read his heart, and gestured to the field. "A name is like a house, Rodney. It takes time to build, but the both of us are building on a firm foundation. We got a lot of work ahead of us, and even when the house is built, it won't be finished for many more years after that."

"What happens when a name is finished?"

"A good story never ends."

They turned to look on the little gathering. Lucasta had Peter in her lap and was trying to clean his face while he squirmed. Darius was down in the grass and nipping at Peter's flailing heels.

"I've been meaning to tell you . . . " Ray paused and looked at the ground before finding Rodney's eyes again. "I couldn't have done this without you. I mean the whole higgledy-piggledy with Hell, not the destruction of my home. I coulda done that on my own."

Rodney laughed.

"Lucy Skyskipper over there has been on my case to apologize for dragging you into it all, but I'm not so sure you shouldn't be thanking me?" He gave Rodney a squinty-eyed smirk.

"Thanks, Uncle Ray," he said with a roll of his eyes. "I couldn't have nearly died many times without you."

Ray laughed again and slapped Rodney on the back. "Rod Ness Monster, we make a pretty good team. Now go save Peter. I think Lucy is about to lick her thumbs and go after his eyebrows."

Rodney looked back to see the angels still tussling, Peter bobbing and weaving his head while Lucasta moistened her thumb. "Too late," he said.

"Eh, might as well enjoy the show."

Peter squealed as though hot irons were being applied to him.

* * *

Later that evening, Rodney and Peter took up bat, ball, and glove, and made their way into the field on the other side of the pond. They'd spent the summer throwing and hitting. In this time Peter had developed quite a home-run trot. After a big looping swing that often sent him corkscrewing into the ground, he'd flip the bat, take a running skip, and stretch out his arms to airplane around their imaginary basepaths. The final stretch to home included cartwheels, but he filled the rest of the run with pirouettes and spins to keep Rodney laughing.

Rodney lost three rounds of paper-rock-scissors, so he won the right to serve up gopher balls for Peter to smack into the darkening woods.

After several home-run trots, when the ball was becoming too hard to find, they retreated to the rabbit pen. Peter began reciting the names of the baby rabbits skittering around. "Robin, Greystoke, Blackberry, Boaz, Maggie, Iggy, Gypsum, and Butterscotch."

"Where did you get those names?"

Peter looked over and smiled. "From all over. I've been reading books." He crouched down next to Rodney and plucked a bit of tall grass with his fingers.

Rodney looked into Peter's slate gray eyes. "I've been meaning to ask what's going to happen to you."

"What do you mean?"

"Well, you're an angel now. Don't you have, like, angel things to do?"

"Yeah."

"So what are you doing? Has Lucasta told you yet?"

Peter's voice dropped as he spoke in raspy eagerness. "I'll be doing what I've been doing."

Rodney's face flashed with puzzlement. "What's that?"

"Ever since, well, as Birthless, I was without anchor and goal. I was lost. A stray before I strayed."

"I've felt that way, too."

"But then I was summoned by Ray to Twin Rivers."

Rodney snorted and smiled. "That happened to me too."

"I was given a mission, to watch over you. That was not my job from Murkpockets or the Old Master. My job was given to me by the Name. I was and I am your guardian angel."

Rodney's eyes went wide and he let his mouth drop. "But, but . . . " His mind rushed over the events of their adventure, Pinwheel's role, his help and protection every step of the way. How everything was leading them to this point.

"I think we're stuck together, Rodney."

Rodney swung his hand around and clasped Peter's. "Peter Pinwheel, it's great to have you on board."

He shook Rodney's hand. "Rodney Niemand, we make a great team."

They were both startled by a burst of dust in front of them as Thundertrump landed with a deep thud. She knelt down and raised her haunches, wiggling her tail. Without warning she jutted side to side.

Rodney looked over at his guardian. "Up for a little rabbit wrangling?"

"Yeah, whoever catches her gets the other's ice cream on his apple cobbler."

"You know Lucasta will give us as much ice cream as we can eat."

"Yeah, you're right." They both stood.

"Okay, new deal. Whoever catches Thunder first gets to bat for the rest of the week."

"Then you better save up your energy for chasing my homers." He gave Peter a shove.

Thundertrump juked and bolted into the open field. Peter and Rodney stumbled and clambered after her.

In the shadow of that great mount—wearing the crushed stone serpent like a crown—and in the darkness where the Snake wended its way toward the Wine to be usurped, the city of Twin Rivers found rest, and as night descended the stars came out to watch the rolling earth.

THE END

AFTERWORD

Can Demons Be Saved?

trays was born out of a little fairy tale that I told my young sons called "The Little Lost Demon." It was about a boy who convinced a lost demon that sunshine is glorious and baseball is fun. It was a tale meant to teach my son about the transformative nature of love and the fun nature of baseball.

As this was scaled upward into a novel, the mechanics of plot required a form of realism that a fairy tale ignores; therefore, the demon of "The Little Lost Demon" could no longer be an allegory for the unloveable and unenlightened among the world, but (seemingly) a minion of Hell who sides with the angels. The question is then raised: Could this be a true story?

As I see it, there are three possible answers explaining how Pinwheel could be among demons, but be Rodney's guardian angel.

The first is, Yes, demons can repent and be saved.

Obviously the Bible is not concerned with giving this information, but I will say, without delving into deep theological discourse, that evidence given to the contrary is greatly exaggerated. The only definitive response to such a question is that we don't know. Every treatise on the matter that I've read is too quick to assume that *angel* in the Bible means *Divine Being*. The word translated as *angel* in both Hebrew and Greek first and foremost means *messenger*, and any time you see it in Scripture, you ought to think of a human being until it becomes absolutely clear that there is no possible way it can be a human being.

This answer is very pleasing to me and is the simplest explanation for the novel.

The second answer is, No, but Pinwheel is not a demon; he is an angel among demons.

While resolving one sticky theological aspect, it raises its own questions and it would, I imagine, require its own book to explain.

But it also pleases me, because, obviously, I love stories about the gulling of the devil. This new story would have the marks of a spy thriller: deep undercover alias, amnesia, crossings and double-crossings and maybe even triple-crossings. Good stories seem to climax with three crosses.

The third answer, and perhaps the most palatable, is that the story functions in places as an allegory and not as a theological treatise.

As an example, to take Narnia as entirely orthodox would be tragic at best and heretical at worst. Lewis himself makes this distinction in his letters:

> I did not say to myself, "Let us represent Jesus as He
> really is in our world by a Lion in Narnia": I said "Let
> us suppose that there were a land like Narnia and that
> the Son of God, as He became a man in our world,
> became a Lion there, and then imagine what would
> happen." If you think about it, you will see that it is
> quite a different thing.

In like manner, if it please you, say, "Let us suppose demons can find themselves in the service of God," and imagine this is such a story. You may take as a model the words Aslan expresses to Emeth, the servant of Tash, at the end of *The Last Battle*: "Beloved . . . unless thy desire had been for me thou wouldst not have sought so long and so truly. For all find what they truly seek." Or, in the words of J.R.R. Tolkien, "Not all those who wander are lost." Both of these quotations seem fitting to apply to Pinwheel.

With the first option, you get a story of shocking redemption. With the second, you get to imagine another exciting adventure. And with the third, you may ponder the significance of such a vessel of wrath straying into the hands of the Name above all names.

Taking the Name

I have written a novel for Christians that is certain to make Christians feel uncomfortable. What's worse is that I wrote a young adult novel that could potentially offend Christians. The book is titled Strays and I've described it as "A Screwtape Adventures Story" after C.S. Lewis's brilliant, but diabolical book, *The Screwtape Letters.*

Rodney, the hero of the book, encounters a small demon named Birthless. It is a frightening event. He kicks out of his bedsheet with a series of oh-my-god's and after a particularly gruesome threat, Rodney mutters: "Jesus, oh, Jesus."

A friend told me that when he was reading it to his children, he instinctively censored it.

"Thou shalt not take the name of Yahweh thy God in vain, for Yahweh will not hold him guiltless who takes His name in vain," saith the Ten Commandments. This has been taken to mean, "Be careful when you use the name of the Lord" and

"Do not say the name without meaning." But while I might counsel you against stubbing your toe and crying out, "Jesus Christ!" it is not because it breaks the third commandment.

Calling upon the name of Jesus, in a crisis of Legos and barefeet or upon your pious knees, accomplishes the same thing: the attention of Jesus. Thereby you see my reasoning for avoiding the Name in times of irritation. Calling on Jesus to pay attention to you over toe pains and table legs, hopping one footed in the dark, is probably not your best moment. In a moment of surprise—SPIDERS! popping out of a pinecone! in your hand!—the Name may burst from your lips with fear and fury, I dare say, but I suspect the Almighty will look askance at you chucking a perfectly good pinecone crawling with some of his most interesting creations.

What the Third Commandment prohibits is not the verbal use of his Name, but the bearing of it vainly. The word translated "take" means "to lift" or "to bear" and is used by Cain in Genesis 4:13 when he says that his punishment is "greater than he can bear" and by Yahweh in Exodus 19:4 when He tells Israel that He bore them on eagles' wings. To "not bear the Name vainly" means that those who are baptised into His Name are living according to His requirements.

Rodney, at the beginning of the novel, is wondering about his name. His mother is returning to her maiden name, his uncle names things left and right, baseball bats and cars, and they discuss the name change of the nearby river. Inadvertently, Rodney subjects a tormenting demon to the Name, the Name above all names, which leads to the uncovering of a plot that looks to be the ruin of the world. Rodney must learn what it means to bear the Name and bear it wisely as we all must do.

I should add that my friend, when he began to see the theme of names in the book, apologized to his children for skipping something and returned to the chapter so that Rodney's use of the Name was included. It's a dangerous word. Jesus. Gee-zus. It sometimes erupts out of people without prompting, both in secular and sacred use. I like that there is a reverence toward it. I like that it is a weighty thing on our tongues. Even the unbelievers recognize its power (for nobody calls upon the name of Horus). And yet, it ought to be easy on our tongues, for he is light and what is lighter than light?

I fear that our mis-emphasis on speaking the Name has curbed our use of it, but what I hoped to show in *Strays* is that speaking the Name has power. For Rodney it had a totally surprising result, but one that is no less miraculous and powerful than the usage available to us daily.

ACKNOWLEDGMENTS

I give my thanks to Lewis and Luther for providing the spark, to Aaron R. for stoking the flame, and to Brian K. and the rest of the Canon crew for striking the iron. I thank my early readers for their feedback, particularly Zachary P., as well as my last-minute reader Nancy D. And thanks to Christian M. for Garglenails. I owe a great debt to my parents for the innumerable stories invested in me; I hope to pay them off with this and future stories. And lastly, I thank my wife, whose creativity is of such prodigality that I was able to have the necessary solitude for my own singular act of creation and still find a home full of rest and joys abundant.

www.ingramcontent.com/pod-product-compliance
Lightning Source LLC
Chambersburg PA
CBHW072122250626
47159CB00007B/2538